T0285305

A St Ives Christmas Mystery

A St Ives Christmas Mystery

DEBORAH FOWLER

Allison & Busby Limited
11 Wardour Mews
London W1F 8AN
allisonandbusby.com

First published in Great Britain by Allison & Busby in 2024.

A CIP catalogue record for this book is available from
the British Library.

First Edition

ISBN 978-0-7490-3193-0

Typeset in 11.5/16.5 pt Sabon LT Pro by
Allison & Busby Ltd.

By choosing this product, you help take care of the world's forests.
Learn more: www.fsc.org.

Printed and bound by
CPI Group (UK) Ltd, Croydon, CR0 4YY

For Alan, in loving memory

Bristol, Today

PROLOGUE

Merrin McKenzie popped two pieces of bread into the toaster. Toast was not her breakfast of choice but the family's African Grey parrot, Horatio, was watching her intently from his favourite morning perch on top of the wine rack. Horatio insisted on toast every morning, or else he sulked. It was Merrin's firm belief that no creature on the planet could sulk so effectively and consistently as a parrot.

She walked over to the sink and gazed out of the window. It was a beautiful spring morning. In the last couple of days, the cherry blossom had flowered in the garden of the house opposite. The contrast of the pink blossom against the blue sky was lovely.

Her mobile rang. She smiled; it would be her husband, Adam, who had left for work that morning before she was properly awake. She picked up her phone. It wasn't

Adam; it was his sergeant, Harry. In all the years ahead, Merrin would never come to understand why she had experienced no sense of foreboding at that moment.

'Hello, Harry,' she said, 'how are you?'

'Mrs McKenzie, the guv's had an accident,' Harry said.

Still Merrin felt no real sense of panic. Adam, now a chief inspector, had been in the police force for over thirty years. Particularly in the early days of his career, he was often coming home with injuries of one sort or another. 'What sort of accident?' she asked.

'I — I'm not sure,' said Harry, 'I wasn't actually there when it happened. He's in an ambulance on his way to Southmead. I've sent a car round to pick you up and take you to the hospital. It should be with you at any moment.'

And then it hit her. It was like being slammed against a brick wall – the breath forced from her body. Whether it was the tone of Harry's voice, or a premonition borne of having known Adam her entire adult life, but she knew in that moment, with absolute certainty, that Adam was dead.

She put down the phone with a trembling hand. In the distance, she could hear the sound of a police siren, presumably the car on its way to collect her.

Mechanically, she went to the toaster, tore off a piece of toast and handed it to Horatio.

CHAPTER ONE

Seven months later, Merrin's footsteps echoed as she walked across the kitchen to the window – for the very last time. She stood in her jeans and padded jacket and stared across the road. The cherry tree was bare, of course, which seemed fitting. All that was left in the house, apart from herself, was a small overnight bag, a tub of parrot seed and Horatio in his travel cage. He was absolutely furious.

Adam and Merrin had met in their first term at university and, apart from the odd falling-out in the early days of their relationship, had been inseparable ever since. They both read law, which had led Adam into the police force. On leaving university, Merrin had joined a firm of solicitors to do her articles and had specialised in family law. Without question, they had always known they would marry one day, and within a year of leaving university they had formed a plan. Adam's parents lived in Argyll, just outside Oban, and Merrin's parents lived in St Ives, West Cornwall. Being so far apart, neither family's location seemed a practical place to settle and so they decided to stay in their university city of Bristol. They found a dilapidated Victorian terraced house, named Arcadia, close to the city centre but not on one of those roads that acted as a rat run during commuter hours. It was delightfully quiet. With help from both sets of parents and an eye-wateringly large mortgage, they moved in on their return from honeymoon and virtually camped for several years, both ambitious and therefore giving priority to building their careers.

It was the imminent arrival of their first and only child, a daughter, Isla, that prompted some serious repair and maintenance work. As a result, Arcadia had gradually morphed into a cosy and much-loved home for the three of them – no, four; one must not forget Horatio.

Standing now in the empty house, memories flooded back. Often, when Isla was tiny, Merrin would bring her down to the kitchen at night in order not to disturb Adam, who worked such long hours. She remembered so many nights, cradling her daughter in an effort to lull her to sleep, standing in front of this very window and staring up at the night sky.

Their kitchen was also their dining room and therefore their party room. And there had been so many parties; in the early days, when most of their friends were still single and childless, the parties involved much loud music accompanied by appropriate quantities of booze;

there was Isla's first birthday party, sitting proudly in her highchair; and the parties Merrin loved best, a myriad of family and friends of all ages – including grandparents, teenagers and rampaging small children. This room had a great many stories to tell.

'Come on, Horatio,' Merrin said, draping a cover over his cage. Normally, Horatio would have tried to tear off the cover, enraged at having the world blotted out. This time, he remained uncharacteristically silent. *He's just as nervous and apprehensive as I am*, Merrin thought.

She put the cage and her bag in the car, then returned to the house and closed the front door. The door was painted a deep red and a small granite plaque alongside displayed the word *Arcadia*. She locked the door and then, after a moment's hesitation, pushed the keys through the letterbox. She took two steps backwards, still facing the house. 'Am I doing the right thing?' she asked.

The house declined to comment.

CHAPTER TWO

Luckily, as it was now late morning, fighting her way out of Bristol was not too painful. Soon, Merrin was on the M5 and settled down for the long journey to the South West.

In many ways, Merrin knew her decision to move back to St Ives – the hometown she had left at eighteen – was an eccentric one. Her parents were both dead and her only sibling, a brother named Jago, now lived with his family in Australia. Brother and sister had been very close as children but distance now meant they saw one another infrequently. She still had contact with a few childhood friends from St Ives, including Max Richards, who had become an estate agent and was responsible for finding her the delightful little cottage she had just bought. She would be meeting him later to collect the key. Trying to keep positive, in between bouts of self-doubt, she felt sure there were still plenty of families with whom she could reconnect. Looking beyond the influx of tourists every year, St Ives was still a very small town.

It was just after 5 p.m. when Merrin started the descent into St Ives. She pulled off the road at the Malakoff, parking her car out of the way of the buses. She walked to the railings, the traditional place to view the town on arrival. It was completely dark, of course, but the Christmas lights were up already, illuminating Fore Street, the harbour and Smeaton's Pier beyond. The tide was in and the sea was very dark, but quiet; there was no wind and so little surf. She took a deep breath of sea air. It felt good. She had spent less than a third of her life here – did it feel like coming home? Not yet, she decided, but the concept was not impossible.

She called Max. 'Max, I've arrived; I'm at the Malakoff.'

'Well done, welcome home, my girl. Have you much luggage?'

'No,' said Merrin, 'just a small bag and a parrot.'

Max laughed. 'A parrot! You never fail to surprise! I suggest you park at the Sloop for tonight. I'll meet you there in five and then we can walk round to the cottage.'

The Sloop Inn, where Merrin, Max and their friends had spent many happy hours in their youth, stands conveniently opposite the slipway leading down to St Ives harbour. Cold and wet after a long day at sea, St Ives fishermen, through the centuries, had only to take a few steps to reach the haven of the bar. One of the oldest pubs in Cornwall, the Sloop began life in 1312.

It is quaint and cosy, like many ancient pubs, but there are added dimensions - a sense of the sea and the huge role it plays in the life of the town. And then there is the art - paintings, old photographs, all with a story to tell.

Immediately behind the building, sits the small, somewhat eccentric pub car park, mostly used by the locals - for good reason. Presumably, in order to maximise the number of cars it can house, the marked-out spaces are so narrow that while it's possible to park in one, it is often quite impossible to open the car door sufficiently in order to get out. Merrin, a veteran of this conundrum, parked sensibly at the end of a row. Max was waiting for her.

Back in the day, Max had always been a big success when it came to girls. He was good-looking, funny, sociable and one of life's enthusiasts. Girlfriends came and went with monotonous regularity. Merrin's moment in the sun came shortly after her sixteenth birthday – she was Max's girlfriend, briefly and innocently, for about three months and then he dumped her. He broke her heart, of course, but, surprisingly, it only took a few weeks to mend. Thereafter, they became friends and had remained so through the years – Max was Isla's godfather.

Despite being something of a lothario, Max could be very kind and thoughtful, as was demonstrated now. He unlocked the cottage door and stood back. 'After you, m'lady,' he said. The lights were on; so was the heating. A fire crackled in the grate and a camp bed was made up in the corner of the room.

'Oh, Max, this is so kind,' said Merrin. 'I hadn't booked anywhere to stay because I didn't think any hotel would take a parrot and I didn't want to leave Horatio alone in a strange house. Thank you so much.'

'There's a price you have to pay for all this,' said Max, producing a bottle of champagne with a flourish. 'I insist you share this bottle with me to celebrate your return home – only plastic glasses, I'm afraid.'

While Max opened the champagne, Merrin removed the cover from Horatio's cage. She topped up his water and seed and whispered a few words of comfort. To no avail, Horatio turned his back on her and fluffed up his feathers in disgust.

They sat on the floor by the fire, backs against the wall. Max handed Merrin her champagne. 'I'm glad you've arrived in time for Christmas, my dear girl. So, here's to you and your new life in St Ives,' he said.

'New life?' said Merrin. 'That sounds daunting.'

'I'm absolutely certain you've done the right thing, Merrin. After such a terrible tragedy, in order to cope without Adam, you have to start a completely new sort of life. Trying to continue living the same life without Adam, I truly believe, just wouldn't have worked. I know it's a dramatic change, leaving your job and your home, but it's something you need to do to stand any chance of moving forward – though I expect at this very moment, you haven't a clue as to whether St Ives is where you want to be. Enough lecturing, apologies – tell me, how are you coping and how is Isla?'

'One has to cope; most people do eventually because

there's no alternative – the world over, nearest and dearest are being lost all the time,' said Merrin. There was a defiant edge to her voice and a very clear message to Max: *don't go there.*

What followed was a long, very awkward silence, during which they sipped their champagne. Surreptitiously, Max glanced at Merrin, who was frowning into her glass. She had always been slim, but now she was definitely thinner than Max ever remembered. Otherwise, she had changed very little through the years; her colouring was typically Cornish, dark hair, which she wore to her shoulders, and a bright, fresh complexion, pink cheeks and big blue eyes. She was not beautiful but now, even in her fifties, she was very pretty – a pleasure to look at. Finally, Max pulled himself together. 'Look, my girl, you and I have been friends all our lives. If you can't talk to me about Adam, then I doubt you can talk to anyone. Come on – spill.'

CHAPTER THREE

There was another long pause and Max was starting to think he had made a serious mistake in raising the subject of Adam, when Merrin suddenly started to speak.

'You must know how he died from the newspapers.'

Max nodded.

'He was stabbed, just once. Whoever was responsible must have known what they were doing; the knife went in between his ribs and straight into his heart. I think the doctor was telling me the truth when he said Adam would have known very little about it. Death was virtually instantaneous.'

She was trembling slightly. Max topped up her glass and threw another log on the fire. 'Surely, he should have been wearing some sort of protection – what are they called – body armour?'

Merrin rallied. 'Yes, of course he should have. And

more to the point, he shouldn't have been chasing after some villain in the first place, given his age and rank. That's what constables and sergeants are for – it was ridiculous. The trouble is, he was always the same: he had to muck in; he couldn't stand by and just give orders.'

'From what you have just said, I assume they haven't found the person responsible? I bet everyone is trying hard; the police look after their own, I believe?'

'No arrests as yet – apparently there was a scuffle between two criminal gangs and Adam ended up in the middle. I very much doubt they will find the perpetrator now; it's been too long. Anyway, I'm not sure it matters – losing Adam is the only issue so far as Isla and I are concerned. We don't, or maybe can't, look beyond that.'

'So,' said Max, 'are you ever going to answer my question: how are you coping?'

Merrin hesitated. 'In a practical sense, I'm doing OK. I've sold a house, bought a cottage, made the decision to move back to St Ives and given up my job. Having been a solicitor all these years, I had no problem sorting out all the associated paperwork; the police force have been good and granted me Adam's full pension, so financially I will be able to support Isla until she leaves Oxford and lead a modest but comfortable life down here.'

'So, what about emotionally?' Max asked gently.

'I loved him, he was my life, but strangely, it's not the big happenings in our life that I miss; it is the minutiae.' Merrin frowned in an effort to explain herself. 'Sharing a beautiful sunset, a goldfinch in the garden, Isla being

impossible but infinitely lovable all at the same time.'
She glanced fondly at the cage. 'Horatio's antics. The
list is endless, Max, but it is the interwoven fabric of
two people's lives together – just gone – which I find so
hard to take.'

'This, without doubt, is a completely stupid and
inappropriate thing for me to say.' Max hesitated. 'It
sounds crazy, but I envy you. I have never felt like that
about anyone. To have lost him is terrible, I can't even
imagine the pain, but to never have experienced that
sort of love – that's a tragedy, too.'

That silenced them both again but it was Merrin who
recovered first. 'This is dreadful; we need to cheer up
– fill our glasses and let's talk about something happy.
As soon as I have unpacked everything, my guests of
honour should be you and Bridget. Why don't we fix a
dinner date now and then I'll have a deadline to work
towards?'

'I'm afraid that's another drama,' said Max. 'Bridget
has gone.'

'Gone?' said Merrin. 'But she adored you!' She
studied Max for a moment or two. 'You cheated on her,
didn't you?'

'Well, yes,' said Max, having the grace to look
ashamed.

'You're a bloody idiot,' said Merrin. 'Bridget was a
keeper; she was just what you needed.'

'I am a bloody idiot, I can't deny it,' said Max.

Merrin smiled. 'How many times have we had this
exact conversation over the years?'

19

Max smiled back. 'I don't know but please don't try to count.'

'I couldn't possibly,' said Merrin. 'There are far too many.'

Suddenly, they were both laughing. Max raised his glass. 'To life,' he said, 'with all its twists and turns.'

'To life,' Merrin echoed.

CHAPTER FOUR

The following morning, as good as their word, the removal men arrived promptly at nine-thirty, and an hour later, they had gone. Selling, or giving away, most of the contents of Arcadia had been the hardest part of the move for Merrin. It had been necessary since she was moving into a space that, in its entirety, was about the same size as Arcadia's kitchen. Her new home was called Miranda's Cottage but it was not really a cottage. To reach it, you had to climb up a flight of outside stone steps, for the cottage was actually perched on top of a baker's shop – so it was, in reality, a flat. It consisted of a small kitchen/dining room, complete with log fire, a tiny sitting room and, upstairs, two small bedrooms and a bathroom. What had sold the property to her was that leading out of the larger of the two bedrooms, there was a balcony with stunning views of the harbour, and which enjoyed nearly day-round sunshine.

With the removal men gone, it was to the balcony that Merrin was drawn, a cup of coffee in hand. A garden table and four chairs had been unloaded from Arcadia, but she did not sit down. Instead she leant against the balcony rail, looking this way and that, to see what she could spy from her own personal crow's nest. Immediately below her was Fore Street, the main shopping street of St Ives, and although it was not yet eleven, crowds were out in force, presumably hunting for Christmas presents. Although there were one or two chain stores dotted around the town, it delighted Merrin to realise that every single shop, bar and bakery she could see from where she stood was privately owned. Directly in front of her was the harbour, the tide now way out, revealing a large expanse of golden sand, dotted with fishing boats. It was the particular colour of the sand, Merrin knew, which had attracted artists to the town over several hundred years. Not only was the sand itself amazing but it was the effect it had on the water which was so special. The sea flowing into the harbour, on a sunny day, was an extraordinary colour combination of deep blues and greens, translucent and sparkling – quite unlike anywhere else.

She could already imagine that this view from the balcony was going to be a serious time waster. 'Pull yourself together,' Merrin said out loud, 'there's work to be done.'

By lunchtime, the kitchen/dining room was unpacked and Horatio had been moved into his big cage, as a result of which, Merrin now sported a plaster on her

22

finger. Horatio did not normally bite his family and just this once, Merrin had found it in her heart to forgive him since moving house was known to be stressful for everyone – so why not for a parrot? She moved his cage into the window, which gave him much the same view as that from the balcony. 'There you are,' said Merrin to Horatio, 'this should be much more interesting for you than the view from Arcadia.' She was rewarded with an icy stare.

She was just contemplating the idea of going out to get something to eat when there was a knock on the door. Before she could even reach to answer it, the door was flung open. 'Pearl, my dear little Pearl, welcome home.' Merrin was swept into a huge hug.

'Clara, how lovely to see you. Do I smell pasties?' said Merrin.

'You do, my Pearl. Let me have a look at you.' Clara studied her friend. 'Thinner but we can soon put that right. One thing we Cornish are good at is providing the means to pile on the pounds, aren't we, my love?'

Clara and Merrin had met at nursery school and had been friends ever since – indeed inseparable friends until Merrin had left St Ives to go to university. Clara had always been tall for her age; Merrin had always been tiny, hence Merrin's nickname 'Pearl', because '*merrin*' is the Cornish word for 'sea pearl'. Although they had seen very little of one another in the intervening years, whenever they met, it was like they had never been apart, and Clara was Isla's godmother.

'I have plates and glasses and a bottle of white wine

in the fridge,' said Merrin triumphantly, delighted to see her friend.

'Perfect,' said Clara and then did a double-take. 'Who's this?' she asked, staring at Horatio.

Clara and her husband, Tristan, had never been to Bristol so had never met Horatio. Every summer, Adam, Merrin and Isla had come down to St Ives for a couple of weeks but Clara and Tristan were never free to leave town. As well as a fish restaurant, they also had two holiday lets to manage.

'This is Horatio. Normally, he behaves like a perfect gentleman when meeting new people but he is very upset and angry about the move and is going to sulk, I imagine, for some days.'

Clara went up to the cage. 'I don't normally like the idea of caged birds but he is rather splendid. Slightly odd name, though. Horatio is not very . . . well, not very Amazonian.'

Merrin laughed. 'Actually, his species originates from Central Africa, but I agree, Horatio is a very English name. I didn't much like the idea of caged birds either, although he will be let out to fly about once he is used to his new home. He was a rescue parrot; that's how he ended up with us.' She began laying out plates and glasses.

'What's the story?' Clara asked.

'Ages ago, while Isla was still little, in fact Adam was still a sergeant, he was called to a house where an old lady lived. The neighbours had rung in because they were worried they hadn't seen her for a couple of days. Adam had to break in and, unfortunately, the poor old dear was dead. Horatio was sitting in his cage in a corner of the room, looking very forlorn. The suggestion was that the parrot should be carted off to some rescue centre but Adam got it into his head that the parrot was very sad about his mistress's death and needed some TLC, at least until the relatives could be contacted.'

'Typical Adam,' said Clara.

'Yes, indeed,' Merrin agreed. 'Anyway, the relatives were contacted, and no one wanted the parrot. We learnt that his name was Horatio because the old lady came from Norfolk. In fact, she was born and brought up in the same small village as Lord Nelson – Burnham Thorpe – so obviously she thought she should name her companion after the great man.'

'Nice story,' said Clara. 'He's looking quite perky now.'

'That's only because he knows we're talking about him.'

They toured the cottage, not a lengthy process, but Clara clearly loved it, particularly the balcony. 'I can just see us out here on a summer's evening, watching the sun go down over a bottle of cava.' They then returned to the kitchen and gossiped over their pasties. They had met briefly when Merrin had come down to view the cottage but otherwise had not seen one another since Adam's death.

'Max was surprisingly helpful last night,' Merrin said.

'Did he tell you that he and Bridget have split up?'

Clara asked. Merrin nodded. 'Well, you watch it, my Pearl, he will be after you next.'

'He won't,' said Merrin firmly. 'We did all that nearly forty years ago and anyway, there is never going to be another man in my life, not after Adam; it's just not possible. Also, even if I was tempted, which I shan't be, Isla would go absolutely mad if I even looked at another man. She is cross enough about the move as it is.'

'So,' said Clara, 'tell me about my goddaughter and how she's doing.'

CHAPTER FIVE

'OK,' said Merrin, 'she's doing well at university; she's a clever girl, always has been.'

'That's my excellent influence, absolutely nothing whatever to do with her parentage,' said Clara, helping herself to another glass of wine.

'Naturally,' said Merrin. 'Actually, it's good to be able to talk to you about her. I'm worried; we seem to be drifting apart just at a time when we should be particularly close and supporting one another.'

'Why is that, do you think?' asked Clara.

'We used to be so close and share everything; we were each other's best friend really. But since Adam's death, there is a sort of distance, between us, as if we don't know what to say to one another. Also, she's furious about me moving down here. I can completely understand that. It was easy to pop home to Bristol from Oxford but it's too far to come down here just for a weekend. Also, Arcadia is the only home she has ever known so, of course, she didn't want us to leave it.'

'The fact that you are not as close as you were could be nothing to do with Adam – it could just be that she's growing up, a natural process, living away from home, making her own life. What made you decide to leave Bristol anyway?'

'I had become increasingly fed up with my job even before Adam died. The family court process almost exclusively deals with marriage and relationship break-ups. It is extremely stressful always dealing with other people's problems and so many of the parents drove me mad. They are so often consumed with the desire to score points off one another and to fight over the family assets; they do not even consider their children's feelings. The whole process has become so selfish and ugly and many solicitors advise the clients very badly, just adding fuel to the fire – to increase their fees, no doubt.'

'Oh, dear Pearl, it sounds awful. I'm surprised you stuck it so long.'

'I am too,' Merrin admitted. 'I suppose I just kept putting off making a decision. Then Adam was killed and I just knew I couldn't continue with the job without his support, nor could I bear the idea of living alone in that big old house, the home Adam and I had created. I have friends in Bristol, of course,' she smiled fondly, 'but not like you, obviously – much more sensible and therefore a little dull, by comparison. Anyway, as a result of the move, Isla is threatening not to come home to St Ives for Christmas, which is awful. Our first

Christmas without Adam; I just can't bear it.'

'She'll come, I promise, she's just flexing her muscles in protest. So, tell me, if you're not going back to being a solicitor, what are you going to do? You're not the sort to sit around.'

'I don't know,' said Merrin.

'Well, Tristan and I are really up against it at the moment. Costs keep rising and our profit margins keep shrinking. We have laid off our chef in the restaurant; Tristan does it now and I do front of house, with one extra waitress to help out at busy times. Tristan just manages with a kitchen porter to help him. Then there are our two letting cottages and to crown it all, our changeover cleaner, Jenny, has left us with absolutely no notice. She left this morning, the weekend's coming up and then we are into the Christmas rush. Honestly, we're going mental.'

'Is there anything I can do to help?' Merrin asked, falling neatly into the trap.

Clara regarded her thoughtfully for a moment. 'You could do the changeovers; that would be an absolutely marvellous help – except, as I recall, my dear Pearl, you're not very domesticated, are you?'

'I could learn,' said Merrin valiantly. 'What's involved, exactly?'

'We have two cottages; the changeover is on Friday for one, that's Rupert's Cottage, and on Saturday for the other, which is Elsie's Cottage.'

Merrin smiled. 'Named after your parents, that's lovely, Clara.'

'When Mum died, she left me enough money to buy outright both cottages. Since then, sadly, we've had to mortgage them both but we still make money from the holiday lets, though obviously not as much. I know it's supposed to be bad luck to change the name of a house but I see them as a sort of memorial to my parents, who were so great.'

'They certainly were, like second parents to me,' agreed Merrin. 'I think it's a lovely idea. Now tell me what's involved in this cleaning lark?'

'It's just a question of cleaning up after the last visitors and making up the beds and putting out clean towels. It's all pretty obvious, really, and I can show you what to do. We'd pay you too.'

'OK,' said Merrin, much to her own surprise and to Clara's. 'I'll give it a go as long as you promise to sack me if I'm no good, or allow me to leave if I hate it.'

'A deal,' said Clara. 'I am very grateful, if a little bemused.'

'Me too,' said Merrin. 'I mean I'm bemused, definitely not grateful. My good nature has been taken hideous advantage of, obviously.'

CHAPTER SIX

Tristan and Clara were quick to demonstrate their gratitude by helping Merrin settle in. Tristan arrived with screws and a drill. The walls of the cottage were all made of granite, at least two foot thick, so picture hooks were out of the question. He put up all Merrin's pictures, which immediately made the cottage feel more like home. He also strategically fixed the wine rack to a piece of wall that both Merrin and Horatio thought would be a suitable location for his morning perch. In fact, Horatio took to Tristan in a big way. He had been Adam's parrot, always preferring men to women, and he clearly approved of Tristan. 'See,' said Merrin to Horatio, 'you're going to love it here; you're already making friends.'

On Friday morning, feeling surprisingly nervous, Merrin presented herself at the front door of Rupert's cottage, which, like her own, was really a flat with outside steps leading to the first floor, and was just round the corner. She had weaved her way through the crowds on Fore Street, turned right into the Digey and then veered off left into Virgin Street. Immediately, the years rolled away because further up the street on the opposite side from Rupert's was the home in which she and Jago had grown up. It had been a fisherman's cottage but her family had occupied all three floors so there was plenty of room for the four of them, and the beach was their garden. While at school in St Ives, she had never been teased about living in Virgin Street, which was named after St Ia, the patron saint of St Ives. It was just a street like many others in St Ives, which sported some truly eccentric sounding names – like Teetotal Street, Salubrious Place and Court Cocking.

Actually, Merrin would always be deeply grateful for the somewhat unusual name of her street. In her first term at university, she was in the student bar having a drink with her roommate. A particularly odious boy, named Martin Thomas, had been in her year at school and had also been granted a place at Bristol University. So far, she had managed to avoid him until that night. He was drinking with a rowdy group when he suddenly spotted her across the bar. 'Look,' he shouted, 'there's Merrin, she lives in St Ives, near me. In fact, she lives in Virgin Street. Are you still a virgin, Merrin?'

'And are you still a plonker, Martin?' Merrin shouted back.

There was general laughter, clearly aimed at Martin. A young man detached himself from the bar and came over to Merrin. 'It would give me enormous pleasure to give the plonker in question a good hiding, if you would like me to.'

'Thank you, but no need, he's not worth it,' said Merrin.

'Then let me at least buy you a drink to congratulate you on dealing so brilliantly with such an idiot. My name's Adam McKenzie, by the way.'

This was the reason why Merrin would always think on the address of her childhood home with the greatest fondness.

Clara was waiting for her with a big bundle of bedding and some cleaning materials. Merrin immediately felt daunted.

Clara clearly picked up on her friend's apprehension. 'So, when did you last clean your house and change the sheets on the bed?' she asked, not unkindly.

'It's not really what I do,' said Merrin, 'or rather, did,' she corrected herself. 'Both Adam and I worked very long hours so we had this wonderful mother's help, called Betty. She was in charge of all that, fetched Isla from school and looked after her in the holidays. However, since Isla went to university, Betty has been working only three mornings a week, so I have been doing quite a lot more domestic stuff,' she added, a little defensively.

'It sounds like it's Betty I really need,' said Clara. 'Still, a steep learning curve is what we're facing and I am sure you will be up to the task.'

'Of course I will,' said Merrin crossly, to cover up her mounting panic.

Clara unlocked the front door and let them in. It was a cheerful cottage, full of colourful pictures, rugs and curtains and painted white throughout, which made it feel bright and airy. However, in the hallway, the floor was covered in sand and through the open door into the downstairs bathroom, Merrin could see a huge pile of towels left on the floor.

'What's with all this sand in December?' she asked, turning to Clara.

Clara sighed. 'It goes with the territory. People who don't live by the sea rush to the beach regardless of the weather – you must remember that. Children make sandcastles all year round and this is the result. Listen, before we start, I have something to tell you, Pearl. Isla called me last night to see how you were.'

'I don't believe you,' said Merrin. 'I bet you called her.'

'OK, I admit I was going to, but she beat me to it. Honestly, she called me.'

'Is everything alright?'

'Yes,' said Clara. 'She's absolutely fine but worried about you, oh, and Horatio as well. I told her all about the cottage and I was very enthusiastic, which was not difficult – Miranda's Cottage is lovely. I told her that Tristan had put up all her favourite pictures in her bedroom, being careful not to call it the spare room. I also said Horatio was fine, loving Tristan and his new view of Fore Street. I did say you were missing her very much and I said we were all looking forward to seeing her at Christmas, as if it was a done deal. She didn't disagree, which has to be a good sign. Then, I slightly blew it.'

'You were doing so well, Clara, how could you possibly have messed it up?'

'I told her you were helping me by doing the changeover cleaning in the cottages.'

'So what?' Merrin asked.

'She went ballistic; she said you must have gone mad to go from being a solicitor to becoming a cleaner. Unfortunately, that annoyed me; there is nothing wrong with being a cleaner. I told her that in Japan, everyone's job is equally respected. A good road sweeper is valued as highly as a good CEO of a huge public company, and valued much higher than a bad CEO, and that's exactly how things should be in this country. I told her she needed to get over herself and not be such a snob and just because she is an Oxford University undergraduate, it doesn't give her the right to look down on cleaners.'

'Blimey!' said Merrin. 'How did that go down?'

'Well, being your girl, she put up a good defence. She argued that she wasn't being derogatory about cleaners, just about you being one. I have to say, she was not very polite about your domestic skills and she said I would be regretting my decision to employ you within the week.'

'She could be right,' said Merrin.

'So, let's prove her wrong,' said Clara, with more confidence than she felt. 'You start brushing up all this sand and I'll get the towels in the washing machine.'

The two women worked fast and furiously for two hours. It was a messy changeover. It took three washing machine loads just to clean the towels. 'Why did four people need thirteen towels?' Clara grumbled. Everywhere was covered in sand – on the sofa, the chairs and even the children's beds. There was washing-up in the sink, the oven needed cleaning and the fridge was full of out-of-date food.

'It's not usually this bad,' said Clara. 'Look, I'm sorry but I am going to have to leave you to it now. The restaurant is just opening and I can't leave Tristan on his own.' She handed Merrin two sets of keys and became suddenly very business-like. 'I've checked that there are keys in the key safe for the guests, so these keys are yours, for Rupert's today and for Elsie's tomorrow. I won't be able to join you tomorrow. As it's Saturday, it will be very busy in the restaurant and so I have to prep for Tristan. Anyway, you know what to do now. Tomorrow, Elsie's sleeps four but only one couple have been staying there this last week so you may only have to change one bed. Clean sheets are in the airing cupboard. Today, all that's left to do here is the oven to clean, clear out the fridge and put away the last lot of towels that are in the dryer. Oh, and there's the bathroom. I've done the floor but not the loo, shower and basin. You must be out of here before three. Good luck.'

After Clara had left, Merrin felt overcome with weariness. Then, concentrating on the very unappealing thought that her daughter believed she would be hopeless at the job, she set to. The oven took over an hour to clean; it took her a while to work out that she had to turn the dryer to 'off' before being able to open the door; the contents of the fridge filled a whole dustbin liner, which then burst all over the kitchen floor, and, in Merrin's eyes, the bathroom looked slightly worse than it had done before she started cleaning it.

By three o'clock, Merrin was done. On her return home, Horatio was subjected to a tirade on the horrors of changeovers. She opened a can of soup, lit the fire and collapsed in front of it with her mug and a piece of slightly stale bread. Remembering Clara's story about Japan, in Merrin's view, cleaners should be paid at least double the earnings of the world's most efficient CEO. Suddenly, being a family solicitor seemed positively attractive.

CHAPTER SEVEN

Merrin was woken the next morning by a text message. Clara informed her that she'd forgotten to mention the guests staying at Elsie's Cottage had booked to leave the previous morning, rather than stay the full week. Merrin, therefore, could start cleaning as early as she liked. 'Oh great,' muttered Merrin. She lay in bed for a few minutes and then realised the sooner she attacked the cleaning, the sooner it would be over.

She found the cottage easily enough in one of the streets leading down to Porthgwidden Beach. *It's bound to be full of sand, being so close to the beach*, she thought, but to her delight, when she opened the front door, the cottage looked immaculate. She checked the ground floor to find practically nothing needing doing, other than a quick wash of the kitchen floor and a bit of dusting. She chose some bedding from the airing cupboard and was about to go upstairs when her phone rang. She looked at the phone – it was Isla.

'Darling, how lovely to hear from you. How are you?'

'I'm fine, thanks, Mum. I spoke to Clara yesterday and she says you are fine too, but I didn't believe her. What's all this about you cleaning her cottages? You're not having a breakdown or something, are you?'

'I nearly did yesterday,' Merrin admitted. 'The guests had left the place in an awful mess but today's guests are absolute saints; there is practically nothing to do.'

'Mum, you're not making me feel any better. You hate cleaning and you're very, very bad at it. This can't be a job you're enjoying. Tell me you're just suffering from a temporary blip in your sanity and in a moment you will return to your normal self.'

'Thanks for the vote of confidence, darling,' said Merrin, without rancour. 'I am just helping out Clara and Tristan in the run-up to Christmas. Their cleaner left suddenly, giving no notice and the poor things are rushed off their feet. As soon as they find someone permanent to do the changeovers, I'm out, and I will admit to you, and to you alone, I can't wait.'

Isla laughed. 'That sounds more like you.' There was a pause. 'Mum, I am sorry for being so angry about your move. It's just that I didn't, still don't, understand it. Bristol has so much to offer – you had

39

a great career, plenty of friends, a lovely home and you were close to your only child's university.' There was a slight catch in her voice.

'I'm sorry, too, for hurting you, Isla, which is the last thing I would ever want to do. I just couldn't stay on in the house, with Dad gone and you at university. And, if I couldn't stay in the house, I felt I couldn't stay in Bristol. It would have been awful to live in the city but not in Arcadia. St Ives just seemed the right place to go; though, of course, I realise now I should have talked much more to you about the idea before making the decision to move. It feels odd being here, like I'm on holiday, but I think I have done the right thing. I am very tired all the time, at the moment, as I don't sleep well but that's no excuse for not consulting you properly about the whole idea – Arcadia was your home, too.'

'I miss him so much, Mum,' said Isla.

'Me too, darling. When you come down, can we have a proper talk about Dad? I'm frightened to ask but are you coming down for Christmas? Only it being our first Christmas without him, it feels like we should be together.'

'Yes, of course I'll be down. I was only lashing out. I can be with you the week after next, on Monday, 19th, I thought. Would that suit?'

'It's your home, Isla, come whenever you like, the sooner the better. Monday the 19th will be wonderful. I can't wait.'

Merrin pocketed her mobile and felt as if an

enormous weight had been lifted off her shoulders. She had lost her husband and, for a while, it had seemed as if she might lose her daughter, too. Now, she felt more positive than she had done in some months. She had Isla back and this changeover was not going to take long. She would go back to Miranda's Cottage and unpack some more boxes. The place had to look perfect for Isla's arrival.

She picked up the bedding and headed up the stairs. The bedroom on the left contained a double bed, which had obviously been slept in. Suddenly full of energy, she stripped the bed and remade it in double-quick time. The carpet needed vacuuming, plus a quick dust, and then the room would be done.

Hoping that the other bedroom had not been used, as Clara had suspected, she crossed the landing and opened the door. The room was in semi-darkness as the curtains were drawn.

It was a twin-bedded room. The first bed was perfectly made up. Merrin walked into the room and pulled back the curtains. She turned to look at the second bed and gasped. There was someone in it. She moved closer; it was a young man, not much more than a boy, lying on his back. He was neatly tucked into the bed, so neatly that the duvet was completely uncreased. It looked almost as if he had been laid out after death. Images flashed unbidden into her mind of the moment she had identified Adam's body. Adam had looked just like this, so perfect, only very cold. She had longed to take him in her arms to warm him and bring him back to life.

She shook her head to clear the image and moved to the bedside. He was a very good-looking boy but he was too pale and his lips very slightly blue. Carefully, she leant forward and put two fingers to his neck, just below his ear. His skin was icy to the touch and there was no pulse. He was quite dead.

CHAPTER EIGHT

Merrin was sitting on a chair by the bed when the doorbell rang. After the initial shock, she had dialled 999 to be told that a local member of the police force would be with her very shortly. She had made the call out on the landing but instead of going downstairs to wait for the police, she had returned to the bedroom, pulled up a chair and sat down beside the poor, dead boy. Somehow, it didn't feel right to leave him all alone. She knew it was odd but she just felt she should be keeping him company.

Her mind kept shifting back to Adam. *How quickly the world can change,* she thought, *and become an alien and frightening place.* In the days immediately after Adam's death, she felt she no longer belonged anywhere, that nothing was familiar any more. She could feel herself slipping back into that dark place again, now. Five minutes ago, she had been happily planning to make a home for her daughter, and now . . .

The doorbell chimed again and pulled her into reality. With one last look at the boy, she stood up and hurried down the stairs. A rather bedraggled figure greeted her; it was pouring with rain. 'Come in – you're getting soaked,' said Merrin.

'Just for a moment, thank you, but I'll have to go back to my car. I left my warrant card in my jacket when I put on my waterproof. You're Mrs McKenzie?'

Merrin nodded.

'I'm Sergeant Eddy. I was here in town when we got your call. My inspector will be along directly; he's in Truro at the moment.' He paused for breath. 'Have you really got a dead body here? Only you seem very calm, Mrs McKenzie, and we don't have much call for dead bodies in St Ives.'

In different circumstances, Merrin would have been amused. 'I know St Ives is pretty crime-free, compared with most places,' she said patiently, 'but I can assure you that there is a dead body upstairs.'

The sergeant seemed in no hurry to examine the body. 'Are you local, then?' he asked.

'I was once, and hope to be so again,' Merrin replied.

The sergeant stared at her, frowning. Suddenly, his expression cleared. 'You're not Mrs McKenzie at all, you're little Merrin Tripconey, old Harry Trip's maid. I used to go out with your dad when I was a boy, when he ran his boat out of Hayle. I used to help him bring in the crabs, lobsters, too, sometimes. Damned heavy, those pots, did my back in good and proper, never been right since. Well, I never, little Merrin Tripconey has come home. I used to play footie with your brother, Jago; I was the year above him at school. Whatever happened to Jago? I think he went to foreign parts, didn't he?'

It was Merrin's turn to stare into the face of the sergeant and try to peel back the years. He looked a lot older than her brother, he had lost most of his hair and he was rather overweight for a policeman. But looking into his face, she could suddenly see the young lad who had helped her father – thin as a rake then, with a shock of dark hair and always cheerful, cheeky too, particularly with the girls. 'Jack,' she said, 'yes of course, Jack Eddy, I remember you, too.'

'As this is official business, we ought to shake hands,' said Jack, 'but as you're little Merrin Tripconey, I'm going to give you a hug.' They embraced a little awkwardly.

'Now I'd better go and fetch my warrant card,' said Jack. 'I need to be here when the inspector arrives, or there will be hell to pay.'

Merrin smiled. 'Honestly, Jack, I really don't think we need to bother with your warrant card, do you? We've known each other most of our lives and it's chucking it down out there.'

'Right-oh,' said Jack, 'you'd better show me this body, then, little Merrin.'

As she led the way up the stairs, Jack puffing and wheezing behind her, Merrin was struck with the bizarre notion that maybe there wasn't a body at all, that she'd imagined it, which was why, as Jack had suggested, she was so calm. When they entered the bedroom, it was almost a relief to see the body was still there.

Jack stood at the end of the bed and stared down at the boy. 'Poor young lad,' he said at last. 'He must have killed himself; there's a lot of it about among this age group, I'm told. How old would you reckon he is?'

'I would say eighteen at the very most, but he couldn't have killed himself, Jack.'

'Why ever not, Merrin Trip? There is no sign of violence on him.'

'That's the whole point,' said Merrin, 'there is no sign of anything. Look how neatly he's tucked up in bed. He couldn't have done that himself and there are no pills or anything else that could have contributed to his death. It's almost as if he has been laid out, like for a funeral. Someone has been very careful with him, almost tender.'

'You're making a lot of assumptions there,' said Jack, a little huffily.

Merrin was aware she had ruffled his feathers but that didn't stop her from speaking her mind. After all her years with Adam, it seemed to her that Jack was the victim of some pretty sloppy thinking for a policeman. 'I think he has been killed, or at any rate, died somewhere else and then the body has been placed here by someone who cares. It's very odd.'

'I wonder why that chair has been placed by the bed,' said Jack.

'I did that,' said Merrin. 'I moved the chair from under the window so that I could sit with him until you arrived.'

Jack gave her an odd look. 'You shouldn't have done that, my maid. You're not supposed to touch anything at a crime scene, if it is a crime scene. You must know that from the telly.' Jack was clearly trying to re-assert his position.

'I'm sorry,' said Merrin, as tactfully as she could. 'I felt his pulse too, just to make absolutely sure that he was dead.'

'You should have waited for us to do that, too,' said Jack, his good humour now restored since it appeared that Merrin was in the wrong.

'How could I wait for you to arrive? I had to make sure he was dead. Supposing he'd been still alive, could have been saved and I'd done nothing? He could have died while I was waiting for you to arrive.'

Merrin was now visibly upset and Jack rallied, putting an arm round her shoulders. 'What we're going to do now is to go downstairs and make a nice cup of tea while we wait for the inspector. You're all shook up; we can't have that, poor little Merrin.'

Merrin had brought some milk and tea bags with her to the cottage and Jack insisted on making the tea, clucking over her like a mother hen. Once seated at the kitchen table with their mugs of tea, Jack started reminiscing.

'I think I saved your life, once upon a time, little Merrin Trip.'

'Did you?' said Merrin, frowning. 'I don't remember that, Jack.'

'It was one afternoon, us kids were all pier jumping – off Smeaton's Pier that day. You were a tiny bit of a girl, too small really to be jumping with us lads, but Jago was there so I expect you didn't want to be left out.'

'So, what happened?' Merrin asked.

'I was watching you. It was quite a high jump from the top of the pier. Some of the younger kids used to jump off the steps, but not you, little Merrin. Straight in you went but when you came back up to the surface, you were right beside a seal. Well, as you know, they don't do you no harm but they are big buggers up close, even if you're a grown up. You were such a tiny little maid, and not surprisingly you were frightened half to death. You panicked and went under water again and when you came up you were choking. So I dived in after you and pulled you out. Jago was jumping the other side of the pier but when he heard what had happened, he was so worried. Anyway you were alright and look at you now.'

'I do remember it now, it's a bit hazy, but I can still see that gigantic seal. I thought it was going to eat me!' said Merrin. 'I think I must have blanked out the whole incident but I never did enjoy pier jumping – I expect that's why. It was bodyboarding for me, that's what I liked best. Anyway, thank you, Jack, a little belatedly, I clearly owe you one.'

'I loved pier jumping,' said Jack, 'all us lads did and

in the summer the visitors' kids used to join in. Happy days.'

'Not so happy today, though,' said Merrin, soberly. They both went silent, thinking of the poor dead boy upstairs, who probably would have loved pier jumping, too.

CHAPTER NINE

Inspector Louis Peppiatt was livid. The traffic was terrible, there was a dead body in St Ives and his sergeant wasn't answering his phone. To top it all, he had been forced to sit in his car in a layby off the A30 for at least fifteen minutes, arguing fruitlessly, as it turned out, with his ex-wife, Stephanie.

He and Stephanie had been separated for over six years ago and had been divorced for four. It was obviously sensible that Stephanie should have custody of their two children – Daisy now aged thirteen and Edward aged nine. It would have been impossible, in his line of work, for Louis to have operated successfully as single parent – they both recognised this, and it had never been an issue between them. Stephanie still lived in the marital home in Falmouth, so the children's school and social life had not been affected by the marriage break-up. Louis now lived in a tiny Victorian terraced house on the outskirts of Truro, which was actually very convenient and just large enough for the children to come and stay.

In the early years of their separation, there had been a satisfactory degree of harmony regarding Louis's access to his children. Now and again, a crisis had arisen at work that meant he had to cancel or change arrangements, but Stephanie was well used to that, having been a policeman's wife. Everything changed two years ago, when Stephanie met Andrew, who owned a building firm in Falmouth. Swiftly, much too swiftly in Louis's view, Andrew moved in with Stephanie and the children and that's when the trouble started – the children suddenly appeared to have prior engagements on the day they were supposed to spend with their father and over time Louis began seeing them less and less. Now Andrew had arrived, it seemed as if they were a complete family unit again and Louis was no longer needed.

The last two Christmases the children had spent in Falmouth with Stephanie and Andrew. This year, however, Louis had negotiated to have Christmas off work and the children were going to spend it with him. That is, until today. Stephanie's name had appeared on his mobile, so he had pulled into the layby to hear that the children had decided they would rather spend Christmas in Falmouth so they could see their friends.

'But I've taken the time off, it's all arranged and now you're wanting to cancel everything less than three weeks before Christmas? It's not right; you've had them for Christmas two years running,' Louis had argued, trying to keep control of his exasperation.

'Surely, at Christmas, of all times, the children's wishes should take priority?' replied Stephanie coolly.

'Steph, we've always decided when the children should come to me. Of course, when they're older, then they will decide where they want to spend their time, but Edward is only nine. We should still be making the decisions.'

'Exactly,' said Stephanie, 'and given that the children want to spend Christmas in Falmouth, I have made the decision that they should do so. You can have them for the New Year.'

'I am working over New Year,' said Louis, not quite believing what he was hearing.

'That's not my fault,' said Stephanie.

'Of course it's your fault; it's you who's changing the plans with almost no notice.'

And so, it raged on. Louis accused Andrew of being behind it all, Stephanie accused Louis of being jealous and paranoid, the call became increasingly nasty, which had never been their style in the past.

'I'll ring Daisy tonight and see what she really wants to do,' Louis said, finally.

'So long as you don't shout and upset her,' said Stephanie.

'I never shout,' shouted Louis.

It had taken him several minutes to calm down before it felt safe to rejoin the A30 and by the time he finally dropped down into St Ives, Louis had reluctantly accepted the situation. He was just very sad – sad, yes, because he would now not be seeing his children over Christmas, but also because of his deteriorating relationship with their mother.

Ironically, as it turned out, Louis and Stephanie had first met at the scene of a very nasty domestic punch-up. Louis, still a constable in those days, was trying to stop the warring parties from killing each other, and Stephanie, as the social worker involved, was trying to remove the children from the mayhem. When a degree of peace was restored, with both parents in the cells and the children safely in foster care, Louis had suggested to Stephanie that they both deserved a drink and that maybe they should drink it together.

It was a true love match and despite the fact that being a policeman's wife is renowned as a difficult role, they remained deliriously happy – that is until Daisy was born, when cracks began to appear in the marriage. Daisy was very premature; Louis was not at the birth, nor very supportive in the weeks that followed, while Daisy fought for her life. This was not callousness on Louis's part; his boss, at that time, was not a pleasant man and being childless made him less than sympathetic to Louis's requests to spend more time with his wife and daughter.

Their relationship never really recovered its former glory. Stephanie's parents died within a few months of one another and, as an only child, she inherited a substantial property in Exeter and a big wad of cash. Even after paying off their mortgage, it was obvious that, from a financial point of view, Stephanie did not need to return to work. She gave up her job, the birth of Edward followed, and she threw herself wholeheartedly into being a parent. Her resentment towards Louis's job grew alongside his promotion. By the time he became an inspector, Louis had started to delay hurrying home in order to avoid another barrage of recriminations from Stephanie.

Yet once they had recognised that the marriage had become unworkable and they started living apart, a strange new friendship had grown. And occasionally, when their eyes met, perhaps in amusement at a remark from one of their children, or the reminder of a particularly happy memory, the ghost of their love still hovered about.

All that had changed with the arrival of Andrew. He was not a bad man; he clearly loved Stephanie and was kind and attentive to the children. But it changed the dynamics – they were now a family and Louis was the outsider.

CHAPTER TEN

While Merrin and Jack Eddy waited for Inspector Peppiatt to arrive, it suddenly occurred to Merrin that she should ring Clara and tell her what had happened. Clearly, alternative accommodation would have to be found for the incoming guests. Merrin looked at her watch – it was almost midday and the guests were allowed into the cottage any time after 3 p.m.

The restaurant was full and there was a queue outside. At first, Clara refused to come to the phone but eventually Merrin managed to convey to the young girl who had answered it that there really was an emergency.

'What is it, Pearl?' said Clara irritably. 'We're going mad here; surely you can sort out the problem, whatever it is?'

'I found a dead body at Elsie's this morning,' said Merrin.

'Very funny. Look, I haven't time for this. What do you want?'

'I really did find a dead body, Clara. Jack Eddy is here but the main reason I'm calling is because there is no way anyone can stay here for several days, I imagine. It's a crime scene; at least it may be. You need to get hold of the guests who are booked in and try and find them a hotel room for a few nights.'

'You're actually being serious? Who is it? Do we know what happened?'

'We don't know anything yet. It's a very young man, there's no sign of trauma and there's also no obvious sign as to the cause of death. He doesn't seem to have been living at the cottage; there's no luggage, in fact no possessions of any sort so far as we can see. We are waiting for the inspector, the police doctor and forensics to arrive.'

'How awful,' said Clara. 'I don't want to sound callous but this couldn't have happened at a worse moment. I'll look up the booking, contact the guests and try and find them a room somewhere, which is not going to be easy so near to Christmas. I'll let you know what I've arranged and please keep me in the loop so far as the police are concerned. I'm glad you have an inspector coming. Jack is an absolutely darling, but not blessed with many little grey cells, is he?'

Luckily, Merrin had moved into the sitting room to make the call. 'No,' she agreed, 'but I'm so very glad he's here.'

'Poor darling Pearl, what a shock. Are you alright?

I'm so sorry, I should have thought about you first. Look, I must go, take care, love you.'

The police doctor had arrived while Merrin was on the phone to Clara. Jack took him straight upstairs and, from her seat in the kitchen, she could hear them talking but could not make out what they were saying. She boiled the kettle once more in case the doctor wanted a hot drink, and then sat down and waited. She shivered; the room was not particularly cold but she supposed shock was starting to set in. The whole situation seemed unreal.

Eventually, the two men came downstairs and Jack Eddy introduced the doctor as Dr Graham Bennett, a bad-tempered-looking man, in his middle years, with an unruly shock of ginger hair.

'Would you like a tea or coffee?' Merrin asked.

'No, I need to go home and change before starting work. It's going to be a long day since our revered inspector is bound to want the postmortem results in double-quick time. Why do these things always happen at a weekend?' He gave Merrin an accusing look, as if it was her fault. 'Did you move the body at all? I assume it is you who found him?'

'Yes, it was me,' said Merrin, 'but no, I didn't move the body but I did feel for a pulse to make absolutely sure he was dead.'

'I would have thought it was obvious he was dead.'

'Not to me,' said Merrin, who'd had enough of this doctor already. 'I think I behaved sensibly. Obviously, I had no idea how long he'd been here and I wanted to be absolutely sure he was not still alive and perhaps could have been saved.'

Dr Bennett was unrepentant. 'And so having given him a medical examination, you then tucked him up in bed, I assume?'

'No, I did not,' said Merrin. 'I checked for a pulse but otherwise he is just as I found him. I agree it's odd. Someone must have put him in that bed; he couldn't have tucked up himself like that.'

'Thank heavens we have such an expert in our midst,' Dr Bennett said nastily. Mercifully, before Merrin could formulate a reply, there was a ring at the door. 'I'll go; it will be our inspector. I'll speak to him on the way out.'

Jack pulled a face at Merrin as the doctor left the room. 'He's not always that rude, it's just he likes his golf at the weekend.'

From the hallway, they heard Bennett say, 'Hello, Louis. The body's upstairs. He's had a blow to the back of the head but not enough to kill him, though he was probably unconscious for a few moments. I've left the body where it is so you can study the whole scene, which is slightly strange. I also replaced the bedclothes more or less as they were, because they could be important. My lads will be along to collect him in about fifteen minutes. I should have some results for you by this evening; who needs weekends anyway, when work is such fun.'

'Thanks, Graham.' Inspector Peppiatt entered the kitchen and nodded at Jack.

'This is little Merrin Tripconey; she is the lady who found the body,' Jack explained.

'I thought the body was found by a Mrs McKenzie,' said Louis, frowning.

'That's my married name,' said Merrin. 'Jack and I have known each other since we were children and he hasn't quite got used to the idea I am no longer Merrin Tripconey.'

'Come, Eddy, let's take a look at this body,' said Louis. Then he paused at the doorway and smiled back at Merrin. 'It's hard to believe Jack was ever a child,' he said.

CHAPTER ELEVEN

The two men were back downstairs surprisingly quickly. 'I need to ask you a few questions,' Louis said to Merrin.

'Would you like a coffee?' she asked.

'Thank you, that's very kind. I'd love one, black, no sugar.'

A welcome change from Dr Bennett, Merrin thought.

'Sergeant Eddy tells me that you didn't touch anything except for feeling the young man's pulse to make sure there was no chance of saving him. Is that right?'

Merrin nodded.

'Although I also understand that you did move a chair to sit by his bedside.'

'Yes, I did,' said Merrin.

'Wasn't that a rather strange thing to do, Mrs McKenzie? I understand you don't know this poor young man and you'd established he was dead. Why did you want to sit with him?'

Merrin thought for a moment. 'As I told Jack, I just didn't feel he should be left on his own. I can't explain why; it just felt right to sit with him.'

'So, if you felt the need to comfort him, did you also straighten the bedcovers and effectively tuck him up? That would seem a natural extension to keeping him company.'

'No, Inspector, I did not. As I have repeatedly said, the only contact I had was to feel his neck for a pulse. The bed is exactly as it was when I found him. I can only tell you what I told Jack and the doctor: someone must have put him in that bed, but it certainly wasn't me.'

It seemed to Merrin that Inspector Peppiatt still looked somewhat sceptical. 'And have you found anything around the house that could have belonged to the deceased, anything that might help us to identify him?'

'I don't know,' said Merrin helplessly.

'What do you mean, Mrs McKenzie?'

'I mean that today is the first time I have ever set foot inside this cottage. How could I possibly know who owns what?'

'My apologies,' said Louis, 'I assumed this was your home. If it isn't, what are you doing here?'

'I'm helping a friend. The person who normally does her changeover cleaning has let her down. This cottage is a holiday let and I came here today to prepare it for the arrival of today's guests.'

'Good Lord, what time are the guests arriving?' Louis said, looking at his watch.

'It's alright,' said Merrin. 'I've spoken to the owner, Clara Tregonning, and told her what has happened. She is contacting the guests and arranging hotel accommodation for them.'

'Then I need to speak to Clara Tregonning urgently to establish the identity of everyone who has stayed at this cottage recently. Can you give me her contact details, please?'

It took a while for Merrin to explain to Inspector Peppiatt that Clara could not talk to him immediately because she was working flat-out in her restaurant. It took a while for Inspector Peppiatt to explain to Merrin that he had to talk to Clara right away, even if it meant her having to close the restaurant. It took a while for Inspector Peppiatt and Clara to persuade Merrin that she should take over the role of waitress to free up Clara and still keep the restaurant open.

These various conversations resulted in Merrin finding herself standing in the middle of a crowded restaurant, wearing a navy-blue sweatshirt emblazoned with the words *Tristan's Fish Plaice*. Clara was once again in organisation mode. 'These are your tables, numbers one to twelve; those are Alice's tables, thirteen to twenty-seven. Here is your order pad – one copy goes to Tristan in the kitchen, one goes on the clipboard under the appropriate numbered table for billing, one goes to the bar and the fourth copy stays in your pad. Got it? Here's Alice; Alice, this is Merrin, show her what to do, I'll be as quick as I can. Oh, and, Pearl, don't be rude to customers, even if they're rude to you. Count to ten, think beautiful thoughts, think of angels.' And she was gone.

Over the next hour, Merrin was in a whirl of confusion as she tried to cope. Alice was kind but a little condescending and looked about twelve, which didn't do much for Merrin's dwindling self-confidence. She made mistakes. However, she found that by telling customers she was very sorry but was helping out her friend and learning on the job, most people were very understanding. That is, until the customers from hell arrived in the form of mother, father and two teenaged sons.

Merrin forgot to bring the boys' extra chips to the table. She apologised but it wasn't enough for the ill-mannered father. 'We've been waiting in the rain for nearly half an hour to eat in this overpriced, inefficient, so-called fish restaurant. Bring my sons' chips now, I'll have another beer, and I don't expect to find those chips on my bill.'

'I'll bring your sons' chips now, they will go on the bill and I'll bring your beer when I have served the next two tables who are waiting,' said Merrin, who was perilously close to losing her temper completely.

'I'm not putting up with this,' thundered the father. 'I want to speak to the manager now.'

Merrin tried counting to ten, gave beautiful thoughts a fleeting try, then turned on her heel muttering 'angels' under her breath and bumped straight into Inspector Peppiatt, who looked somewhat out of place in his dark suit and tie.

'Angels?' he said, smiling. 'What on earth is that all about, Mrs McKenzie?'

'The customers behind me are being impossible,' she whispered, 'and Clara told me to think of angels if I was tempted to answer back. I must not be rude to customers, Inspector, but sometimes it is not at all easy.'

'Hey, you!'

Merrin turned back to the table; it was the irate father again.

'Yes, you, I said find the manager now and I mean now!'

'Leave this to me,' said Louis. He walked over to the table and produced his warrant card. 'I'm sorry you're not happy with the service, sir, but you are causing a disturbance. I suggest you either allow the waitress to do her job, or else leave now and there will be no charge for your meal.' He turned on his heel and winked at Merrin as he passed. 'Come on,' he said, 'your ordeal is over; Mrs Tregonning is back. I'll wait outside for you; I've just a couple more questions.'

Merrin handed over her tables to Clara and was amused to see that the 'table from hell' had quietened down and the occupants were now eating their meal without complaint. It was with huge relief to slip out of the front door. The rain had stopped, and Inspector Peppiatt was waiting for her.

'I'm definitely not waitress material,' she announced.

'I don't think that's anything to fret about. Where do you live? I'll walk you home while we talk. I imagine you must be exhausted.'

'I live just along the Wharf and up Bunker's Hill. Thank you for saving me from my customers and, I suppose, saving them from me.'

'A pleasure, it was largely my fault you were put through that ordeal,' said Louis. 'I've just one question really. Can you think back to the moment you first walked into the room to find the body. Was there anything unusual, however insignificant – a smell perhaps?'

Merrin was silent for a moment, deep in thought, reliving the moment. 'Not a smell,' she said at last, 'but there was one thing I forgot to tell you – the curtains were drawn. It was not until I drew them back that I saw the body; the room was almost in darkness although it was daylight outside.'

'That's very helpful, Mrs McKenzie.'

'I suppose what it means is that the body was moved after dark, which would be logical if you didn't want to be seen by anyone.'

'Assuming there was a body to be moved. The young man could have walked into the cottage himself. Anyway, thank you for your help, Mrs McKenzie. Here's my card; call me any time if you remember anything else, and may I have your number in case we need to contact you again?'

They parted at the slipway and Merrin watched him go. He was a nice-looking man, not handsome exactly but well-preserved and he had a dependable, honest sort of face, which turned warm and kindly when he smiled. His hair was mostly grey but he still had plenty of it.

He was not particularly tall and of stocky build. *I bet he was a rugby player*, Merrin thought. A complicated man, she suspected, and not a very happy one; there was an air of melancholy about him. Perhaps it was just his job. Merrin certainly knew enough about the police force to believe this was indeed possible.

She reached the stone steps leading to Miranda's Cottage and all thoughts of Inspector Louis Peppiatt disappeared. All she could think about was a hot bath and an early night.

CHAPTER TWELVE

It was just after seven on Sunday morning when Dr Graham Bennett telephoned Inspector Peppiatt with the news that the inspector probably had a murder on his hands.

'Sorry for the delay, Louis. I need the test results to confirm cause of death but I believe someone killed that lad,' said the doctor. 'As well as the blow to the head, I found the site of a recent injection in his upper thigh. I have sent off a number of blood samples to the lab and I have insisted they work on them today, although it's Sunday.'

'You must be popular,' said Louis.

'I'm not flavour of the month but, in the circumstances, it's a reasonable request. Do you remember, about two or maybe three years ago, we had a dead body washed up at Mullion Cove. You weren't involved; you were on another case.'

'I remember,' said Louis, suddenly serious. 'I was

heading up the search for that missing child in Penzance at the time – that was an awful business.'

'Yes, of course, terrible. Anyway, the Mullion body is still an open verdict, but the idiot judge insisted on saying that in his view it was a case of suicide. The man in question was a local fisherman. Like our body in St Ives, he had been bashed over the head and then injected in the thigh. The cause of death was an overdose of insulin. He was not a diabetic and neither was any member of his family nor immediate friends – not that he had many of either, as I recall. As the injuries to the two bodies are so similar, I have requested the lab to urgently test for insulin in the blood. As you may know, insulin is a killer for a non-diabetic and becomes increasingly less detectable the longer it remains in the body, hence the urgency. If it is insulin, I just hope we are in time to find it. It's not normally included in postmortem investigations because it's so tricky. We found the insulin in the Mullion body quite by chance because I was demonstrating postmortem procedure to some students and I wanted the lab to cover all possibilities for cause of death. Then, amazingly, insulin turned up in the results.'

'So, are you saying, Graham, that in your view the boy in the bed was killed by whatever was injected into his leg, whether it is insulin or something else?'

'He was a fit young man in his mid to late teens. There was no trace of alcohol or drugs in his system. His organs were all perfect, except that his heart had just stopped. So yes, without a doubt, whatever was put into his bloodstream killed him.'

'I suppose he could have injected himself, a suicide maybe, or simply an overdose by mistake?' said Louis hopefully.

'My dear Louis, how on earth would he have injected himself with a lethal dose of whatever, disposed of the needle and put himself neatly to bed? Though it pains me to admit it, that extremely annoying Mrs McKenzie is right – someone else put him in that bed.'

'What on earth has Mrs McKenzie done to upset you?'

'Oh, I don't know; she seemed rather too sure of herself for my liking. Do we know anything about her? After all, she did find the body and seemed rather protective towards the boy. Somewhat peculiar to become attached to a corpse, don't you think?'

'Come on, Graham, you become attached to corpses all the time, particularly those whose autopsies baffle you!'

'It's my job,' said Graham huffily.

'Alright, well, following your legendary instinct, I will ask Jack Eddy about her. They have known each other since they were children, apparently.'

'I can't imagine Jack ever having been a child,' said Graham.

'That's exactly what I said! On the strength of your findings so far, I will get forensics back in to pull the cottage apart and we'll take Mrs McKenzie's fingerprints – but for the purposes of elimination, in my view.'

'You do whatever you like, Louis. I'm off for a round of golf.'

* * *

Merrin had anticipated a lie-in on Sunday morning, but it was not to be. Firstly, Clara had called to make sure she was alright and to find out if there was any news from the police. Merrin told her she'd heard nothing from the police and didn't expect to do so – but she stressed that it would have been delightful to have been able to sleep a little longer.

'Sorry, darling Pearl. Just as I started to call you, I realised I might wake you up.'

Merrin did not trust herself to reply to this.

Wide awake now, Merrin staggered out of bed and made herself a cup of coffee and Horatio his morning toast. She had just returned thankfully to her bed, clutching her coffee, when her phone rang again. This time it was Jack Eddy.

'The boss needs access to the cottage; forensics are going to do a full sweep of the place. Can you let me have your key, Merrin?'

'Wouldn't it be more sensible if you used the key in the key safe? Then you can all come and go as you please. If you ring Clara, she will give you the code number,' said Merrin, snuggling deeper into her bed.

'I don't have her telephone number. I rather have my hands full here. Would you mind giving her a call and then text me back with the number. Thank you, Merrin. Oh, and we need your fingerprints, for elimination purposes only, of course. I will be at the station for the next hour. Could you pop down, my girl, as soon as you can. There's a bit of a flap on.'

* * *

By the time Merrin returned to Miranda's Cottage with her ink-stained fingers, it was still only 10 a.m. but it felt like bedtime. She made herself some more coffee and tucked into the croissant that she had bought from the bakery below. Horatio eyed her breakfast and then began strutting up and down his cage, banging his bell.

'OK, I'm coming,' said Merrin. She tore off the end of her croissant and handed it to him. 'I can't imagine you'd find too many croissants where you came from, spoilt bird,' she grumbled as Horatio tucked into his piece with gusto.

She tidied up the kitchen, swept the grate and lit a fire. It was a cold, windy day. A walk on the beach was what she needed but she was just too tired. She considered calling Max and then thought better of it. She didn't need company; she just wanted a chance to relax and absorb all that had happened the day before. She put another log on the fire and settled down in the Windsor chair. It had been Adam's chair, in which he had always sat beside Arcadia's log-burning stove. It was perhaps a little too large for this kitchen but she had to keep it.

She was just drifting off to sleep when there was a knock on the door. *Now what?* she thought as she struggled out of the chair and opened the door. It was Jack Eddy.

'Sorry to trouble you again, Merrin Trip, but could I have a word? I'm a bit worried, in a bit of a state to be honest.'

'Yes, of course, Jack,' said Merrin, with a sinking

heart. 'What can I get you – tea, coffee?'

'Nothing, my maid, thank you. This is very irregular; I would probably lose my job if the boss got to hear of it but your dad was good to me and I was very fond of you when we were young – you and Jago – so I have to say something or I wouldn't be able to sleep at night.'

Jack looked genuinely worried and suddenly rather old and confused. Merrin pulled out one of the chairs from round the table and put it beside the fire. 'Come and sit down, and tell me what's bothering you.'

'It's the boss, Inspector Peppiatt – he seems to think you are involved in some way with the body in the cottage.'

'What do you mean?' Merrin asked, alarmed.

'Well, he asked me a lot of questions about you, most of which I didn't know the answers to. "I only knew little Merrin Tripconey," I kept telling him. "I don't know anything about her life since she left St Ives."' Jack hesitated. 'Do you promise on the grave of old Harry Trip, you won't tell anyone what I'm about to tell you?'

'I promise,' said Merrin solemnly, 'except possibly Clara; the body was found in her cottage, after all.'

'Well, I suppose it doesn't matter telling Clara,' said Jack. 'We've now been told the postmortem suggests that the boy was probably murdered and they think he might have been injected with insulin. They're just waiting for the results.'

'How awful, poor boy, and rather peculiar,' said Merrin. 'I suppose that means the killer could be a diabetic. At least it means the boy probably didn't suffer.'

'The boss thinks you behaved very oddly. You didn't seem in as much of a state of shock as you should have been on finding a dead body. He also thinks it was strange that you sat by the bed until I turned up and also, he wonders whether maybe you tidied up the boy's bed. You didn't, did you, Merrin?'

'No, of course not. Inspector Peppiatt has already asked me all these questions; I don't know why he needs to go through it all again.'

'Very often, the person who calls in the crime is the person who committed it. That's what he must be thinking. But I told him, "Merrin would never do anything bad; she was always a good, truthful girl, tender and kind."'

'And what did he say to that?' Merrin asked, amused despite the circumstances.

'I would rather not say,' said Jack, avoiding eye contact.

'Please, Jack, I need to know what I'm up against.'

'He just said that people change,' mumbled Jack reluctantly. 'You're not a diabetic, are you, my maid?'

'No, I'm jolly well not,' said Merrin angrily.

After Jack had left her cottage, Merrin found she couldn't settle. She knew enough about police work from Adam to appreciate that everyone connected to a serious crime had to expect to be on the end of some pretty searching questions. However, she also knew that she could explain her behaviour in a way that would completely satisfy the Inspector. But frankly, her explanation was personal and, she felt, none of his business.

And then it occurred to her – the only person she really wanted to speak to was Isla.

CHAPTER THIRTEEN

'Isla, it's Mum,' said Merrin, unnecessarily. 'Is it a bad moment? I can call back later.'

'Mum, of course it's not a bad moment. It's Sunday afternoon and Saturday night was a blast, we didn't get home until . . . well, actually, I'm not sure what time we got home.'

Isla was a July baby and clever, so she was the youngest in her year at school. She'd had absolutely no interest in a gap year and was beyond excited to take up her offered place at Oxford. This meant that in her second year at university, she was still only nineteen. This also meant that Merrin was always having to fight the desire to start telling her to be careful and to give her yet another lecture about spiked drinks, boys and life in general. With commendable restraint, she said nothing, which produced a lengthy silence.

'So, Mum, what's up?' Isla asked.

'I found a dead body yesterday,' Merrin managed.

'You're kidding!'

'It's not something I'd joke about, Isla.'

'Of course not, sorry, Mum. Who, when, where?'

'I understand his identity is still unknown,' said Merrin, 'but he's definitely not local – Jack knows everyone.' Merrin then told her daughter everything that had happened the previous day. It made her feel tired and fraught just explaining it all.

When she had finished, Isla exploded. 'I don't think Clara, and Tristan come to that, behaved very well. After finding the body and coping with the police, to then expect you to be a waitress – it's ridiculous, and unkind. Clara is supposed to be your friend and she knows what you have been through in the last eight months. It's an appalling way to behave. They should have shut the restaurant and spent the evening looking after you; you must have been in a real state of shock. How are you feeling now, Mum? Do you want me to come down? You're clearly not getting much support in St Ives.'

'I'm fine now, darling, thanks to you. To be able to tell you everything and to know you are in my corner makes all the difference. I just needed to unload to the person I love most in the world. Sorry to be the bearer of such weird news in the middle of your relaxing Sunday and don't think of coming down, honestly, I'll be seeing you very soon anyway.'

'If you're sure, I must admit I'm behind with my essay for this week. Of course, if you lived in Bristol, it would be a lot easier to pop over – scrub that, definitely below the belt!' They both laughed, the tension easing. 'I would like to call Clara, though, and tell her to stop taking advantage of you.'

'Please don't, Isla. I'm a fifty-four-year-old lawyer; I can take care of myself, honestly.'

'A fifty-four-year-old lawyer who has just lost her husband. OK, I won't say anything to Clara but please chuck in that cleaning job as quickly as you can and don't get roped in for any more waitressing,' said Isla firmly.

'I'm not doing any more waitressing, I absolutely promise. They wouldn't want me anyway; I'm absolutely hopeless at it.'

'Well, just remember you're absolutely hopeless at cleaning as well,' said Isla.

There were more gales of laughter. 'Thanks a bunch for the vote of confidence, darling,' said Merrin. 'For some extraordinary reason, it has made me feel so much better!'

They said goodbye, with Isla promising to ring her mother in the next couple of days. It was a huge relief to share the awful events of yesterday with her daughter. Merrin had told her everything, except, of course, for one thing – Inspector Louis Peppiatt apparently seemed to think she was a suspect.

The following morning, Clara was once again responsible for waking up Merrin, who admittedly had slept in rather late. 'Can I come and see you, Pearl? There is something I want to ask you.'

Buoyed up by her conversation with Isla the previous

evening, Merrin immediately responded. 'Clara, I really can't do any more waitressing and even the cleaning is a bit much. I've just moved and I have to get my cottage straight before Isla arrives.'

'My Pearl, I promise I will never, ever ask you to do any more waitressing. Also, the police have told me to cancel bookings for Elsie's cottage over Christmas and possibly even the New Year. It is going to make a big hole in our income but it does mean there is only Rupert's to clean on Fridays, and I promise it will only be for the next couple of weeks, three at the most. Pearl, I keep thinking about the body of that poor young man – in Mum's cottage of all places. Mum was such a kind, easy-going person, who loved everyone, pretty much. She would be horrified that someone had died in the cottage that is named after her.'

'I've been thinking exactly that as well,' said Merrin. 'I'm so sorry, Clara, but it looks as if the boy was murdered; at any rate, according to Jack Eddy. He was injected with something that killed him and they think it might be insulin. It's unbelievable, really; I find it hard to accept it's actually happened – in St Ives, too, of all places.'

'Tristan and I had sort of assumed it could be murder but given that the boy was a young teenager, we did also wonder if it might be suicide. Miserable,' said Clara.

In an effort to lighten the mood, Merrin changed the subject. 'It will be good to see you, Clara, but why are you coming round? Nice though it will be to have a visit from you, I can't help suspecting an ulterior motive – no more waitressing, only one cottage to clean, so what's the snag?'

'Wait and see,' said Clara. 'I will be round in ten minutes.'

It was only after she had ended the call that Merrin realised Clara had not actually denied having an ulterior motive.

She had just managed a quick shower, to dress and fill a cafetière of coffee when there was a knock on the door, followed by Clara bursting in through it. 'Morning, darling Pearl, isn't it a lovely day?'

Merrin turned from her coffee-making, about to reply, when a movement by Clara's feet caught her eye. 'What is that?' she said, staring down at the most extraordinary dog she had ever seen.

'It's a dog, Pearl, obviously. He's very sweet. His name is William, not Bill or Will and certainly never Billy.'

Merrin studied William. He seemed to be two dogs, rather than one, or maybe even three, or perhaps four. The front half of him was quite different from the back half. His face looked rather like a labrador but his ears were definitely poodle. His front legs were sturdy, his back legs spindly, his coat was quite long but curly. He had largely white with brown markings that were reminiscent of a Jack Russell, the size of whom he favoured. His tail was the final straw – it was long and flowing but stood straight up in the air, like a flag.

Merrin liked dogs. There had always been dogs around during her childhood. However, despite Isla's pleading, she and Adam had made the decision not to have a dog as they did not think it fair, bearing in mind the unpredictable hours they both worked. And in any case, they had Horatio, who had more character and attitude than a pack of dogs, in Adam's view.

Merrin bent down and held out her hand for sniffing. 'Hello, William,' she said. William responded by displaying a formidable set of teeth. 'He's not very friendly,' Merrin suggested.

'He's smiling,' said Clara.

Merrin leant in a bit closer and William added a significant growl to the bared teeth. She stood up and went back to preparing the coffee. 'I didn't realise you had a dog; he certainly wasn't with you last time we were down here.' Deeply regretting her own words, Merrin tried forcibly to remove the memories of their last summer holiday together as a family – it was only eighteen months ago; it seemed more like a lifetime. She pulled herself together. 'I don't want to be rude, Clara, but what possessed you to take on William? He is, well, very odd to look at, and aggressive too.'

'He's not aggressive,' said Clara. 'The growling is him talking; he was actually saying "How do you do, Merrin."'

'I'm afraid I'm failing to be convinced,' said Merrin, not unreasonably.

'Look,' said Clara, 'you go and sit down in that chair, and I'll let him off the lead. Then, just pat your lap and call him.'

'If I get savaged by your bloody dog, that will be the end of our friendship, I kid you not,' said Merrin, nonetheless sitting down. She patted her lap, as instructed. 'Come on, William.'

William dashed across the room, the eccentric tail madly wagging. He made two attempts to jump on Merrin's lap, during which he growled ferociously. On the third attempt, he made it, licked her nose, without permission, and then snuggled down happily on her lap.

'See,' said Clara triumphantly, 'he loves you!'

'A damn funny way of showing it,' said Merrin, leaning across to the table to reach for her coffee. From her lap came a deep growl. 'What's that about? It's certainly not love.'

'He was just complaining because you were disturbing him,' said Clara.

'How very thoughtless of me,' said Merrin sarcastically.

From across the room, Horatio let out a squawk, followed by a wolf whistle and then, clearly, in Adam's voice, said, 'What are you doing?'

'That's Adam's voice; I haven't heard Horatio speak before. Do you find it creepy, Pearl?'

'Not at all, I find it oddly comforting, which, I accept, might seem peculiar. When I'm alone I suppose it makes me feel that Adam may have gone but is not forgotten, not just by me but by Horatio as well. Anyway, Horatio clearly doesn't like William either and as well as growling at me, he smells. Can you get him off my lap before he either bites me or I am asphyxiated by the pong, and then tell me why you're here.'

'Ah,' said Clara, 'my visit is actually about William.'

CHAPTER FOURTEEN

It took Clara quite a while to explain William's story. Clara's aunt lived in Hayle and William was her pride and joy. Over the weekend, which had already not been without its dramas, Auntie Janet had suffered a major stroke. Obviously, when Auntie was carted off to hospital, Tristan and Clara had rescued William and brought him back to their home. This had all happened on Sunday evening. 'I did try to call you yesterday, but the phone was always engaged,' Clara said plaintively.

'I was talking to my daughter and just telling her I'd found a dead body.'

The irony was clearly lost on Clara, who persisted with her tale. Apparently, she had spoken to the hospital this morning to be told that Auntie Janet's stroke was indeed massive, and it was unlikely that, at ninety-one years old, she would survive it. If she did, there was no way she would ever go home again.

'So, this leaves poor William homeless and I was wondering, Pearl, whether you might take him in for a few days, just until we have dealt with Christmas and the New Year and then we can decide what to do. I know Auntie Janet would be absolutely devastated at the idea of him going to a rescue centre.'

'There is a slight anomaly there, Clara,' said Merrin coolly. 'You mentioned me having William for a few days but in the same breath you added "until after the New Year". That is going to be nearer three weeks.'

'I know it's a lot to ask, Pearl, but with the restaurant being run on a skeleton staff there is no one at home from early morning until about midnight. We can't leave him alone all that time. Also, now we have lost three weeks' rent on the cottage we can't possibly take on any more staff. Please, Pearl, you love dogs. When you were a child, your family was never without a dog – remember dear Joe, and Timmy, oh, and that little corgi – what was her name, Jilly?'

Merrin was not even slightly moved by the reminiscences. 'If I wanted the complication of a dog in my life – which, incidentally, I don't – I certainly would not choose William, who looks weird, growls, appears to want to kill me, smells and, significantly, Horatio doesn't think much of him. Anyway, I don't have a garden.'

'Please, please, Pearl, I'm desperate. I've picked up his bed, bowls and some food; they're in the car outside. Could you just have him even for the next couple of days? The doctor said Auntie is either going to pull through or die in the next few days. Supposing she regains consciousness, I need to be able to tell her that William is being looked after in a nice home, safe and secure. It'll be all she cares about.'

There was a long silence. Isla would say that, once again, Clara was taking hideous advantage of their friendship, which was probably true. Merrin looked down at William, who, despite her request to Clara, was still sitting on her lap. She gave him a tentative stroke and this time, he didn't growl, as if he knew his future was hanging in the balance.

'Alright, I'll keep him for a few days because I do recognise you are in a difficult position. However, there are conditions. Firstly, if he bites me, or anyone else, while he is in my charge, he comes straight back to you. Secondly, if he is not house-trained, ditto, straight back to you. Thirdly, for God's sake don't tell Isla; she'll go mad.'

'I thought Isla loved dogs; she was always trying to persuade me to persuade you to get a puppy.'

'She already thinks you're taking advantage of our friendship and she's very angry about it.'

'And she's right,' wailed Clara, suddenly bursting into tears. 'I am so, so sorry, Pearl, I just don't know how we would have managed without you in the last few days. Trying to run the restaurant without proper staff, the cleaner leaving, the dead body of that poor young man and then Auntie and her dog, it's just too much – and coming all at once, it's a nightmare. It's so hard. Our bank manager is hassling us all the time, with good cause – if we don't have a spectacular festive season, we may well go under, things really are that bad.'

Merrin pushed William off her lap, to the sound of significant growling. She ignored him and took Clara in her arms. 'It's OK, you and Tristan are going to get through this, I just know it. Things are clearly difficult for you at the moment, but the last few days have been truly shocking. Let's fetch William's stuff and then you can get off to the restaurant.'

William watched as all his worldly goods were brought into the cottage. Merrin put his basket by the fireplace and immediately William climbed into it and buried his nose in his paws.

The two women hugged again. 'Off you go,' said Merrin. 'Oh, is there any dog shampoo in that bag?'

Clara shook her head.

'Don't worry, I'll use mine. He'll smell of lily of the valley, which will be a vast improvement.'

After Clara had left, Merrin went upstairs and ran a shallow, tepid bath. When she returned, William was still in his basket and Horatio was watching him with interest. 'What are you doing?' he asked.

'God knows, Horatio, because I certainly don't.'

Surprisingly, William enjoyed his bath, he allowed Merrin to dry him with her hairdryer, wolfed down his breakfast and returned to his basket. Merrin then lit the fire, which definitely met with William's approval.

After tidying up, Merrin clipped on William's lead and took him down to the Harbour Beach. Then they walked across Porthgwidden Beach and up onto the

Island, stopping to sit on a park bench, above Porthmeor, to watch the surfers – at least Merrin watched the surfers while William studied a nearby seagull, with what looked like evil intent.

The Island is not really an island but is a lovely place with stunning views out to sea in all directions. This is why it has been a lookout point since Napoleonic times up until the present day – Coastwatch now preside over all the coastal activities in St Ives Bay from their lookout on the island. At the top of the Island is St Nicholas Chapel. Merrin remembered her mother telling her that St Nicholas was the real Father Christmas and he was the patron saint not only of children but also sailors. 'So,' she had told Jago and Merrin, solemnly, 'St Nicholas looks after you two and your Daddy.' Maybe it was because of that, Merrin had always loved the Island. In Spring, it is a mass of wild flowers and a stopping-off point for migratory birds of all sorts. Merrin remembered once seeing a puffin. It is a magic place, full of life.

Realising she was becoming stiff and cold, Merrin stood up, but instead of returning to Miranda's Cottage, she found herself walking the full length of Porthmeor Beach and really enjoying it, despite a cutting wind. Originally, Merrin had intended to take him out for ten minutes or so; instead, the walk had taken just over an hour and she had thoroughly enjoyed it. She took William out twice more during the day and on the third walk, she nervously let him off the lead. He ran round the beach in mad circles before returning to her side, and when they reached the road, he stood by her, waiting for the instruction to cross. Poor old Auntie Janet had clearly trained him well.

That evening, having emptied several packing cases, she made supper and then decided on an early night. The fresh air and exercise had made her sleepy. She covered up Horatio's cage, settled William in his basket and went upstairs to bed.

She was just drifting off to sleep when there was a movement at the end of the bed. William had jumped up and was settling himself down on her feet. She knew she shouldn't allow him on the bed, but his warm little body was oddly comforting. She went on to have the best night's sleep since Adam's death.

CHAPTER FIFTEEN

Inspector Peppiatt walked into his office and was pleased to find Sergeant Eddy already waiting for him. Eddy was not famous for his time keeping. Graham Bennett had just delivered the results of the postmortem and there was a great deal to do.

Sergeant Eddy struggled to his feet as his boss entered the room. 'How did you get on, sir?' he asked.

'As we feared, it has now been confirmed that we do have a murder on our hands, Eddy. Dr Bennett's hunch that the injection could be insulin has been proved right as well. So, the boy was hit over the head, injected with enough insulin to cause heart failure and then put to bed in the Tregonnings' cottage. Why?' Clearly not expecting an answer, Inspector Peppiatt continued. 'The main problem we have is that we can find no identity for the boy. Nothing, absolutely sod all – it's as if he was dropped into St Ives from outer space. No dental records, no fingerprint records. His photograph has been already widely circulated but there are no matches with missing persons. Without a name, it's going to be hard to make any progress. However, the boy does have the same murder profile as that of the fisherman in Mullion about three years ago. You were on that case, weren't you?'

Jack nodded.

'Then dig out the file for me. Also, are there any results from Mrs Tregonning's guests?'

'Nothing so far, sir. We're checking the guests who booked both Tregonning cottages going back to June, as you requested, and also the people who booked for this week and over Christmas, again in both cottages. All the guests in the most recent bookings have been interviewed and so have future bookings where the guests have already been provided with the key-safe codes. I don't know why we are bothering with Rupert's Cottage, though, sir. The code for Rupert's won't help them get into Elsie's, where the body was found. It seems pointless, to me.'

'It is just to cover all bases, Eddy; we have so little to go on.'

'In which case, sir, we ought to be interviewing the guests in every letting cottage in St Ives?' said Jack Eddy, looking rather pleased with himself.

'Don't be ridiculous,' said Louis. 'Mrs Tregonning has confirmed that sometimes large families book both cottages and, therefore, could have access to both key safes. This could also apply to two lots of friends, holidaying together. Right now, I'm going back to St Ives to talk to the Tregonnings again. Incidentally, I also meant to ask, did you get any useful information from Mrs McKenzie?'

Mutinous now at having been called ridiculous, Jack replied, 'No, nothing, and we shouldn't be troubling little Merrin. She lost her husband a while back; she's a good woman – of course she is not involved in this murder. That really would be ridiculous.'

'That's quite enough, Sergeant. Get that file on the fisherman for me and also start checking to see if anyone close to this murder is a diabetic and therefore has access to insulin – and that includes Mrs McKenzie.'

It's time Jack Eddy retired, Louis thought as he climbed into his car. Jack had never been an imaginative policeman, but in his own way, he was methodical, and his knowledge of St Ives and its surroundings was positively encyclopedic. But he was becoming pedantic and he had a medical coming up in the spring, which there was no way he could possibly pass. Yet what would become of him? Being a policeman defined Jack, and by all accounts his wife was something of an old battleaxe, so how would he fill his days? *And what applies to Jack applies to me, when my time comes*, thought Louis. *These days, being a policeman is pretty much all I am – certainly not a husband and barely a father.*

Louis had tried over the weekend to ring his daughter, Daisy, but she was always too busy to talk. It was either a hockey match, or rehearsals for the school Christmas concert, or out with friends. Was she avoiding him or was Stephanie not passing on the messages? It was hard to tell. In any event, he was not going to put up a fight about Christmas. Stephanie was right about that – Christmas was for children; it was certainly not a time to have a tug of war over which parent they should be spending their festive season with.

It was still only mid-morning by the time Louis arrived in St Ives, so Tristan's Fish Plaice was quiet except for a few customers having coffee. Clara was peeling potatoes at a table by the serving hatch. Seeing him, she stood up and wiped her hands. 'Good morning, Inspector, would you like a coffee?'

'I would, thank you, just black. I imagine you must be heartily sick of peeling potatoes?'

Clara smiled as she handed him his coffee. 'You're right, of course, I should be but I survive it by simply zoning out and thinking about something else, anything else really except bloody spuds. How are you getting on?'

'I'm afraid I have to tell you that we now know it was murder.'

Clara went very pale. 'That's awful; Merrin says the boy was very young. The thought of that poor young man being murdered in our cottage is just too awful. How did he die?'

'I can't tell you that, I'm afraid; it's important for our enquiries to keep as much detail to ourselves as possible at this stage. However, I did want to tell you myself that we are treating the death as murder before the news gets out. I wanted to make sure that you and your husband were the first to hear about it. Do you want me to fetch him? You're looking a little, well, peaky, which is hardly surprising.'

'No, it's fine,' said Clara. 'I felt a bit shocked hearing the news officially from you, but I already knew you were treating his death as murder.'

'How could you possibly know that, Mrs Tregonning?' said Louis, genuinely puzzled.

'Inspector, St Ives is a small town. In my case, Jack Eddy told Merrin and Merrin told me, but you can be sure everyone local will know about it by now. I won't fetch Tristan if that's alright with you. He's always so busy with prep at this time of the morning. I will tell him you called with the official news after the lunch trade has quietened down.' Clara reached for a chair and sat down. 'I do just hate the idea of our lovely little cottage being a murder scene.'

'Well, there is some good news on that score, if one can rate any news as good news in such a tragedy. It may be that the boy wasn't murdered in your cottage. Shortly, forensics will be able to confirm this, one way or another. However, it does seem as if someone really cared about him. As Mrs McKenzie pointed out, it appears as if he was sort of laid to rest.'

'Trust Merrin to have worked it all out. Don't worry, though, thanks to me she is not going to turn into an interfering Miss Marple figure and start telling you how to run your case.'

'Why thanks to you?' Louis asked, amused.

'I have put her in charge of a totally ghastly dog, which belongs to an aged aunt of mine who sadly had a stroke over the weekend. William, the dog in question, is absolutely hideous and growls at everyone. I do feel guilty, honestly I do, Inspector, but not guilty enough to take him back. So, in a nutshell, she has her hands full.'

'I am very sorry about your aunt, Mrs Tregonning, but I must admit to having a passing sympathy for Mrs McKenzie. I thought you two were friends?'

'We are,' said Clara firmly. 'Best friends, really. It's the sort of thing you can only do to a very good friend.'

'Women never fail to amaze me,' said Louis. 'I'll keep you informed of developments. Forensics have done their initial sweep of the cottage. It shouldn't be too long before you can have access to it again. I'll leave you to your spuds. Good luck.' He raised a hand in a farewell greeting as he started to leave the restaurant.

'Inspector!' Clara called after him. 'So it was an insulin injection that killed him, wasn't it?'

'Oh, for God's sake,' said Louis, as he walked out onto the Wharf. Clara took that as an affirmative, and, with a sigh, she picked up the potato peeler and returned to work.

After leaving the restaurant, Louis walked across town to Elsie's Cottage and let himself in, using the key safe. Forensics had left the place reasonably tidy. He walked upstairs and into the twin-bedded room. The sheet and duvet had been pulled back to remove the body. Otherwise, the room was immaculate. He sat down on

93

the chair where Merrin had sat three days before and looked around him, trying to absorb the atmosphere. It was oddly peaceful and Louis suddenly had an inkling as to why Merrin McKenzie had wanted to sit with the body. Even before having confirmation from forensics, Louis had felt on his first visit to the cottage that no violence had taken place in this room. Whoever had brought the boy here had somehow cared, even if he or she had been responsible for the boy's murder – which, of course, made no sense at all.

With a sigh, he stood up, let himself out of the cottage and retraced his steps to the Wharf, where he had left his car. The walk back to the Wharf took him past several art galleries. He was hugely tempted to stop and browse, he loved art and liked to think he had a small talent for watercolours. He peered in the window of the Penwith Gallery, fighting the temptation to go in. The Tate and the Barbara Hepworth museum were the obviously destinations for art lovers, but Louis loved best the little galleries dotted around the town. 'I have a murder to solve,' he told himself, firmly, and reluctantly tore himself away from the window.

As he neared the Wharf, Louis was fairly sure his return journey took him past Mrs McKenzie's cottage, for she had pointed it out to him. When he passed a little hand-painted sign saying *Miranda's Cottage* with an arrow pointing up some stone steps, he was sure it was where she lived; he remembered the address. For a moment, he hesitated, tempted to knock on the door, but what had he to say to her? News that the boy in the bed had been murdered, she now knew, thanks to his sergeant not being able to keep his mouth shut. There was nothing else he needed to say to her, so, reluctantly, he walked on down the street towards the harbour.

CHAPTER SIXTEEN

By Wednesday morning, Merrin and William were starting to like one another and Horatio was positively besotted with William. He cooed at William through the bars of his cage and Merrin was beginning to suspect that there must have been a dog in Horatio's life before. Maybe the old lady from Norfolk had owned a dog, which had died before she did. After several days of walking the beaches of St Ives, Merrin was feeling clearer headed and more positive about life. She was eating and sleeping better. 'It can't be anything to do with you,' she said to William. 'It must just be the sea air.' It might have been her imagination, but William was looking particularly smug.

Merrin was just about to go out for their morning walk when her phone rang. It was Isla. She never called during the day. Merrin grabbed the phone. 'Isla, are you alright, darling?'

'Stop panicking, I'm fine, Mum.'

'I wasn't panicking, it's just unusual for you to call during the day. Are you really OK?'

'Stop, I am perfectly OK. I just want to tell you something, but I haven't much time. I have a lecture across town in about twenty-five minutes.'

'I'm listening,' said Merrin.

'You know I'm always going on about our eccentric landlady, Roberta? Well, she has a missing nephew and I am wondering whether it could be your dead body.'

'I don't think that's very likely, is it, darling?'

'Let me just tell you the whole story. Roberta has a brother. He and his wife live in Singapore and are tax exiles, which means they can never come back to the UK. They have one son whose name is James, James Allnut, the same surname as his aunt – she never married. It was decided that James should come to the UK to go to university. He has just finished his first term at St Andrews, you know, in Scotland. He is supposed to be coming here to spend Christmas with his aunt but first he decided to have a few days in St Ives – apparently, he's surfing mad. He was due to be up in Oxford last Friday – us girls were getting excited about his arrival, as you can imagine! However, he never turned up and his phone appears not to be working. He's nineteen; didn't you say your body was about nineteen? It really sounds like him, doesn't it? And you said the police can't trace his identity.'

'It just sounds like one big fat coincidence to me,' said Merrin. 'There must be masses of teenage boys down here at the moment. I expect Roberta's James is having too much fun and is not exactly looking forward to Christmas with an aged aunt. As for his phone, he's probably just run out of battery.'

'Mum, you're not listening properly. You told me the police were having difficulty tracing the boy's identity. James doesn't have a UK passport because he was born in Singapore. There won't be any dental records or indeed any records of him in this country. He has been in Scotland for one university term and that's all. It seems to me very likely that he has so far slipped under the radar, so to speak.'

'Well, there's an easy way to solve this, darling. Can you text over to me a photograph of him?'

'I'd already thought of that and there's a problem. Roberta only has a newborn baby photo of him. Roberta and her brother don't get on and so there has been virtually no contact for years. I have suggested she ask her brother for an up-to-date photograph but she is reluctant to do so. She doesn't want to worry James's parents, if there is no need. You can see her point.'

'So, what do you want me to do?' Merrin asked.

'I wondered if you could talk to the police, maybe to this Jack person who you and Uncle Jago were friends with as kids. If you tell him the story, then maybe they could take it further. I don't know much about these things but perhaps Roberta could do a DNA test to see if she and the body are related. Sorry, that sounds awful – to see if she and the poor dead boy are related. What do you think?'

'I still think it is all a bit far-fetched. Does Roberta know where James was supposed to be staying, and also, when did he arrive in St Ives? As much detail as possible would be helpful and might make the police take it seriously. I suppose the easiest thing would be for her to come down and identify the body, if there really is a chance it's James.'

'I'm afraid that doesn't work either. You see, Roberta has never actually met James. They have spoken on the phone and made arrangements about Christmas, but he went straight to St Andrews on his arrival in the UK and then directly down to Cornwall.'

'Goodness, there's not much to go on. I wonder if he came down to surf alone, or with a friend. See if there are any more details you can extract from Roberta. In any event, it seems to me to be a bit premature to raise the alarm just yet – after all, James could be on his way up to Oxford, even as we speak.'

'OK, Mum, it just seems a bit odd to me. I hope it's not James for Roberta's sake but he does tick a lot of boxes, you must admit. I will text you later, after my lecture, if I can find out any more details. Take care, love you.'

Merrin said her goodbyes and then headed for the kettle. 'Well, Horatio, what do you think of that?' she asked. His response was a wolf whistle. Merrin made a coffee, then went and sat by the fire. William jumped on her lap, without growling. Being practical, the chances of the body she had found being the nephew of her daughter's landlady seemed extremely unlikely. On the other hand, it did explain the absence of any identity for the young man she had found – assuming, that is, she realised, his identity was still unknown. For all she knew, by now the police may have discovered exactly who he was.

She would wait for Isla's text. If she did decide to contact the police, she knew it was no good approaching Jack Eddy. She was fairly certain he would not know where to start with an investigation into the missing boy, James Allnut, supposedly in residence either in Oxford or St Andrews – Jack was a very local policeman. No, she would have to contact Inspector Peppiatt. He had seemed so kind when he had rescued her from the restaurant. However, now she knew he had been making enquiries about her, behind her back, she was not so sure about him. Not sure at all, in fact.

Isla sent her mother a text during the afternoon. There were no more details to add except that James had travelled down to Cornwall by car. Roberta naturally had no idea as to the make of car, never mind the registration number, having never actually met James.

Should I contact the police about James then? Merrin texted back.

Can't do any harm, though Roberta doesn't seem very worried about him. Odd, really, she seems very detached, was Isla's reply.

Merrin spent Thursday evening thinking about James Allnut. She had been quick to dismiss the matter as a coincidence. However, the only coincidence was that she had found a body, who could be related to her daughter's landlady. Strip that away and suddenly the two separate incidents started to make sense – the body of a young man with no identity and a missing young man who, as Isla had described, was someone who could have 'slipped under the radar' – and, of course, the common denominator was St Ives.

CHAPTER SEVENTEEN

The following morning, Merrin took a deep breath and telephoned the number Inspector Peppiatt had given her. He answered straight away. Merrin started to explain about Roberta's missing nephew but Louis stopped her in mid flow.

'Mrs McKenzie, I'm just about to leave to come over to St Ives to interview someone who might have seen the victim. Are you in all morning? Perhaps it would be easier if I came to your cottage and you can explain everything then.'

'That would be fine, Inspector.' Merrin then gave him directions for finding her cottage and Louis did not admit to already knowing where she lived.

Merrin spent the morning emptying the last of the packing cases, which was a very satisfactory feeling. She had just tidied up the kitchen and lit the fire when there was a knock on the door. She ushered in the inspector, feeling slightly nervous. Over the last few hours, as she had worked on the packing cases, she kept rethinking what she had to tell him – the more she thought about it, the more ridiculous it seemed.

'Do sit down, Inspector,' she said. 'A coffee, black without sugar, if I remember correctly?'

'Thank you, yes, perfect,' said Louis, sitting himself down in Adam's chair. Merrin tried not to mind – and failed.

Louis looked around him. 'This is a charming cottage,' he said, 'and who is this?' He gestured towards Horatio.

'Horatio,' said Merrin, handing the inspector his coffee. 'He's a rescue parrot, extremely bossy and demanding but a family member we wouldn't be without. Are you OK with dogs? Only I have one visiting at the moment.'

'Fine,' said Louis, intrigued to see the creature Clara Tregonning had bestowed on her friend.

Merrin opened the door to the sitting room and out trotted William. 'I know he's not a thing of beauty,' she said, 'and he growls a great deal, but Horatio likes him and Horatio is usually a very good judge of character.'

Merrin and Louis studied William in silence for a moment, then looked at one another and laughed. 'I am trying really hard to think of something complimentary to say about William's appearance. How do you feel about "unusual"?' Louis asked.

'I think that is a valiant attempt at striking the right note, Inspector – polite, without telling a downright lie, which would not be appropriate for a policeman.'

'Quite,' said Louis, suddenly sobering. 'So, you'd better tell me about this missing boy – James, did you say?'

Having established that the police had still not been able to identify the boy in the bed, Merrin retold her conversation with Isla in every detail. Louis appeared to be listening intently, but she formed the firm impression that he was not overly interested in what she had to say.

When she had finished, she waited while he drained is coffee cup. He let out a sigh. 'One of the things I have learnt in my years of police work is that coincidences very rarely happen. They are nearly always just too neat and often cause misguided suspicion. You found a body and now your daughter, in Oxford of all places, thinks she is in a position to identify him. If this really is the case, then I feel forced to ask you again whether you were responsible, or in any way involved, in the death of this young man?'

Her nervousness completely vanished and Merrin was suddenly very angry indeed. 'How dare you make such an accusation. Until I left Bristol, just over a week ago, I was a practising solicitor and my husband was a serving police officer until he was killed nearly eight months ago. Ours is not the sort of family who go round murdering people. Of course I told Isla about finding a dead body – I needed to tell her; I was naturally very upset. Then, the following day when her landlady told her that she had a missing nephew, it naturally rang alarm bells so far as Isla was concerned. And what's particularly relevant, Inspector, is the location. St Ives is a small town and I believe your blanket dismissal of coincidences may well be misplaced on this occasion.'

Louis Peppiatt stared at her in silence. Merrin could see he was shocked. Perhaps she had gone too far, she had been rather rude, but the arrogance of the man – how dare he suggest that she and Isla could be capable of murdering anyone! Finally, he spoke. 'Oh my God,' he said, clearly very shocked. 'Bristol, McKenzie, I should have realised: you're Adam McKenzie's widow, Chief Inspector Adam McKenzie?'

'Yes, I am,' Merrin managed in a small voice. The anger drained away; she suddenly felt inexplicably close to tears.

'I am so very sorry. I can see I've upset you and I wouldn't want to do that for the world.' Louis hesitated. 'I met him once, your husband; he was so impressive. Ever since, I've aspired to be the sort of policeman he was. In fact, I have held him in my mind as a sort of yardstick as how to behave.'

There was a tense silence. Merrin recovered first. 'Tell me about when you met him,' she said. 'No, wait a minute.' She put another log on the fire and then, going to the fridge, poured out two glasses of white wine, handing one to Louis. 'I know you're on duty but it's a small glass and I think we've both had a bit of a shock.'

'Thank you,' he said, taking the glass without argument. 'We met at a conference held at the Met, some years ago now. The subject was the increased grooming of young girls for prostitution. I was stationed at Newton Abbot at the time, still a sergeant. Your husband was an inspector and was one of the speakers. His speech was brilliant, impassioned, heartfelt without being melodramatic. It was very well received.' Louis sipped his wine. 'Afterwards, we met in the bar and had quite a long chat. Policemen have an increasingly poor image these days, don't they? We come across, at best, as insensitive brutes and of course at our worst – well, just too awful, as is rightly documented in the press. I imagine your husband could be tough but he also appeared to be compassionate and very aware of the frailty of human life – the fact that none of us are all good, or all bad. Most of us just struggle to do our best; sometimes we succeed, sometimes we don't. Sometimes we do bad things for good reasons and good things for bad ones. I was devastated to hear of his death. I can't believe I am sitting here with his widow – I am very, very sorry for your loss, Mrs McKenzie.'

Merrin was moved by his words but felt the need to lighten the mood. 'So, what you're saying, Inspector Peppiatt, is the reason you so kindly rescued me from the worst effects of the "table from hell" the other evening was entirely due to the influence of my husband.'

Louis smiled, obviously relieved by the change of mood. 'Actually, that would be about right. But for your husband, I definitely would have left you to be shouted at all night long.'

'Look, Inspector,' said Merrin. 'I am sorry I was so angry just now; you were only doing your job, I know that. Also, the fact that you've had your doubts about me is also understandable, without knowing about my recent background. It's not who I am or who my husband was that is relevant, it's what happened after his death. You see, I obviously had to identify his body and, like our boy in the bed, Adam looked perfect. I felt all I had to do was just hold his hand or hug him and he would wake up – ridiculous, of course. When I saw the boy, initially common sense took charge, which made me check his pulse and call 999. Then I went back into the bedroom and all I could think about was seeing Adam's dead body. I had at least been with Adam, to mourn him, to say goodbye. The boy, so very young, had no one but me – so I pulled up the chair to sit beside him and keep him company. I don't know whether I was thinking about him or Adam in the time it took for Jack to arrive; it's all a bit of a blur. I just didn't want him to be alone. Do you understand?'

'Of course I understand; to witness another death, so soon after your husband's, must have been unimaginably awful.'

'No, that's not it,' said Merrin. 'Seeing Adam dead was unimaginably awful, but the poor boy – I cared, I assume, or I wouldn't have sat with him. But the worst thing that could possibly happen to me had already happened, so the boy's death didn't shock me, as it should have done in normal circumstances. And that's what surprised you, wasn't it, Inspector, that I appeared to be so comparatively calm?'

'I jumped to conclusions – I shouldn't have done.'

'No, you didn't do anything wrong, that's what I'm

trying to say. Take my behaviour out of the context of losing Adam and it is easy to see how it could be misconstrued. Sitting by the body of someone unknown to me is odd; appearing not to be shocked is odd. Was I sitting beside him out of a sense of guilt or remorse? Was I not shocked because I'd had time to recover from his death because I'd been involved in it? Having calmed down, I see where you were coming from, of course I do, and I'm sorry for not understanding your concerns.'

'Look, this might not be appropriate but if you have the time, would you feel like telling me a little about Adam – only if you don't mind?'

'I don't mind at all,' said Merrin. 'I love talking about him, it's surprising the number of people who simply cannot talk about death, even quite close friends. Would you like another glass of wine?'

'I'd better not,' said Louis, standing up, 'but let me get you another one.' Having filled Merrin's glass, he sat down and almost immediately, William jumped on his lap.

'Good heavens,' said Merrin, 'you are honoured. I don't think he even growled at you, did he?'

'No,' said Louis. 'Should he have done?'

'Definitely,' replied Merrin. 'Quite extraordinary. Maybe you are one of the good guys, after all, Inspector.'

Over the next half an hour, Louis and Merrin swapped life stories. All antagonism had gone and they found it surprisingly easy to talk to one another.

'I'm sorry you see so little of your children; that must be hard,' said Merrin.

'It is hard but then I think I've brought it on myself. I resent Andrew and it may well be because he is a far better and committed partner and father than I ever was. A policeman's lot. Did you ever resent Adam's work?'

'No, not really. I always wished we could spend more time together, particularly now – now we have no more time left. But I worked as a family solicitor and I was always having to rush off to emergencies, so I couldn't really complain about his various work dramas. Can I get you another coffee, tea, anything?'

Louis glanced at his watch. 'Look at the time; I need to go. About James, I will ask Thames Valley Police to pop in and see Roberta Allnut. If there is still no sign of James, at least we can resister him as a missing person for her, even if he's not our boy. Could you text me Roberta's address and I'll get that organised.'

'But you said . . .' Merrin began.

'I know what you're going to say and I can promise you I'm not going to ignore the possible connection because of – what did you call it, oh yes – my "blanket dismissal of coincidences". Let's see what Thames Valley turn up and take it from there. Incidentally, I did interview a barman in the Sloop today who remembers our boy. He came in a couple of times for a pint, apparently, but was always alone.'

'Have you talked to the regular surfers on Porthmeor Beach?'

'Not personally but yes, we've had a couple of constables going round town asking questions. No one remembers him, except the barman. It's a pity it's winter.

If the lifeguards were still on the beach, they would probably have remembered him.' Louis walked towards the door and then turned back to Merrin. 'I'm so sorry again about my crass remarks earlier on,' he said.

'And I'm sorry I shouted at you. I should have remembered to think about angels, shouldn't I?'

They smiled at one another and shook hands. 'I will keep you in the loop,' said Louis.

CHAPTER EIGHTEEN

The tide was way out and despite the fact that it was December, the sun was surprisingly hot. Merrin sat on a rock at the far end of Carbis Bay Beach; William was busy sniffing at a large pile of seaweed. They had walked on the cliff path from St Ives and then along the beach to where, at low tide, there was still the remains of an old shipwreck. She let out a sigh and for the first time since Adam's death, while it was going too far to say she was happy, she did feel a kind of contentment. She was starting to believe she might have done the right thing coming home, even after all the years away. Maybe it was fanciful, but it felt as if the familiar beaches, sea, rocks and cliffs were helping to heal her. She would never fully recover from Adam's death, she knew that – nor, come to that, did she want to – but she could now envisage the possibility of learning to live with it.

'Come on, William, we'd better head home.' They

started walking back along the beach when William suddenly stopped, waded into the sea, his nose up in the air. He could obviously smell something. *It must be seals*, thought Merrin, and then suddenly the fins of a small pod of dolphins appeared and in seconds, they were leaping out of the sea. The sun glistened on their skin as they played, their lovely smiling faces seeming to confirm the wonderful time they were having. 'Oh, magic!' said Merrin and it was perfect – the sun, the sparkling sea and the joy of the dolphins. She stood, transfixed – and then her phone rang.

'Pearl, how are you, where are you?' It was, of course, Clara.

'I'm on Carbis Bay, watching dolphins – it's wonderful, and such a beautiful day.'

'I'm sure it is. I never have time for the beach any more.' Clara sounded decidedly miserable. 'Honestly, the way Tristan and I are living at the moment, it's absolutely ridiculous. Bad news, I'm afraid: Auntie Janet died in the middle of last night.'

'Oh, I'm so sorry, Clara, poor you, poor Auntie Janet.'

'To be honest, Pearl, we weren't close. She was a bit of an old tyrant and pretty miserable with it.'

'She certainly trained her dog well, though,' said Merrin. 'When we're out and about, he never puts a paw wrong.'

'It's about the dog I'm calling. Tristan and I have had a long talk and there is absolutely no way we can take on William. I think the best thing is if we come and collect him tomorrow morning and take him to the Animal Welfare Trust in Hayle. I have spoken to them and they will look after him and try and find a home for him. I have told them that he is not the best-looking dog in the world but they are willing to have a go at finding someone who will take him. I am grateful to you for having him during the last few days while Auntie was still alive.'

At that moment, a cloud passed over the sun and the dolphins stopped their playing and disappeared as swiftly as they had come. William was out of the water now and came running up to her, before shaking vigorously and covering her legs in sand and sea water. 'OK, what time will you be coming to collect him? Only it's Friday tomorrow and I have that wretched changeover at Rupert's to do, if you remember.'

'Of course,' said Clara, 'we'll be over about nine-thirty. And another thing, Pearl.'

'Yes?' said Merrin.

'No dead bodies this week, please.'

'That's not even slightly amusing,' said Merrin.

The joy had gone out of the day. It wasn't just the disappearance of the sun and the dolphins. As Merrin and William trudged along the sand together, Merrin could not ignore the sense of companionship that had grown between them in the last few days. By the time they climbed up onto the cliff path, Merrin decided she did not want to spend the evening alone, so she called Max.

'Are you free tonight?' she asked.

'I'm always free for you, my darling girl,' was the reply.

'Oh, for heaven's sake, Max, enough of all that nonsense. Would you like to come to supper this evening? I'm feeling fed up.'

'You're making the idea of spending an evening with you sound so enticing, how can I possibly refuse? What time?'

'Seven o'clock,' said Merrin.

'I'll be there,' said Max, 'and I will concentrate all my efforts into cheering you up – quite a tall order, by the sound of things.'

By the time Max arrived, Merrin had lit the fire, a casserole was in the oven and she was already on her second glass of wine. She was sitting in Adam's chair with William on her lap.

Max helped himself to a glass and sat down opposite her. 'What's up?' he asked. 'Apart from the fact that your husband recently died, I understand you found a dead body last weekend and Clara has saddled you with that appallingly ugly mutt.'

Merrin started to laugh, which rapidly turned into crying and finally to sobbing. William, clearly worried, started licking her face.

'Dear God, what have I said?' Max produced a handkerchief but as he leant over to give it to Merrin, William showed some impressive teeth, followed by some serious growling. 'I don't think he likes me,' said Max.

Merrin accepted the handkerchief and mopped her face. 'Of course he doesn't like you,' she said at last. 'You've just called him an appallingly ugly mutt. You hurt his feelings – just imagine how you would feel if someone called you something like that.'

'It would never happen,' said Max confidently, 'not with my peerless good looks.'

'Oh, Max, you are just who I needed tonight.'

Over supper, Merrin told Max all about the boy in the bed, about Isla thinking the body might be that of James Allnut and her various conversations with Inspector Peppiatt.

Max was outraged. 'How could the idiot policeman possibly think for one moment that you and Isla could be mixed up in a murder?'

'I don't believe he did really,' said Merrin. 'I think he was just on a fishing expedition.'

'In my view, he's still a prat and he can't be very bright either.'

'No, you're wrong there, he's a clever man,' Merrin insisted. 'He met Adam once and was incredibly impressed by him. It's rather touching, actually, he clearly idolised Adam and wants to be like him.'

'Damn, so I suppose in that case, we'll have to forgive the wretched brute,' said Max.

'I think so,' said Merrin.

After Max had gone, Merrin cleared up and then called William for his last walk before bedtime. They went down onto the Harbour Beach, picking their way between the fishing boats. There was enough of a moon, which, together with the Christmas lights, meant there was no need for a torch. A pall of depression still hovered over Merrin, which even Max had been unable to shift. They walked back home together, she gave William his treat and covered up Horatio, who had been uncharacteristically quiet all evening. She got ready for bed and once she had climbed in, William jumped up, as usual, and settled himself at her feet.

This time tomorrow night, Merrin thought, *where will he be – will he be frightened, will he be lonely, will he be missing me?* She lay on her back, staring up at the ceiling and found herself crying again. Immediately, William shuffled up the bed, licked her face and then snuggled down beside her. She put an arm round him and fell into a deep sleep.

First thing the following morning, Merrin phoned Clara. 'There's no need for you to come round this morning. William is staying with me.'

CHAPTER NINETEEN

Inspector Louis Peppiatt shut down his phone with a heavy sigh. He had been speaking to Sergeant David Brownley of Thames Valley Police and the news was not especially good. The Sergeant and a WPC, Jessie Andrews, had visited Roberta Allnut earlier in the day. Their reception had been decidedly frosty. Roberta was angry on many levels – that Isla had told her mother about James's apparent disappearance; that Isla's wretched mother had the temerity to contact the police; that the police seemed to think it was their business to become involved at all.

'It was all rather peculiar,' said Sergeant Brownley. 'You would think Miss Allnut would be very anxious about her nephew. He was due back in Oxford a week ago, he's not answering his phone and he has made no attempt to contact his aunt. Also, he is new to the country. Although he was born of English parents, he has only been in the UK since September and then up in Scotland under the umbrella of his university. He is only just nineteen and away from home for the first time. I would have thought he could be quite vulnerable, sir.'

'I don't disagree with you, Sergeant. So how did the meeting end?'

'Miss Allnut said she didn't want James's parents to be unnecessarily worried at this stage and absolutely refused to give us their address in Singapore. I have someone in the office trying to track them down right now. She confirmed she had no photographs of James, except as a newborn, so I asked if we could take a DNA sample to check whether she is related to your body in St Ives. At first she refused point blank but my colleague, Jessie, who, I have to admit, has much more patience than me, talked her round. So, we have the sample and it's on its way by courier to your lab. We are checking out his college at university to make sure he has not returned there. Oh, and another thing – we have James's mobile number and we've tried to put a trace on it but it seems to have disappeared.'

'Well done, Sergeant, you've done a great job, I'm most grateful. Will you contact the parents if you can track down their address?' Louis asked.

'I thought we should wait until we see if we have a DNA match. If there is no match, then James is purely a missing person. If it is a match, well, it's a whole different ballgame, isn't it, sir?'

'I agree,' said Louis. 'I'll be in touch the moment we get the results.'

'I wouldn't want to be Isla McKenzie when she comes home from university this evening,' said Sergeant Brownley. 'Miss Allnut has a real temper on her and she is not at all pleased with Isla.'

After the phone call, Louis sat at his desk, staring out of his window at the unhappy view of a dilapidated brick wall and broken drainpipe, which were the primary features of the adjacent property. Should he warn Merrin that her daughter was in for trouble when she got home? No, he decided, he shouldn't meddle; Isla would call her mother if she needed support, which, by the sounds of it, she probably would.

Roberta's reaction to the police visit worried him, though. It made no sense. Roberta may not know her nephew but presumably she was *in loco parentis* as his parents were trapped abroad. Why was she angry? Why hadn't she already contacted the police herself to report that James was missing? Why, too, had she resisted giving a DNA sample – surely, she should have wanted to know if the body in St Ives belonged to her nephew.

It all pointed to something being not quite right, which in turn made him recognise that Merrin McKenzie had probably been correct in contacting him about James Allnut.

For Isla McKenzie, it had been a foul day at university. She had handed in her essay the previous day, confident that it was a good one – it had involved a great deal of work and thought. She disliked her tutor, Christopher Barlow, but it never occurred to her that he would not be pleased with her efforts. Instead, he had rubbished both the essay and her in front of the whole tutor group. It had made her feel angry, humiliated and frustrated, because she was still confident that her work was good.

Isla was a pretty girl who had inherited her father's blonde hair and her mother's big blue eyes and petite figure. She had dated a few boys during her first year at university but no one special. Frankly, she was so exhilarated by being awarded a place at Oxford University she was immediately focused on her work. Her first year at Oxford had begun extremely well – her tutor was inspiring and her essays very well received. Initially, she was terrified at being surrounded by so many clever people, but as the year progressed, she had started to gain in confidence. And then, on 12th April, her father was killed and everything changed.

The university was enormously supportive, giving her as much time off as she needed, offering counselling and tutorials by Zoom. However, after a couple of weeks at home, following her father's funeral, both Isla and Merrin decided they should try going back to work. Throwing herself back into studying worked for Isla but she found she simply could not socialise. If someone made her laugh, she felt guilty – how could she enjoy herself when her father had so tragically died, well before his time?

Even before Adam's death, Isla had become very friendly with a girl named Maggie Faulkner. They were both reading history and loved their course. When Isla returned to Oxford, Maggie was the only person she wanted to spend time with. Maggie seemed to understand, to be able to fit in with Isla's moods, knowing when to be cheerful and when to keep quiet. The girls were in the same college and when they decided to find accommodation outside college in their second year, Isla couldn't bear the idea of living in a flat with a lot of other people. It seemed the obvious solution that they should seek accommodation together and they had been extremely lucky to find the two rooms in a small house in Jericho, belonging to Roberta Allnut.

The autumn term had begun well. Isla's new tutor, Christopher Barlow, had seemed to appreciate both her hard work and her essays, until the last few weeks of term, when he had been absolutely vile to her. It was such a shock to the system to suddenly find herself an apparently poor student. So far, since her early days at school, Isla's academic life had been a breeze – she loved learning and had always been extremely able. Without a doubt, her commitment to study had helped her through the dark days following her father's death – until now. She just did not understand what was going on.

Isla and Maggie had arranged to meet for lunch at a café in Oxford's Covered Market. Maggie was already there, sitting dejectedly over a coffee. Isla could see at once that she had been crying. Maggie had not been herself recently and had admitted to Isla that she was seeing an older man, who was married but in the process of divorcing his wife. Isla did not like the sound of him and certainly he was not apparently making her friend very happy.

'What's up?' Isla asked, sitting down at the table.

Maggie raised her head and Isla gasped. One of Maggie's eyes was bruised and very swollen.

'Maggie, what has earth's happened?' Isla asked, horrified.

'I fell over,' Maggie muttered.

'Well, I suppose that's slightly more original than saying you walked into a door. Did he do this to you? Because if he did, you must never see him again.'

'He didn't mean to, Isla; it was a mistake. He's very sorry and he wants me to stay up in Oxford for Christmas, which is fantastic, isn't it?'

'It's absolutely not fantastic. Who is this guy? Is he really getting a divorce or is he just using you for a bit of fun on the side, and a punch bag as well, by the look of it? Honestly, darling Mags, you are such a lovely person and you deserve so much better. It doesn't feel right, it really doesn't. Anyway, you said you were going home for Christmas.'

'I'm going to tell them I can't come home, they won't mind at all, probably won't even notice. But he wants me to be here for Christmas and I want to be with him. There is nothing to discuss, Isla. It's what I'm going to do.'

'Well, I'm not leaving you in Oxford on your own over Christmas with a middle-aged married man who has given you a black eye. Does he have any children?'

'Yes, two,' said Maggie.

'Then I bet you he will be spending Christmas Day with his children.'

'He's explained all that. He is going to spend part of the day with the children and then we will be together all evening,' said Maggie defensively.

'So you will be spending most of Christmas Day on your own? Honestly, Maggie, this is a relationship you really have to bin.'

'I'm not going to bin it, Isla. I love him; he is the best thing that has happened to me in my whole life.'

Isla left the café having totally failed to change Maggie's mind. She felt wretched. Whoever this man was, he had some sort of hold over Maggie; coercive control came to mind. And now he had started hitting her, Isla felt pretty sure he was not going to stop. She decided not to go back to the library, which had been her original intention. Instead, she would go home and work there. It would give her the opportunity to ring her mother. If necessary, she would delay going down to St Ives for a couple of days and see if she could persuade Maggie to spend Christmas in Cornwall. Merrin really liked Maggie and she was sure her mother would not mind including her in their festive celebrations. She would call her as soon as she got home.

CHAPTER TWENTY

Roberta's home was a charming little house, close to the canal in Jericho, just a two-up-two-down, but with room for them all. Roberta lived on the ground floor, the former sitting room acting as her bedroom in which she had installed a shower room and loo. The second room was her kitchen/dining room, to which Isla and Maggie had access. They lived on the first floor with a bedroom each and their own bathroom. It was ideal. Both being studious girls, Roberta appeared happy to have them; they were no trouble. Recently, though, Maggie had been coming in at all hours, sometimes not until early morning. It was annoying because although Maggie was as quiet as a mouse, her arrival often woke up Roberta, who, as old age approached, had become a light sleeper.

Still, all in all, they were good girls – or rather they had been, but the honeymoon period was now well and truly over.

Roberta heard the front door open and someone come into the hallway. It was too early for either girl to come home normally but she judged it to be Isla since Maggie had slept in late. 'Isla!' she called. 'Is that you?'

Isla popped her head round the door of the kitchen, where Roberta was sitting at the kitchen table. 'Hello, Roberta, it's only me. I've come home early today to start this week's essay. Creepy Chris didn't like last week's, in fact he was horrible about it, so I'm really going to try and knock him dead with this week's essay.'

'Creepy Chris isn't a very polite way of referring to your tutor,' said Roberta. Her wide range of friends included many academics, Christopher Barlow being one of them.

'It's what you call him,' said Isla defensively, coming further into the room. 'Would you like me to make you a cup of tea?'

'I would like you to come and sit down,' said Roberta; her voice was icy.

Only then did Isla realise that Roberta was not in the best of moods. 'Yes, of course,' she said. 'Is something wrong?'

'Is something wrong, is something wrong?' Roberta mimicked. 'Yes, of course something's wrong. You and your bloody mother sent the police round here this morning. What on earth made you think you had the right to do that? How dare you interfere with my family, my life and have the nerve to involve the police without even asking me. And the questions they asked – you'd think it was me who murdered my nephew, the way they went on. Well, what have you got to say for yourself?'

Isla was stunned but recovered quickly. 'I don't understand. We discussed your missing nephew, James, and we decided together I should check with my mother to see if there was any way the body she had found could be James. You knew perfectly well I was going to talk to my mother about it.'

'Sneaky! That's what I call it – sneaky! I certainly didn't ask you to call in the police, did I? I don't know how you dared to do that without my knowledge.' Roberta was now very red in the face and her several chins were wobbling with agitation. She was a formidable sight.

Isla, however, was not intimidated; she was too angry. 'I wasn't being sneaky; I wasn't listening at keyholes. We had a discussion about James and I suggested I should speak to my mother and you did not disagree. I was only trying to help, for heaven's sake.'

'A bloody funny way of showing it. Don't you dare tell your mother anything more about my nephew – he's my business, not yours. Not that you will hear anything more about him from me. I want you out of here in a month, you and your wayward friend. One month's notice from today. I'd kick you out now but for the fact it's Christmas and I'm a charitable person by nature.'

Isla had the good sense not to challenge the suggestion that Roberta had a charitable nature. Instead, she said, 'What do you mean – my "wayward friend"?'

'That Maggie, she's out until late most nights, sometimes not back until morning. You must have noticed. She had a black eye this morning, serve her right. She must be messing about with some particularly unpleasant man.'

'I don't think it's any of our business,' said Isla stoutly.

'What, you mean like my missing nephew being none of yours? Just get out of my sight, Isla, and keep your nose out of my business until you leave here.'

Anger sustained Isla up the stairs and into her bedroom and then shock set in – shock and confusion. She could not believe she had so wrongly judged the situation. She sat down on her desk chair, feeling a little wobbly. The thought of having to find new accommodation in the middle of the academic year was not a good one. She and Maggie had been so lucky. Jericho was a lovely place to live and so near their college and the other university buildings. Most of the students lived out at Cowley, which involved either a bus or a long walk into town. A wave of sadness suddenly overtook her – she missed her father so much. He would have been particularly better than her mother at helping her sort out what to do next and there was something about his reassuring presence that had always made her feel safe.

She needed to ring her mother, if for no other reason than to tell her she might not be home on the 19th. As well as Maggie, there was now the problem of finding somewhere else to live. She badly needed a coffee before making the call but not for one moment did she dare go back downstairs to the kitchen.

Merrin listened carefully to everything her daughter had to say. When she had finished, she could sense Isla was close to tears. 'Darling, it's not your fault. If it is anyone's, it's mine.'

'No,' wailed Isla. 'It was me who suggested you should get hold of your chum in the police force. I suppose I thought you would have a chat about it with him, and just bear James in mind if the police drew a blank in finding out the identity of your dead boy. I didn't imagine that they would send round two policemen to interview Roberta. She said the questions they were asking sounded like they thought she had murdered her nephew. I admit, she was probably exaggerating that bit but she was so very angry.'

'Would you like me to talk to Roberta and explain it was all my fault? Hopefully, she might change her mind about asking you to leave.' said Merrin.

'No, I don't think so, not yet at any rate. Hopefully, she'll calm down but I don't think she'll change her mind. Honestly, it has been such a shit day.'

Isla then told her mother about her horrible tutor, about Maggie and her black eye and the fact that she felt she might need to stay up in Oxford for a few more days.

'Do bring Maggie down to us for Christmas, if you can,' Merrin said, before Isla had even asked, 'and try to be down by the 22nd at the latest. I have someone I would like you to meet.'

'Oh God, Mum, not a boyfriend at your age and so soon after Dad? That really would be the final straw.'

'No,' said Merrin hurriedly, 'we now have a dog in the family, who I am dying for you to meet.'

'A dog, a puppy? What breed? How exciting, tell me everything, I need photos now.'

'His name is William, he is not a puppy, I am told he is about five years old and he's a rescue dog.' At this point, Merrin decided to omit the fact that Clara had been involved. 'As to his breed, I am afraid it's a question of taking your pick. He has a look of most popular breeds and he seems to be a dog of two halves, the front half being rather different from the back. Am I selling him to you, darling?'

'Looks aren't everything, Mum. The thing is, do you love him?'

'I rather think I do,' Merrin admitted, 'and equally important, so does Horatio.'

After mother and daughter had ended the call, Merrin made herself a cup of tea and sat at her kitchen table, deep in thought. She felt terrible that it looked as if Isla and Maggie had lost their accommodation. It was all her fault – she should have asked Inspector Peppiatt to hold off the Thames Valley visit until she'd had time to tell Isla, and presumably Roberta, what was happening. However, it had been hard enough trying to persuade the inspector that there could be a possible link between James Allnut and the boy in the bed, without asking him to delay pursuing any further enquiries. Anyway, she wasn't in a position to start telling him how to run his investigation.

Something wasn't right, though, she was sure of it. Why was Roberta so angry? Any normal person would have been pleased that the police were taking seriously the fact that their nephew was missing. It felt as if the police visit was a worry for her, which, surely, could be because there was something she didn't want them to know about.

Then there was Merrin's new tutor. Just at the moment, Isla needed all the encouragement she could get. Up until now, the university had played a major role in helping her cope with her father's death. And then poor Maggie and her highly inappropriate relationship, which sounded a real worry as it had become violent. Too many troubles coming all at once was absolutely not what Isla needed right now, while her mother was in St Ives, so far away. Suddenly, leaving Bristol seemed a very irresponsible decision to have made.

Remembering that Isla wanted photographs of William, Merrin stopped fretting and concentrated on trying to portray him in his best light. Sitting in his basket, William did not look like a dog of two halves but he would not stay in his basket once he realised he was the centre of attention. So, in the end, Merrin sent three photos of William, warts and all.

A text message came back straight away. *He's sweet, I love him already.*

Crazy girl! Merrin thought proudly. *Foolish, but brave.*

CHAPTER TWENTY-ONE

For the next few days, Merrin continued to worry about Isla. The nagging feeling persisted that all was not right so far as Roberta was concerned. Merrin just could not get it out of her head that the woman was a threat in some way. She had rung Isla several times to make sure she was alright and clearly Isla was uncomfortable, too, as she seemed pleased to have her mother fussing over her, which was certainly not the norm.

On the third day after Roberta's outburst, Merrin received a call from Inspector Peppiatt asking if he could come and see her again. Much to her surprise, she felt relieved to have the opportunity of meeting him – perhaps he would be able to allay her fears where Roberta was concerned.

He arrived looking very grave and Merrin, suddenly anxious, tried to be flippant. 'You're looking very serious, Inspector. Please don't say you've come to arrest me.'

Louis was clearly not amused. 'No, Mrs McKenzie, I haven't. But I do have some news that I thought I should tell you about in person.'

Merrin immediately conjured up the appalling image of Roberta standing over Isla with a carving knife. 'Is Isla alright?' she managed.

'Isla?' said Louis. 'Isla's perfectly alright, as far as I know. May I sit down and I will explain why I'm here?'

He sat in Adam's chair again, but Merrin barely noticed. She drew up a chair opposite him and sank into it, waiting for her heartbeat to return to normal.

'Are you feeling alright, Mrs McKenzie? You seem a little agitated.'

'No, I'm fine, please do go on.'

'We have the DNA results and our boy in the bed is definitely related to Roberta Allnut, which makes it almost certain that he is James Allnut. We have contacted James's parents and their DNA is on its way to the UK now, which will confirm the boy's identity for certain. However, they have emailed over an up-to-date photograph of James and everyone involved in the case is quite sure we have a match.'

'Oh, the poor parents,' said Merrin. 'I don't approve of tax exiles but not being able to come and see their son is an awful thought. Also, even when, hopefully, the case is solved, it will still be months before the body can be shipped home to Singapore, I imagine?'

'Yes, I was thinking the same,' said Louis. 'I share your view about tax exiles. I just cannot imagine sending off one of my children to university on the other side of the world, to a country they have never visited before, without accompanying them. Oh, and to an aunt who doesn't exactly sound maternal. How can money be more important than that?'

'The root of all evil, so they say,' said Merrin. 'So, what happens now?'

'We know from Roberta that James drove down to St Ives so we are currently searching for his car. Of course, we have no idea what sort of car, nor the registration number. We are just hoping that it's either parked illegally or has run out of paid parking time in one of the car parks.'

'There might be a quicker way to find it,' said Merrin. 'Why not start by looking at cars with surfboards, either on the roof or more likely inside the car? It's fine travelling with a board on a roof rack, but leaving it on the roof in a car park, the board is likely to get nicked – that is unless he was packing the car ready to leave for his journey back to Oxford when he was killed.'

Louis stared at her. 'Why on earth didn't any of us think of that? Give me a moment, I'll just make a phone call.' He let himself out of the front door, returning moments later. 'All done. Honestly, Mrs McKenzie, I think you should be running this investigation – first you find us the connection to James, which we might never have done without the help of you and your daughter, and now this, which should have been obvious.'

'It's often more successful to be able to tease out a problem from the outside looking in – much easier than being in the thick of it.'

'You're too kind.' Louis gave her an astute look. 'When I arrived and said I had something to tell you, I got the feeling you were worried about Isla. Am I right?'

'Oh, it's nothing,' said Merrin.

Louis sat down again. 'It's not nothing, Mrs McKenzie. I don't know you well but well enough to know you are a very sensible, grounded and intelligent person. If you're worried about Isla, you must have cause.'

'It's more of a feeling, typical mother worrying, nothing more. I don't have anything tangible to tell you, anything of any value.' Merrin was looking down at her hands, avoiding eye contact.

'Well, your daughter is of great value, and so far in this case, your feelings, your instincts, whatever you like to call them, have been of great value, too – and, incidentally, have also proved to be correct. Come on, tell me what's worrying you.'

She gave in. 'I don't know if Thames Valley told you but Roberta was absolutely furious to receive a visit from the police. She is angry with me, but far angrier with Isla. She implied that Isla had been spying on her but nothing could be further from the truth. It was Roberta who told her about James and Isla suggested she should contact me to see if the body had yet been identified. Admittedly, Isla did not tell Roberta that the police would be visiting her because she didn't know that would happen. I should have warned them, of course, when you told me you were contacting Thames Valley, but I'd imagined that Roberta would be relieved the police were taking an interest in her missing nephew.'

'So, your worry is what exactly?'

'There is something wrong with Roberta's anger at having a police visit, as if she is hiding something. She now hates Isla. I suppose I imagine Roberta might be violent, that's what's worrying me. Also, she has given Isla and her flatmate notice so they are having to find somewhere else to live. It's such an over-reaction – I know you'll think I'm being stupid, and who could blame you?'

'I don't think you're being stupid. I nearly called you when I heard that Roberta was so angry and then I thought better of it, assuming that Isla would contact you, if she was worried. I don't think Roberta is likely to hurt Isla. From what I understand, she is an extremely large elderly lady, suffering from arthritis and finds it difficult to move about. She doesn't sound much of a threat. In any event, Isla must be coming home for Christmas soon, isn't she?'

'You're right, of course. Isla will be down in St Ives by the 22nd at the latest.'

'And for the record,' said Louis, standing up, 'while I don't think Roberta will hurt Isla, I do agree that there is something very odd about her reaction to the police investigation. Thames Valley are going to tell her about the DNA match this afternoon. It will be interesting to learn of her reaction. When they call me, I will tell them about your concerns and get their view.'

* * *

Louis Peppiatt drove slowly back to the office, deep in thought. The previous evening he had spent reading the file on the fisherman found dead at Mullion Cove three years ago. The investigation had been scant, to put it mildly. Every available member of the force had been involved in searching for the little girl who had gone missing in Penzance. He had headed up that investigation and had also been the person to find her – drowned in a water trough on her parents' farm, just outside town. She was only seven and had been murdered by her stepfather, after years of abuse. It was a terrible case that he knew he would never forget.

The fisherman, George Jenkin, kept his boat at Porthleven but the boat had been wrecked somewhere between Gunwalloe and Mullion Cove. His body had washed up at Mullion. He had sustained an injury to the back of his head, which, it was assumed initially, could easily have occurred when the boat sank, or later when he was in the water and maybe dashed against some rocks. There was no explanation for the insulin injection. It emerged at the postmortem that George had no water in his lungs, which meant that he was already dead when he entered the water. The rather sloppy conclusion, in Louis's view, was that he could have been hit on the head by some fallen rigging while still on his boat and only fell into the sea when his boat sank. There was no satisfactory explanation for the insulin in his bloodstream.

George was a local man in his forties, who kept himself very much to himself. He was unmarried and was only survived by an elderly mother, who had dementia. So, there was no one to fight his corner and demand further investigations into his death. Louis made a mental note to talk to Graham Bennett again about the postmortem.

Killing someone by an insulin injection was an extremely unusual murder weapon – there had to be a link to James Allnut; the injuries were too similar. Louis smiled to himself remembering how dismissive he had been of Merrin McKenzie's insistence that there could be a link between James Allnut and the boy in the bed. Here he was trying to make a similar connection between James and George Jenkin. There had to be one, and finding that connection would surely lead them to the person responsible.

CHAPTER TWENTY-TWO

It was to be a day of several major developments.

Merrin woke early and, having taken William for a walk, she came home but found she could not shake off her worries. She knew the source of her anxiety revolved around wondering how Roberta had reacted to learning of the DNA match to James and how it would affect her attitude to Isla. Isla had admitted that she was finding it very hard to live under the same roof as Roberta. Merrin was very tempted to ring her daughter but fought off the desire to do so. Isla would call when she was good and ready. If not, Merrin decided she would have to call her later, if only for her own sanity.

Things were not improving for Isla. She was struggling with this week's essay, which was due in this afternoon. Even she knew it was not a good one but her confidence had been badly shaken by her tutor and the words were just not flowing. The subject she was studying this term was the development of the Victorian industrial transport systems – the railways, canals and steamships in particular. She was fascinated by the Victorians and the quality of their workmanship, still so visible today. This essay was supposed to be focused on canals but she was really struggling. The situation was not helped by the fact that, having done her research, she normally liked to write her essays in her room, in peace and quiet. However, the atmosphere at home was so awful she was forced to try and complete it in the library. Roberta was blanking her and even dear, gentle Maggie was furious with her. Isla had not been forgiven for her outburst in the café as to the unsuitability of Maggie's relationship, and things had deteriorated still further when Isla had been forced to tell Maggie that they were going to be thrown out of Roberta's in a month's time.

The rubbish essay was completed in all its awfulness by lunchtime. Isla was just packing away her books and laptop when her mother rang.

'Sorry, darling,' said Merrin. 'Is this a good moment to talk?'

'I'm in the library, Mum. I'm just leaving; I have to drop in my essay at college but I should be able to call you back in about ten minutes. We can talk on my walk home.'

'You don't sound like you're walking,' said Merrin when Isla called back.

'Actually, I've stopped off in the pub. It's so cold outside and I'm fed up, so I've treated myself to a large glass of red, which I'm drinking in front of a roaring fire. How does that sound?'

'It sounds perfect; I wish I was with you. How are things? I've been worrying about you.'

'They could be better,' Isla admitted.

'Has Roberta told you about the DNA results?' Merrin asked.

'Not a word. Do we know the results, then?'

'Yes, Inspector Peppiatt told me and said Thames Valley were going to call on Roberta yesterday afternoon. The results are positive in that Roberta and the poor boy are related. DNA samples are on their way from James's parents but they sent over a photograph, from which it appears there is little doubt it is James. So, well done you for making the connection.'

'It's awful, though, isn't it?' said Isla. 'I'm afraid I have no idea how Roberta feels. I have been working in the library because the atmosphere at home is so dire. Surely she can't really be cross with us now, can she? Without us, the missing boy and an unsolved murder in St Ives might well never have been linked and no one would ever have known what happened to James.'

'True,' said Merrin, 'but I suppose a lot depends on why she didn't want police involvement in the first place. Anyway, Inspector Peppiatt is very pleased with us, which is something. Has Maggie thawed at all?'

'No,' said Isla. 'Maybe this news will make her see we did the right thing. I'll tell her this evening if she comes home before I go to bed. I don't even know if she wants us to look for a new place together, or whether she wants us to go our separate ways.'

'I'm sure she will want to stay living with you. Tell me, how did the essay go?'

'Don't ask,' said Isla gloomily, 'and as for Maggie, knowing my luck, she's probably going to use this opportunity to shack up with her ghastly boyfriend.'

It was a grey afternoon; even the Christmas lights could not mask the colourless weather. 'Shall we have a walk round town?' Merrin asked William, who, needless to say, was keen. The tide was high so they walked around the Island, then past the Tate Gallery and headed up the cliff path towards Man's Head – so called because it is a rock of granite in the shape of, well, a man's head. It was also the place to where the lads graduated when pier jumping became too tame. It terrified Merrin. They jumped from a rock beside Man's Head into the sea below. It was a fair old drop but the worst part was the necessity to jump well out to avoid hitting rocks on the way down. Even now, after all these years, it still made Merrin feel queasy and she knew the mere mention of the place made many a mother's blood run cold. But it was tradition, a rite of passage, the boys of the town had been making the jump for as long as anyone could remember.

They had just begun climbing up the cliff path when Merrin heard the sound of a police siren. Looking back towards the town, she could see above the cemetery, into Barnoon car park, where several police cars were parked. 'I bet they've found James's car, William,' Merrin said. 'Come on, I can't resist it, let's go and have a look.'

William was unimpressed; he liked walks on the cliff

path. Still, they plodded back and walked up to the car park. A small blue Peugeot was the centre of attention, the car doors and boot open and a cluster of policemen surrounding it. As they approached, the unmistakeable figure of Jack Eddy detached itself from the group.

'How's my little Merrin?' he asked. 'I hear the surfboard idea was yours; the boss told me. You've always been a clever girl, my lovely. Look, it's over there; that's how we found the car, just like you said, my clever maid.' Jack pointed to a surfboard lying on the ground, beside the car. 'He certainly thinks a lot of you now, my boss, and so he should – by goodness, so he should indeed, after all you've done to help us.'

'Is that James's car, then?' Merrin asked.

'We were pretty sure we'd found the right car last night but fingerprints have confirmed it just now. I don't think the boss will mind me telling you we've found James's car but he won't want me to tell you what's inside it, that's for sure. No, he certainly won't.'

'Not another body,' said Merrin, horrified.

'No, no, little Merrin, nothing like that, don't you fret yourself,' said Jack hastily.

'Thank goodness. It's just that you made it sound like something awful had been found.'

'It's awful in a way,' said Jack. 'I probably shouldn't have said that, so I'm not telling you anything more, just to be on the safe side.'

'That's fine, Jack,' said Merrin, though, of course, it wasn't. She was now dying to know what was in the car. 'I'll see you later.'

She and William started across the car park when Jack called after them. 'Hey, Merrin, what's that you've got on the end of your lead?' He was grinning from ear to ear.

'A dog,' she said firmly. 'My dog.'

Jack's voice drifted across the car park. 'Are you sure about that, my maid?'

'Don't listen,' Merrin advised William.

Merrin had just reached the front door when her mobile rang. She hurriedly fumbled in her coat pocket, thinking it might be Isla again. It was Inspector Peppiatt.

'I must have just missed you at Barnoon; Jack told me he'd seen you there. I have something I need to ask you. Could I pop by in about twenty minutes? It won't take long.'

'Yes, of course,' said Merrin. 'I'll put the kettle on.'

Inspector Peppiatt arrived looking decidedly chilly. 'A fire!' he said. 'May I stand by it for a moment? It's suddenly gone very cold out there.'

'Yes, warm yourself up. Tea, let me guess – a little milk but no sugar?'

'Correct,' said Louis, smiling. He took the offered mug of tea and stood with his back to the fire. 'This is a bit delicate and because I've offended you before, I'm very anxious not to do so again.'

'That sounds very mysterious and maybe a little alarming. Do carry on,' said Merrin.

'In the boot of James's car – I presume Jack could not

resist telling you that we have found James's car?'

Merrin smiled. 'In his defence, I did ask him if it was.'

'Fair enough,' said Louis. 'In the boot of James's car, we found a small quantity of cocaine. It was not in a bag; it looked like a spillage. We know James never made it to Oxford but it was his intention to do so. I think that's a reasonable assumption, since he had accepted Roberta's invitation for Christmas. So was the drug something he and maybe his friends had been using, though there were no drugs or alcohol in his bloodstream? Alternatively, was it something he was intending to take up to Oxford?' Louis hesitated. 'So, the question is whether Isla might have seen Roberta using cocaine or whether she has seen any lying about?'

'So, Inspector, are you really trying to ask me if my daughter takes drugs?'

'No,' said Louis firmly. 'That's why I wanted to ask the question in person. I'm certainly not suggesting Isla is involved in anything to do with drugs. It's just that I'm wondering whether James might have been taking up a supply to his aunt and whether there has ever been any indication that Roberta might be handling drugs, hence her anger at the police visiting her home.'

'You mean like a county lines operation?' Merrin asked, slightly mollified.

'I don't know, could be. All I know is that a young man was murdered and some cocaine, quite a lot actually, is scattered in the boot of his car. I think the two facts have to be linked. I don't want Thames Valley to go charging through Roberta's house on a drugs raid; apart from anything else, the link is so tenuous. Remember, Roberta and James never actually met. I also don't want to put Isla through an interview so close to losing her father, on top of having to cope with all the trauma of Roberta's rages and trying to find herself new digs. I just wondered if you could ask her if she has seen anything suspicious and maybe to keep an eye out?'

'I will ask her but, as you say, she has a lot going on at the moment. Roberta is still not talking to her and has told her nothing about the DNA match. The first Isla heard about it was when I told her earlier this afternoon. Do you know how Roberta reacted when Thames Valley told her there was a match, if you don't mind me asking?'

'No, of course I don't mind; Isla has a right to know. When told, Roberta said "Poor boy" and went very pale. She asked how he died and they told her. They asked if she would like someone with her and she was very adamant that she did not. However, she was very quiet and subdued – very different from their last visit. In fact, Sergeant Brownley from Thames Valley, who gave her the news, said she behaved far more normally than before. She just seemed like an old lady who had received bad news, which had both shocked and saddened her. He told her that they were in touch with her brother and that we were working hard to find her nephew's killer, but she barely seemed to react at all.'

'So perhaps she will be nicer to Isla now,' said Merrin, without much conviction.

'Let's hope so. Thank you for the tea. Pick a moment

to ask Isla when you think it is right for her. There's no rush; we have a number of other leads we're working on.' He walked to the door. 'Thank you again for your help, Mrs McKenzie. Goodbye, and goodbye to you, William, and to you, Horatio.'

'His manners are definitely improving,' Merrin told her companions once the door had closed.

CHAPTER TWENTY-THREE

Merrin hurried through her Friday changeover at Rupert's Cottage. It was an easy one – two female friends on holiday who had left the cottage immaculate. Merrin was in a hurry for several reasons: Tristan was giving Clara a night off and so Clara was coming to supper and Merrin wanted to cook a decent meal; she had left William alone hardly at all since his arrival and he'd looked very forlorn when she left him that morning; and, of course, she hated cleaning.

Clara and Tristan were brilliant cooks, so Merrin decided to make a beef casserole with mashed potatoes and spring greens. Nursery food, which she couldn't get wrong. She bought the necessary ingredients from the Co-op and rushed home to find William sitting happily by Horatio's cage. Neither of them looked particularly pleased to see her and it appeared to Merrin, from their expressions, as if she had interrupted a private conversation. 'Pull yourself together,' she murmured to herself. Clearly living with two such strong characters was starting to tip her over the edge.

As she chopped and cooked, Merrin thought back over the conversation she'd had with Inspector Peppiatt the previous day. He'd seemed to be concentrating on the possible link between Roberta and James as being responsible for the presence of drugs in James's car. But what about the smuggling of drugs into Cornwall? Just as back in the so-called romantic days of Poldark et al, when Cornwall was perfect for landing brandy and tobacco in particular, today those same remote coves were the recipients of a wide range of drugs – smuggling in Cornwall had not changed much through the centuries, except for the nature of the merchandise. Surely, the reason James had been murdered was because, for whatever reason, he was in possession of a quantity of cocaine. Had he stolen it, was he acting as a courier, was he involved in some sort of drugs war, or was he just an innocent victim in the wrong place at the wrong time? Who knew, but surely Inspector Peppiatt should be concentrating his efforts down here to trace the source of the cocaine and then check to see if any one of the potential suspects was a diabetic.

In fact, at the same moment Merrin was tipping chopped onions and garlic into her casserole dish, Louis Peppiatt and Jack Eddy were setting out on their way to Porthleven, where, until his death, fisherman George Jenkin had kept his boat, *Young Nancy*. They had arranged to meet Old Tom Conch at the Ship Inn. Louis had it on good authority that Old Tom knew everything there was to know about boats and seamen from Porthleven round to the Lizard. He was well into his seventies but still went out to sea with his son a couple of times a week.

Louis loved Porthleven. It had always been a picturesque little fishing port, but in recent years it had become something of a centre for good food, spawning a number of excellent restaurants and a food and music festival once a year. Most iconic was the church on the pier. In stormy weather, it was used endlessly by the media to demonstrate the ferocity of the sea, which sent waves crashing right over the top of the church tower. The town was also dear to Louis's heart because it was where he took his children on their most successful outings together since the divorce. On sunny days, with a calm sea, Louis would hire a little motor boat and they would go spinning for mackerel. Then, triumphant with their catch, they would build a barbeque on Porthleven beach. Nothing tasted better than mackerel straight from the sea, in Louis's view, and armed also with fresh crusty bread, a lemon and a delicious salad, the three of them had a meal fit for a king. Then a wander back round the harbour in search of an ice cream completed the day. It was perfect.

'With a bit of luck, we'll have at least two more summers together before the children decide they would rather be with their mates,' Louis mused as they arrived at the Ship Inn, forcing him to concentrate on the job in hand.

Old Tom was already up at the bar, regaling what looked like a couple of tourists with stories of the sea. Louis was amused to see they appeared to have already bought him a drink and were on the brink of ordering him another. He stepped in quickly; he needed Old Tom to have a relatively clear head. 'My round, I think,' he said, smiling at the couple. 'I have a meeting with this gentleman, so if you wouldn't mind, I'll drag him away for a few minutes.'

Old Tom appeared to like being called a gentleman. 'Most kind of you, sir, mine's a pint of Proper Job.'

Jack had found a table in a secluded corner of the bar, which, in any event, was not yet busy. The three men sat down.

Old Tom took a hefty swig of his pint. 'So, you want to know about George Jenkin. Why's that, then?'

Louis saw no point in being too cautious as to what he disclosed. Porthleven, like St Ives, had a jungle telegraph. The news that two policemen were in town would already be doing the rounds. 'My name is Inspector Louis Peppiatt and this is Sergeant Jack Eddy. You may have heard that there has been a recent murder in St Ives. The young man's cause of death was very similar to that of Mr Jenkin. We are of the opinion that there may be a link between the two deaths, and if we can find that link, we should be able to solve both crimes.'

'George Jenkin died at least three years ago; the case

was closed. I don't see why you want to rake up all that again,' said Old Tom, having another go at his pint.

'I'll be blunt, Tom. Do you think George Jenkin could have been involved in smuggling? I'm thinking drugs here.'

There was a very long silence during which Old Tom appeared to be gazing into space. Just when Louis was about to ask the question again, Old Tom began to talk.

'He was a rum bloke, George was. No friends, no wife, no kiddies, just an old mother who was as nutty as a fruit cake. I knew him as a little lad. His father was a deep-sea trawlerman and died at sea when George was just a boy. You would have understood if he never wanted to go to sea himself after that, but he was obsessed.'

'What do you mean, Tom, by obsessed?' Jack asked.

'He was always at sea in that little boat of his, *Young Nancy*. Mind you, he had nothing to be on shore for, except his mad old mother. He made a living of sorts from his fishing and he and his mother lived simply. You never saw him in the pub and their cottage had been in the family for donkey's years, I doubt there was a mortgage.' He downed his pint and motioned to Jack to fetch him another one.

As soon as Jack had left the table, Old Tom nodded in his direction. 'He was on the case, wasn't he, looking into George's death?'

Louis nodded.

'A right mess the police made of it. Apparently, George was injected with something but no one ever followed it up. You weren't there, were you?'

'No,' said Louis. 'I was on another case in Penzance; a little girl went missing.'

'I remember that, terrible. It was an inspector who found her – was that you?'

'Yes, that was me,' said Louis. 'It was not a good day, one I'll never forget.'

'For a copper, you're not such a bad lad. Get that man of yours to fetch you a drink and tell him to take his time. I'd rather not have him here while I tell you what I know.'

Without much prompting, Old Tom told Louis everything he knew, which was not much but confirmed Louis's suspicions that there had been some very sloppy police work surrounding George's death. No one locally could understand what had happened. George was a surly individual but an excellent seaman. The night *Young Nancy* went down, there was a clear night sky with an almost full moon. The sea was calm and there was absolutely no reason for the boat to be wrecked.

After the event, rumours flew around claiming that George was involved with some smuggling gang, and, according to Old Tom, the police were well aware of the rumours but did nothing about them. It was recognised that there was no way of telling how George had received his head injury but no one believed he'd simply had an accident. When, at the inquest, it was reported that he had died of an injection of insulin, the court seemed to believe he had injected himself, which was what caused his boat to be wrecked. He was an oddball, a loner and the sad fact was that no one missed him.

'What was he injected with? I forget,' Old Tom asked as Jack returned to the table with a pint for Old Tom and a half for Louis.

'Insulin,' said Louis. 'It's what diabetics take to help them stay healthy. Do you know anyone in town who is a diabetic?'

'I can't say I do,' said Old Tom. 'Was George a diabetic, then?'

'No,' said Louis, 'and that's the point. It was because he wasn't a diabetic that the insulin killed him.'

'Then I think he must have killed himself,' said Old Tom. 'I can't see anyone round here using a needle to murder someone – they'd just belt their victim over the head with a hammer. Simple.'

On that happy note, both policemen rose to leave. 'You've been most helpful, Tom,' said Louis, 'thank you for your valuable time. Would you like one for the road?' Louis nodded at Tom's glass.

'You called me a gentleman just now. I reckon you're a gentleman too, sir,' said Old Tom. 'I hope you get your man.'

'Thank you, there'll be a drink behind the bar for you, when you're ready,' said Louis. 'You'd better drive, Eddy,' he added. 'We're going to the lab now. If you wait in the car, I won't be more than a few minutes.'

Earlier in the day, Louis had called Dr Graham Bennett and asked him to dig out his file on George Jenkin's postmortem. Graham had been his usual grumpy and difficult self, saying it would show up nothing that he had not already disclosed to Louis. 'And I'm busy as hell; everyone's decided to die this week, damned thoughtless of them.'

The file was waiting for Louis when he arrived at the lab. He sat in reception and read the file carefully, making the odd note. When he'd finished, he returned to the receptionist. 'Can I have five minutes with himself? I just have a couple of questions.'

The receptionist smiled. 'On your head be it, Inspector. I think it is fair to say that we are not in the best of moods today.'

'I'm match-ready to beat off any assault,' said Louis, smiling.

Ten minutes later, Graham Bennett appeared in reception. 'This is very inconvenient and, I might say, pointless.'

'If you stop grumbling and let me ask my questions, it will all be over in a couple of minutes.' Graham snorted; Louis ignored him and continued. 'First question – would the injection of insulin, if administered on board, have killed George before the boat sank?'

'God knows,' said Graham. 'It depends on how long it took for the boat to sink.'

'Most helpful, thank you,' said Louis, with just the right amount of sarcasm. 'Second and last question – why was no fuss made at the inquest when you told them he had died of insulin poisoning, not the blow to the head?'

'The judge wasn't interested. They recorded an open

verdict, as you will have seen, but the judge's view was that George had killed himself. He asked me how much insulin would have been needed to kill him. I said a couple of pens would do it and the judge asked if that was the sort of dosage he could obtain from a diabetic mate. I said it was. I made the point about his lungs, that he had been dead when he entered the water, but that only confirmed, in the judge's mind, that it was suicide as there was no evidence that anyone else was on board. I admit it was a poor business. Can I go now?'

In the car on the way back to the station, Jack asked Louis what sort of progress he thought they had made during the day.

'None really, Eddy, other than to confirm my view that a right pig's ear was made of the investigation into George Jenkin's death. If it had been properly investigated and the person responsible caught, then young James Allnut might well still be alive.'

'I wasn't in charge of the case, boss,' said Jack defensively.

'I know, old chap, it's not your fault.' Louis sighed. 'I'm going to have a word with the Border Force to check out the current situation with regard to drug smuggling. They might have some ideas about Jenkin too, though I think I am probably clutching at straws there. To be honest, at the moment, I can't see where we go from here.'

CHAPTER TWENTY-FOUR

When Clara burst into Miranda's Cottage that evening she was very confident that she had some good news for Merrin. Earlier that day, her former cleaner, a young woman named Jenny Rowe, had presented herself at the restaurant. Full of apologies for letting down Clara at such short notice, she asked whether there was any chance she could have her job back.

A first Clara had been very sceptical. Although Jenny had been a good worker for several years, the way she had left was inexcusable and very out of character. Jenny had apologised profusely and said she'd had some serious family problems, which were now resolved. The woman looked tired and drained; she also seemed close to tears and Clara could not help but feel sorry for her.

'So have you somewhere permanent to live now?' Clara had asked. Jenny's accommodation problems had always been an issue, as they were for so many young people in West Cornwall. Rental prices were sky-high, caused, of course, by the tourist trade – both a blessing and a curse. Several times in the past, Clara had allowed Jenny to stay in one of her cottages, if it was empty for the week.

Jenny's expression brightened. 'Yes, I now have a camper van. It's great. I've been camping all over the place and I just book into a campsite for a shower now and again.'

'Camping isn't ideal at this time of year, is it?' Clara suggested.

'No, it's fine. I have a little heater; I'm as snug as a bug, honest.'

So, Clara had given in, knowing it would not have been fair on Merrin to miss the opportunity to replace her.

'Pearl, I need an enormous drink and you're going to love me,' was Clara's gambit.

'White wine?' Merrin suggested, raising an eyebrow. Was Clara suggesting she should be loved because she had another awful new task in mind for her alleged best friend?

'Perfect, a large one, please, darling Pearl.' Once in possession of her wine, Clara raised her glass. 'The toast is to Jenny Rowe.'

'I have absolutely no idea who Jenny Rowe is but I'm also gasping for a drink, so here goes – to Jenny Rowe,' Merrin echoed.

'Jenny Rowe is the cleaner who left at short notice and into whose breach you courageously leapt. Pearl, you never have to do a changeover again. Jenny has her job back and can start next Friday. How wonderful is that?'

'Truly wonderful,' said Merrin cautiously, 'but are you sure she will stay now? After all, she let you down before.'

'She had "serious family problems", poor love. I didn't like to ask what they were but I think her life has always been a bit troubled. She has been homeless on and off but now she has a camper van and all is well. She really was very sorry to have let me down.'

'I'm washing the sheets and towels for Rupert's here because it's easier, so I'll drop them in on Friday and thank her in person. Yippee! Honestly, Clara, I absolutely hate cleaning.'

'That has filtered through,' said Clara. 'Now before I sit down, I had better say hello to William.' William was sitting in front of the fire. Clara approached him; he raised his head and bared his teeth.

Merrin couldn't resist it. 'He's only smiling at you, Clara!' she said.

Clara ignored her and, bending over, started to stroke William, who began by grumbling, which quickly developed into a full-scale growl.

'And now he's just talking to you,' said Merrin, starting to laugh.

Clara stood up and began laughing too. 'I don't know why you wanted to keep him, Pearl, I really don't.'

'It's because of his good looks and lovely nature. Now, come and sit down and stop upsetting my dog.'

Merrin had produced some nibbles and the two women sat round the kitchen table, drinking, eating and above all gossiping. Merrin brought Clara up to date on poor Isla's various problems, Maggie's nasty boyfriend, the odious Roberta and James's car being found to contain cocaine.

'Inspector Peppiatt wants me to ask Isla to keep a lookout for any cocaine around Roberta. It seems a bit far-fetched to me. If she is using cocaine, she is hardly likely to leave it lying about for her tenants to see – particularly now she is throwing them out.'

'My goodness, Pearl, you do live life on the edge. We haven't had this much excitement in St Ives for years.'

'Remember there is a poor dead boy at the centre of it all,' said Merrin firmly.

'Yes, of course,' said Clara, chastened.

They ate supper, which Clara clearly enjoyed as she helped herself to 'thirds', her excuse being she'd not had time to eat all day. The meal finished, Merrin made coffee and they sat down round the fire.

Clara was suddenly uncharacteristically serious. 'Pearl, can I ask your advice? You're a lawyer so you must be a bright button. Tristan and I need some help; we just don't know what to do.'

The sorry tale emerged in fits and starts, poor Clara having to stop now and again to blow her nose and wipe away her tears. Tristan's Fish Plaice was in trouble. Covid, of course, had started the decline. Then they had experienced a bumper year when lockdown had eased but it still wasn't possible to holiday abroad. Although trade was good in that period, it had not compensated for the lack of sales during the height of the pandemic. Their restaurant was not cheap, Tristan was very particular about quality and his ingredients were always top of the range. Also, of course, the business was very seasonal. Costs had gone through the roof, which they could not pass on in total to their customers – in a nutshell, in season, they were just about breaking even; out of season, they were making a loss.

'I can't see any way in which we can increase sales. The locals can't afford us any more and even sales in season are not always great. It's heart-breaking when we've worked so hard,' Clara said, making an effort to calm down.

'What about takeaways?' Merrin suggested.

'That wouldn't work,' said Clara. 'We're a fish restaurant, we can't start serving pizzas and burgers, and there are more than enough fish and chip takeaways in town.'

'What about scallops in a Thai sauce, prawn curry, fish pie, maybe a *bouillabaisse*? In other words, ready meals to take home and warm up for both locals and visitors but not typical fast food, something a bit special. You would have to be very careful with costings and portion control but I can really see it working.'

There was a long silence and then Clara shrieked, making Horatio and William both jump. 'Pearl, you're brilliant, I can really see it working, too. You're so clever. It's going to be difficult to set up quickly enough to save us with Tristan and I both working full-time but you'll help us, won't you, Pearl, now you don't have the cleaning to worry about?'

Merrin looked across at Horatio, who appeared to have been listening intently to the conversation. 'Some people just never learn, do they, Horatio?'

It appeared to Merrin that he nodded wisely in agreement, which was not particularly reassuring.

CHAPTER TWENTY-FIVE

The meeting with Border Force had not been spectacularly helpful so far as moving forward Inspector Peppiatt's case. They were a nice bunch and promised to drop everything and help him if he uncovered any information concerning smuggling in the area. They knew nothing at all about the death of George Jenkin, but then why should they, Louis mused as he drove towards his old marital home. An open verdict had been returned by the judge, who in any event believed George's death was the result of suicide. In the circumstances, it would never have been brought to the attention of Border Force.

Louis had planned his meeting with Border Force to coincide with his children coming home from school. He had telephoned Stephanie on Sunday evening, explained about his meeting and suggested he drop in to see the children and give them their Christmas presents.

Stephanie had seemed happy with the idea but could not resist reminding him that once again he had missed the school Christmas concert.

'I'm so sorry,' he said, 'but I've got a murder on my hands.'

'There's no need to say anything, Louis. I've heard it all before.'

Louis pulled into the driveway. It was a very pleasant house, on the outskirts of Falmouth, with a surprisingly large garden. Since receiving her parents' inheritance, Stephanie had added a conservatory and a heated swimming pool, which attracted the children's friends like bees to a honeypot.

He still had a key, but the house no longer felt like home, so as a matter of courtesy, he rang the doorbell. Daisy was the first to arrive. 'Dad!' she shouted, flinging her arms round her father. Louis attempted to return the hug, while clutching two carrier bags of presents. 'It's been ages since we saw you – missed you, Dad.'

'I know it's been ages,' said Louis. 'I only have to look at you to see that. You must have grown about a foot and I like the haircut; it makes you look very grown up.'

'Now that was the right thing to say, well done,' said Stephanie, appearing in the hall behind her daughter. She stepped forward and kissed Louis lightly on the cheek. 'Come in and I'll put the kettle on.'

'I wasn't just being tactful, Daisy,' said Louis, 'I really like the new look, it suits you.' Since a small child, Daisy's hair had been long, mostly in a ponytail because she was sporty. It was now cut very short and it suited her little elfin face.

The three of them went through to the kitchen and chatted while the kettle boiled. 'Can we open our presents now?' Daisy asked.

'No,' said Louis, hurriedly, 'keep them for Christmas Day.'

'Are you sure?' said Stephanie. 'They could open them now as you're here.'

'No, no, I'm sure it's bad luck to open them before the big day.' In reality, Louis was worried about his choice of presents, convinced that the children would either already have them or they would be something they didn't want. He felt so out of touch so far as his children's likes and dislikes were concerned, and it embarrassed and distressed him.

After a while, Louis said, 'Where's Edward?'

Stephanie looked suddenly slightly awkward. 'He's up in his room; I'm sorry, Louis, but he is being a bit funny about seeing you.'

'Funny how?' Louis asked.

'He doesn't want to see you, Dad,' said Daisy with a thirteen-year-old's candour.

'Well, I want to see him,' said Louis. He set down his mug of tea and headed up the stairs to his son's room.

'Oh dear,' said Stephanie to Daisy, 'I don't think this is going to end well.'

Louis walked straight into Edward's room, without knocking. His son was sitting slumped at his desk. 'What's all this then, Ed? Why don't you want to see your old dad?'

Edward stared down at his desk. 'I just don't.'

'I get that,' said Louis, sitting down on Edward's bed, 'but why?'

There was a long silence. Then Edward swivelled round his chair to face Louis. There was a deep frown between his normally kind brown eyes, so like his father's. 'It's like you've just handed us over to Andrew. He comes to all our matches, parents' evenings, Daisy's Christmas concert, my nativity play, everything. It's like you don't need to bother any more because Andrew's doing it all.'

'Do you like Andrew?' Louis asked. He could hardly bear what Edward was saying because he knew it to be true.

'Yes, he's alright. He's nice and Mum likes him' – he paused – 'but he's not my dad.'

'I've got a murder case going on at the moment,' Louis said.

'I know, Mum told me. I'm proud of you, Dad, it would just be great to see you more often, to feel you were still part of us.'

'I'm so sorry, I will try harder, Ed. It's no excuse, I know, but sometimes I feel awkward, kind of in the way. Mum and Andrew, you and Daisy are a family now and I'm sort on the outside looking in, almost as if I'm interfering.'

'It's not like that, Dad, it's not. I love you.' Edward jumped up and flung himself into his father's arms and they both fell backwards onto the bed.

They lay there for a moment. 'I love you too, Ed,

more than you can ever know.' Louis hesitated. 'Tell me, what was your part in the nativity play?'

Edward sat up. 'I was a sheep.'

Louis, still lying on the bed, looked up at his son. 'The most important sheep, I assume?'

Edward grinned at him. 'Of course, number one sheep!'

Louis began to laugh. 'Was it a speaking part?'

'Absolutely major!'

'What were your lines?

Edward was laughing so hard he could hardly speak. At last, he got it out. 'Baa,' he managed.

'A difficult line,' said Louis, between gasps of laughter. 'I hope you put the right amount of emotion into it; after all, you were witnessing the birth of Jesus.'

'I had to say it twice, Dad: baa, baa. It was tricky.'

'Maybe you should consider acting as a career – after this triumph, I would have thought you're ready to move straight on to Shakespeare.'

'I know some Shakespeare,' said Edward. He laid his hand theatrically on his chest and stared as if into the far distance. 'To be or not to be, that is the question.'

'You've got that wrong, son,' said Louis, starting to laugh again. 'The line is "To baa or not to baa", and you, of all people, should know that is the real question!'

With that, Edward threw himself back down on the bed, father and son yelping with laughter between baas. This was how Stephanie and Daisy found them when they came upstairs to see what all the noise was about.

Stephanie felt a sudden stab of sadness. For a moment, it was just like old times.

CHAPTER TWENTY-SIX

Merrin had spent a quiet, but productive, weekend. She had bought a small Christmas tree and decorated it; she'd also unpacked the nativity set they'd always put up at Christmas time in Arcadia and found a place for it in the sitting room. She'd decorated Isla's room with fairy lights, ordered a turkey, bought presents for both Isla and Maggie and stocked up the wine rack. It was the wine rack that made Merrin wonder whether she dare let Horatio out of his cage but it was William who was making her nervous. They seemed such good friends while Horatio was safely in his cage but how would William react when he had a parrot flapping around? She decided to wait until Isla came home and they could decide together whether to risk it.

On top of her domestic chores, on Monday morning, Merrin presented herself at Tristan's Fish Plaice, having made an appointment with Tristan over the weekend.

Much to her surprise, Tristan was very enthusiastic about her takeaway idea and had already decided on a menu of three dishes initially to keep it simple – fish pie, prawn curry and creamy garlic scallops with crusty bread.

'I was wondering about mussels,' said Merrin. 'What about moules frites?'

Tristan shook his head. 'No, I will never serve mussels or oysters outside of the restaurant. People do such stupid things with them: reheat mussels, leave oysters on a sunny windowsill. Those are two dishes that have to be eaten under supervision!'

'Fair enough,' said Merrin. 'So, you have the recipes and presumably you will do the costings. What do you want me to do?'

'Nothing much,' said Tristan. 'Just source some biodegradable bowls, wooden cutlery, throw-away glasses that aren't plastic, as people may want to buy a bottle of wine at the same time. Then it's just some menu cards and a poster once I can give you the prices. I thought we might head it up "Tristan's Plaice or Your Plaice". What do you think?'

'Good, in fact excellent,' said Merrin. 'I'll get cracking, then.'

Merrin spent a productive afternoon sourcing everything Tristan needed and by early evening, she decided it was time to talk to Isla about Roberta and the cocaine. They had spoken over the weekend but Merrin thought it important to keep their conversations light-hearted. Having surrendered her essay once more into the hands of Creepy Chris, Merrin thought her daughter needed a trouble-free couple of days.

Merrin began by discussing the pros and cons of letting Horatio start flying around again and they both decided she should wait for Isla so they could tackle the problem together. Isla sounded slightly less gloomy – Creepy Chris was away until Wednesday, tutorials were over for the term and, as yet, there was no verdict on her essay. Roberta was still avoiding both her tenants and Maggie was speaking to Isla again but had been away for most of the weekend with her so-called boyfriend.

At last, Merrin could put off the question no longer. 'Darling, Inspector Peppiatt has asked me to ask you whether you think there are any drugs in the house – in particular, cocaine.'

'So, he's still got it in for us, has he? I'm a drug dealer now, am I?'

'No, of course not, let me explain. The police have found James's car and in the boot there was some cocaine. Because he was supposed to be going up to Oxford to see his aunt, the inspector just wondered if Roberta was a user, and if you or Maggie had seen any evidence that she is.'

'She'd hardly leave bags of the stuff lying about on the kitchen table, would she?'

'I realise that,' said Merrin patiently, 'but I suppose he was thinking more of her behaviour, mood swings and, I don't know, white powder round the nostrils?'

'There's a lot of cocaine around in Oxford but I've no reason to suppose Roberta is involved. Mood swings, definitely – she has always been a moody old cow even when she liked us.' Isla laughed. 'Honestly, Mum, cocaine users don't normally walk around with white powdery noses; I think you watch too much telly.'

'I'll freely admit I don't know what I'm talking about, having always been a clean-living girl,' said Merrin tartly.

'I will ask Maggie when she comes in tonight but that's the best I can do and I honestly don't think she will say anything different from me, or we would have talked about it.'

'Now you're back on speaking terms, do try and persuade Maggie to come to us for Christmas, away from her horrid married man.'

'Will do, Mum, and tell Inspector P, the drug squad are reporting for duty.'

Later that evening, Clara rang to say that the visitors in Rupert's Cottage had gone home early because one of them was ill. 'Jenny's free to do a clean tomorrow and so I wonder if you could drop in the sheets and towels, say by about ten-thirty. She's going to give the place a thorough going over, so if you're a little later than that, it won't matter.'

'Are you saying, by any chance, that Jenny is doing a particularly big clean because as I have been in charge for the last couple of weeks, standards have slipped?'

'Of course I'm not saying anything of the sort, darling Pearl.'

'It's OK, Clara,' said Merrin, 'you can uncross your fingers now.'

CHAPTER TWENTY-SEVEN

Merrin and William delivered the laundry to Rupert's Cottage, as planned, on their way out for a walk. Merrin still had her key and so let herself in. However, as she did so, she called out Jenny's name so as not to startle her.

Jenny appeared from out of the kitchen. She was a strange combination, tall and strong-looking – probably a farmer's daughter, Merrin thought – but, by contrast, apparently shy and timid. She stood staring at Merrin like a rabbit caught in the headlights.

Merrin put down the laundry.

'I'm Merrin, a friend of Clara's. I've brought round the clean laundry. I've been helping out while you were away.'

'Thank you,' said Jenny, avoiding eye contact. Her voice was quiet and tentative, another contrast to her large, strong frame.

'I'm sorry you have rather a lot to do today,' Merrin pressed on. 'I know I'm not a very good cleaner. I feel quite ashamed that you are having to clean up after me, as well as the guests.'

There was the ghost of a smile. 'It's not too bad; I've known a lot worse,' Jenny said.

'I tell you what, shall I make us both a coffee by way of a sorry present, assuming there's some milk left in the fridge?'

'There's some milk the guests left behind,' said Jenny. 'I'll finish off the bathroom while the kettle boils.' She hesitated as she walked past William. 'Funny-looking dog,' she said.

'He is,' whispered Merrin, 'but don't tell him; he's very sensitive.'

That smile again. Despite her bulk, Merrin could see Jenny must have been a nice-looking girl. Now in what Merrin imagined was her mid-thirties, Jenny's expression was very strained and careworn. Her pale blonde hair, which badly needed a wash, was pulled back tightly into a ponytail. Strong capable hands picked up the bag of laundry and she disappeared towards the bathroom. *What a strange woman*, Merrin thought.

Minutes later, the kettle boiled and Merrin called out that coffee was ready. The two women sat down at the kitchen table; Merrin put out a plate of biscuits she had found in a cupboard.

'Clara tells me you're living in a camper van,' Merrin began.

'Why'd she tell you that?' Jenny demanded, suddenly hostile.

'Because she knows I have always wanted a camper van,' Merrin lied, astonished by Jenny's violent reaction. 'My daughter is all grown up now, but it would have been fun to have one when she was younger.'

'Have you just got the one kid?' Jenny asked, apparently calm again.

'Yes, we would have liked more but it just never happened. Always too busy, I suppose.'

'I had a kid once,' Jenny suddenly blurted out.

'Did you?' said Merrin. 'A boy or a girl?'

'A boy,' said Jenny, staring down into her coffee. 'He were adopted; I only saw him once, a puny little thing, bawling his head off. I were only fifteen. I wish I'd had more, at least had one I could keep. Got to find the right man first, though, haven't you?'

'True,' said Merrin. 'I'm very sorry about your son; that must have been very tough for you.'

'Well, these things happen, don't they?' Jenny finished her coffee and stood up. 'I'd better get back to work.'

'I'll wash these up,' said Merrin, indicating their mugs. 'It's been nice to meet you, Jenny.'

Jenny started for the door and then stopped. 'I've got to clean Elsie's Cottage this afternoon. I feel funny about it, knowing there's been a dead body in there. Would you come with me, just to see me in and check the house is, well, alright?'

'Of course I will,' said Merrin. 'So, the police have finished in there now, have they?'

'Yes, Clara says they finished at the weekend. I bet they've left a mess. I don't know whether anyone is coming to stay in the cottage for Christmas. Originally, she'd cancelled all the bookings until New Year. I wouldn't want to stay there, not now.'

'Don't worry, I'll meet you there and if the police have made a mess, I'll help you clear up.'

The two women agreed a time to meet again and Merrin let herself out of Rupert's Cottage. Walking round the town with William, lost in thought, Merrin found herself feeling sorry for Jenny. A baby at just fifteen was bad enough but having to give him up for adoption – Merrin could not imagine the pain of having to part with a newborn baby. Still, maybe at fifteen, if she'd had no parental support, it might have been a relief. Jenny was such an odd mixture, looking like she should be a tough, strong character and yet seeming so fragile. She was interesting but rather sad, Merrin thought.

Although Merrin was early, Jenny was already waiting for her at the door of Elsie's Cottage that afternoon. 'I didn't want to go inside until you were here,' she said. Jenny unlocked the front door, and the two women went inside.

First impressions were favourable. The police seemed to have created very little mess. 'I don't know if you are aware, but it was me who found the body,' said Merrin.

Jenny looked startled. 'No, I didn't know,' she said, her voice shaking slightly.

'Let's go upstairs and get it over with. Shall I lead the way?' Merrin said. Jenny nodded.

The room was perfect once more. The bed had been remade and the chair had been returned to its place under the window. It felt slightly surreal, almost as if what had taken place in this room had never happened. Merrin looked round for Jenny. She was still standing on the landing, now very pale and trembling slightly. 'Come on in, honestly, it's fine. Everything is tidied up.' Reluctantly, Jenny entered the bedroom but continued to stare at the floor. 'He was in this far bed,' Merrin said, 'but I guess we should change the sheets on both beds. I'll do this one, if you like, and you do the other one.'

Without speaking, Jenny began stripping the other bed and Merrin did the same to the bed where James had been laid. Neither woman spoke. When they had finished, Jenny said: 'Give me those sheets – I'll put a wash on. You can go now; I'm fine.'

The brief camaraderie they'd enjoyed in the morning appeared to have gone. Before going downstairs, Merrin checked the double-bedded room, which she had made up before discovering the body. Apart from needing a quick vacuuming, it looked fine. She followed Jenny down the stairs. 'Are you sure there's nothing else I can do to help you?' she asked.

'I said no, didn't I?' was Jenny's reply.

Merrin let herself out of the cottage, wondering what she had done wrong.

CHAPTER TWENTY-EIGHT

Merrin returned home, feeling confused. Why had Jenny virtually chucked her out of Elsie's after being almost friendly in the morning – talking about her lost baby? And then it struck her.

Was Jenny the person who had put James into the bed? Merrin considered what she knew. Jenny probably had her own key to the cottages, which meant she could enter them at any time. And even if she had returned them to Clara when she left her employment, she was almost certain to have known the code numbers of the key safe. Jenny had been extremely nervous about entering Elsie's Cottage alone. Why? She knew the body was long gone, yet she had been very reluctant to enter the bedroom. And why had she then become so angry? Was it a reaction to seeing the room and the bed again? However, the more Merrin thought about it, it was Jenny's lost baby who seemed to be the major reason for her placing James in the bed. Clearly, the loss of her son, which had occurred at least half her lifetime ago, still played heavily on her mind – she had to mention him, even to a virtual stranger. And that baby would be about the same age as James now.

Jenny was a complex character but was she a murderer? Merrin thought it unlikely. The more she thought about it, though, the more her theory seemed to fit. One of the reasons the police had spent so much time searching through guests who had stayed at Elsie's cottage was because the entrance had not been forced. So, the only way James could have entered Elsie's was if either he had a key, or someone accompanying him had one – whether at the time James was alive or dead.

Having fed Horace and William, Merrin settled down at the kitchen table. She felt she really had no choice but to ring Inspector Peppiatt.

He answered on the second ring. 'It's Merrin McKenzie, Inspector. I've got something to tell you – have you got a moment?'

'I have indeed, Mrs McKenzie. What can I do for you?'

Merrin explained in detail her two meetings with Jenny Rowe. 'Do you see what I mean? It all fits. You have been looking for someone who had access to the cottage, and here she is, and the fact she lost a son, who would be much the same age as James, has to be significant, don't you think, Inspector?'

'It's certainly possible but there's absolutely no evidence to go on. Just because she has a key to Elsie's

Cottage and had a baby at fifteen, who was adopted, honestly does smack of bending the facts to fit the circumstances of the case. Where does she live?'

'She lives in a camper van. I think she moves around quite a bit from what Clara told me, but she does stay on campsites sometimes. I don't want to sound disrespectful, but she did appear somewhat unkempt, so I suspect the campsites probably don't feature that often. Honestly, I know, once again, you don't believe me but my instincts tell me that this is worth following up.'

'The "once again" in your last sentence reminds me that to ignore your instincts, I do so at my peril, Mrs McKenzie. I will speak to Mrs Tregonning and see what information she has on Jenny Rowe, and obviously check police records.'

'I don't think she's the murderer, but please don't ask me why I say that. I really haven't a clue,' said Merrin. She hesitated. 'One thing, though, Inspector, and please forgive me, you probably have already thought of this – it would be worth checking to see if Jenny is a diabetic.'

'Thank you, Mrs McKenzie,' said Louis, feeling unable to admit that it was not something he had immediately thought of doing.

While Inspector Peppiatt was cursing himself for not being man enough to admit he had not thought of the diabetic angle, and while Merrin was sitting at her kitchen table, muttering her frustrations to Horatio because, yet again, she felt a reluctance on the part of the inspector to take her seriously, a fishing boat was leaving St Ives Bay and sailing up the Hayle Estuary to Dynamite Quay to unload a significant quantity of cocaine into a waiting van.

CHAPTER TWENTY-NINE

After a restless night, Merrin decided that she could not just abandon trying to find out who had killed James when she remained absolutely certain that Jenny Rowe was somehow involved. Without knowing anything about James's background, she felt him to have been very alone and unprotected. His was only nineteen; his parents, by definition, had not demonstrated much support for the boy at the start his university career. His only contact in the UK was an aunt he had never met and who clearly had taken very little interest in him to date. Without any evidence to support her views, Merrin felt that James was the innocent party in all of this and yet had ended up as the victim. She thought of his face on the pillow – nineteen he might have been, but he looked more like a twelve-year-old – small, slight and very vulnerable.

So, if Inspector Peppiatt wasn't going to do anything

to seriously investigate Jenny Rowe, Merrin reasoned she would have to do something herself.

Merrin had every reason to visit Tristan's Fish Plaice as she had to show Tristan details of the various utensils she had hunted down for the takeaway business. She spent half an hour with him and they placed some orders. He also gave her the prices for the menus and posters. Tristan wanted to start the takeaways on Monday 19th December in order to catch some Christmas trade as well as New Year. It was a tall order but Merrin was relatively confident she could get it all together for him in time.

She then made some coffee and took a mug to Clara, who, as usual, was peeling potatoes. She wanted to find out more about Jenny but was very conscious that if she wasn't careful, she could jeopardise Jenny's job. As Inspector Peppiatt had pointed out, she had absolutely no proof at all that Jenny was in any way involved in James's death.

As it turned out, Clara made it easy for her. 'Thanks,' she said as Merrin passed her a mug of coffee. 'I'm glad you popped in. Do you still have any bedding for Elsie's at home?'

'No,' said Merrin. 'Jenny kept it all at the cottage. Why do you ask?'

'Miraculously, we have a Christmas booking for Elsie's. Some people are coming down from Birmingham. Mercifully, our murder does not seem to have made it beyond the local news. So, Jenny is going again to the cottage today to get it ready for them. What a relief to have her back – no disrespect, darling Pearl.'

Merrin smiled. 'No problem, I know my limitations only too well. Has Jenny got keys to the cottages?'

'Yes, of course,' said Clara. 'In fact, she still had them during the period she stopped working for us. I was so shocked at her leaving, I forgot to ask for them back. She is such a good worker.'

'Goodness, that was brave. You must have a lot of trust in her, despite her leaving you in the lurch,' said Merrin, trying to sound casual.

Clara stopped peeling and took a large gulp of coffee. 'She's a funny woman but she's as honest as the day is long. I'm absolutely certain that she would never steal anything and she is very neat and careful with all the contents of the cottages. She is a treasure. Now are you going to help me with the spuds, or not? Some friend you turned out to be, drinking your coffee like a lady of leisure, watching me slave away.'

'I am a lady of leisure, or at least I'm trying to be, no thanks to you. I'll give you a few minutes and then I must go as I have to be somewhere.'

The 'somewhere' Merrin had to be was Elsie's Cottage to try and have another talk with Jenny. Once again, Merrin let herself in and called out to Jenny so as not to alarm her.

Jenny emerged from the sitting room. 'Oh, it's you again. What do you want?'

Not an encouraging start. 'I've come to apologise. I must have said or done something to annoy you last time we were here. I don't know what it was but I am very sorry anyway.'

Jenny seemed immediately mollified. 'It was probably my fault; I was in a foul mood. Shall I make the coffee this time?'

They took their coffees into the sitting room. 'It's warm in here because I've turned on the radiator to air the place for the guests,' said Jenny. 'Honestly, I don't how anyone can want to rent this cottage, knowing what's happened here.'

'Clara says the guests are coming from Birmingham and news of the boy's death has not reached the national press. From what I understand, the police don't seem to be making much progress in finding out who killed him.'

'It must be difficult for them, not knowing where the boy was actually killed,' said Jenny.

'Yes,' agreed Merrin but her mind was in a whirl. She was as certain as she could be that the information about where James was killed was not in the public domain. So, how was it that Jenny knew about it? She took a sip of her coffee, trying desperately to think what to say next.

'Actually,' said Jenny, interrupting her thoughts. 'I'm glad you're here. I want to ask you something, a favour actually, a big one.'

'Go on,' said Merrin, intrigued.

'I've made a decision; I going to leave St Ives for good and make a new life somewhere else,' said Jenny. She hesitated. 'In fact, I'm going tomorrow morning and I wondered if you would tell Clara for me. I just can't face her after all she's done for me and now I'm letting her down again.'

'That's very bad news,' said Merrin. 'Why are you leaving? Clara speaks so highly of you. She told me just this morning that you are a treasure.'

'Don't,' said Jenny, 'I feel guilty enough as it is. It's just so difficult round here, finding enough work and somewhere to live. It's just too hard.' She was close to tears.

'But now you've got a camper van, you've solved your housing problem. Also, I don't know if Clara told you but they are starting a takeaway service next Monday and they are bound to need help with that.'

'Clara did mention it,' mumbled Jenny.

Merrin gave her a shrewd look. 'It's none of my business, Jenny, but I somehow feel your move is about something else entirely besides work and housing. I bet there's a man involved. Am I right?' She tried a smile. 'When big decisions like this are made, there is nearly always some bloody man causing trouble at the heart of it all.'

Jenny smiled back. 'You're right,' she said. 'I'm trying to get away from a bad relationship. I thought I could handle it, which is why I came back to work for Clara, but I've since decided I just can't.'

'I tell you what,' said Merrin. 'I'll help you finish up here with the cleaning and then come back to my place. I have a bottle of wine in the fridge and we can talk things through. If I can't talk you out of leaving, we can at least think up something that will enable Clara to give you a good reference. What do you say?'

Jenny nodded. 'OK,' she said.

Back at Miranda's Cottage, Merrin made every effort to help Jenny feel comfortable and relaxed. She lit the fire, poured the wine and talked about Horatio. The last thing she wanted to do was to give Jenny the impression that she had brought her home to interrogate her – which, of course, she had.

At last, when they were halfway through the bottle, she made her move. 'So, can I talk you out of leaving? Clara is going to be devastated, particularly at this time of year.' She smiled at Jenny, trying to lighten the mood. 'And just think, she'll be back to having me cleaning the cottages – imagine that!'

Jenny tried a small smile. 'I can't stay, I just can't.'

'This bad relationship,' Merrin asked gently, 'is he violent towards you?'

'Sometimes,' Jenny admitted. 'He has a real temper on him, usually when he's drunk too much but not always. He can be very frightening when he's angry.'

'Is he local?' Merrin asked.

'No,' said Jenny. 'He's not from round here. He used to be a fisherman up north somewhere, I think. Now he fishes down here. He likes Cornwall a lot better. I can't stay with him, though; I just don't know what he'll do next.'

'That sounds awful, Jenny. Do you really think he might seriously hurt you or even that your life is in danger?'

Merrin had gone too far; Jenny was immediately on the defensive. 'Why are you asking me all these questions? This is none of your business. I'm leaving Cornwall and that's my decision and nothing to do with anyone else, especially someone I don't even really know.' She fumbled in her pocket. 'Here are the keys to the cottages. Tell Clara I'm sorry.'

'You're not going to drive tonight, are you?' said Merrin. 'It's a beastly night out there and almost dark.'

'I'm leaving at the crack of dawn, not that it's any of your business.' Jenny stood up and hesitated, obviously thinking she had been a little harsh. 'Thanks for the wine – see you around.'

And with that, she was gone.

CHAPTER THIRTY

After Jenny had left, Merrin paced up and down her kitchen for a few moments and then decided she had no alternative but to call Inspector Peppiatt. The call went straight to voicemail. She left a message to say she needed to speak to him urgently. She put away the wine bottle and washed up the glasses – she needed to keep a clear head. She fed both Horatio and William but could face no food herself. Instead, she sat at the kitchen table and made notes.

Jenny had been in possession of the cottage keys when James was killed and his body placed in Elsie's Cottage; Jenny seemed to know that James's murder might not have taken place at the cottage, despite there being no publicity to that effect; Jenny was leaving St Ives, although she now had a camper van to live in, and the promise of more work from Clara; why, because she had a vicious boyfriend who clearly terrified her.

Jenny was a big strong lass – if a man was capable of domestic violence, perhaps he could also be capable of murder; and, finally, the man in question was a fisherman, which meant he could possibly be involved in drug smuggling.

By eight o'clock that evening, Merrin was beside herself with frustration. Why hadn't the inspector called her back? Jenny was leaving early in the morning. In Merrin's view, it was vital to find her before she left Cornwall because Jenny and her boyfriend just had to hold the key to discovering who killed James, even if not directly involved themselves. She was just about to try the inspector's number again when her mobile rang.

'Mrs McKenzie, I am sorry not to have got back to you before now – it's been a busy afternoon,' said Louis. 'What can I do for you?'

'I think it's more a question of what I can do for you, Inspector,' said Merrin. 'It's about Jenny Rowe.'

'I thought we'd exhausted the subject of Miss Rowe.' Louis sounded both tired and slightly irritated.

Merrin was not to be deterred. 'I have a lot more information about Jenny and I think we need to move quickly – I honestly believe you urgently need to talk to her.'

'Go on,' said Louis, without a great deal of obvious enthusiasm.

Reading from her notes, Merrin outlined all that she had discovered during the day. It looked much better on paper. Now, describing what she had found out sounded trivial and she could almost hear the inspector thinking, *circumstantial evidence*, and therefore dismissing all she had to say. When she finished, there was a lengthy silence.

'I'm not too sure where this is going, Mrs McKenzie. We already knew Jenny had kept the keys to the cottages; Mrs Tregonning told us. Also, initially, I told Mrs Tregonning that it was quite possible the murder of James Allnut did not take place in her cottage. We now have forensic evidence to back this up, so I phoned Mrs Tregonning the moment I heard. She appeared to find the information reassuring, so it is not inconceivable that she passed it on to Jenny for the same reason, bearing in mind she was going to clean the cottage. As for the boyfriend, from our experience, I'm afraid there are a lot of very unpleasant men around who seem to think domestic violence is some sort of right. I think Jenny has probably done the correct thing by exiting herself from the situation, and in a camper van she will be difficult for him to trace, should he try.'

'Exactly,' said Merrin, trying very hard to keep her temper. 'I truly believe that Jenny is the key to James's murder. If we don't find her tonight, it's going to be extremely difficult, even for the police, to find her going forward.'

'Do you know where she is currently keeping her van, what type it is or even what colour maybe? I imagine you don't have the registration number?' Louis was not making the conversation easy.

'No, I don't have that information, Inspector, but it is December; I can't imagine there are too many camper vans around at the moment. She can't be all that difficult to find.'

'It's pitch dark and we don't know what sort of vehicle we are looking for. I will get my men to conduct a search in the morning, though on what grounds I can possibly detain Miss Rowe, at this moment I have no idea.'

Recognising that once again she was defeated, Merrin said, 'Jenny told me she was leaving first thing in the morning so your men may well be too late to find her.'

'I'll get them out at first light,' Louis said.

Merrin ended the call. On this occasion, she was certain that thinking about angels was not going to help.

After another fitful night, Merrin rose early, showered and took William out for a walk. It was barely light, raining, windy and very cold. William clearly thought she was mad. Her idea had been to start looking for Jenny and her camper van, but the weather was so awful that in the end she gave way to William's insistence that they should return home. As they were leaving the Island, though, she spotted two police vans arriving at the Barnoon car park, which was encouraging. At least Inspector Peppiatt was as good as his word.

On arriving home, she realised that she was seriously hungry, having eaten practically nothing the day before. She fed William and Horatio and then cooked herself a couple of poached eggs on toast, making sure, of course, that there was enough toast for Horatio. Then, with a heavy heart, she rang Clara and told her of Jenny's decision to leave Cornwall.

'But she can't do this to me again,' wailed Clara. 'Why on earth did she come back, only to leave again? I haven't even paid her. What the hell is she playing at, Pearl?'

'It's about a man, her boyfriend. He knocks her about and she's frightened of him so she is moving to another part of the country to escape from him. I did try to talk her out of it, Clara, but she wasn't having any of it. Since coming back to work for you, I presume something very nasty must have happened between her and the boyfriend to really frighten her.'

'I feel like doing something to really frighten her,' said Clara angrily.

'She gave me her keys and she and I cleaned up Elsie's so it's ready to go,' said Merrin. 'Clara, get yourself a coffee and calm down. You know I will cover for you until you find someone else.'

Merrin lit the fire and settled down in Adam's chair with a book she had been trying to read ever since arriving in St Ives. She must have fallen asleep – the combination of fitful nights and a warm fire. She was suddenly woken by a loud knocking on the front door. Wearily, she stood up and opened the door to find Inspector Peppiatt and Jack Eddy on her doorstep.

'Can we come in?' Louis asked.

'Yes, of course,' said Merrin, standing back to let both men into her kitchen. Having closed the door, she turned to face them and from their grim expressions, she knew immediately that something was terribly wrong. Her thoughts flew straight to Isla. 'What's happened?'

she asked, her voice unsteady.

'We've found the camper van but I am very sorry to have to tell you that we have also found Jenny inside the van,' said Louis. 'I'm afraid she's been murdered.'

CHAPTER THIRTY-ONE

Steve Matthews was in despair. He was sitting at the kitchen table, his head in his hands, crying like a baby. His mother stood over him, her face creased with worry. 'What's wrong, Stevie, tell Mummy.'

Steve shook his head, followed by a fresh bout of sobbing.

'Your breakfast's ready,' said Brenda Matthews, absolutely sure that would cheer him up – Steve had a very healthy appetite. 'Come on, it will make you feel better and it's nearly time for work.'

'I'm not hungry and I'm not going to work,' Steve managed between sobs. This was serious – the two most important things in Steve's life were food and his job.

His mother fetched a box of tissues, sat down beside him and prised one of his hands away from his face. 'Now wipe your face and tell me what's going on. I suppose it's about this woman they've discovered. It is a shock, I'll grant you, Stevie, someone being found dead almost on our doorstep but there is no need to take on so. Come on, you're a big boy now.'

'She was my friend,' Steve sobbed. 'Her name's Jenny; she was very kind to me.'

Brenda was taken aback. 'A girlfriend, Stevie? I didn't know you had a girlfriend.'

'No, no,' wailed Steve. 'I don't have girlfriends. She was just my friend and I liked her very much and it's all my fault she's dead.'

'Don't be silly, Stevie, of course it's not your fault. How could it possibly be your fault?' Brenda was used to this reaction; Steve always thought he was to blame for everything.

As a baby and a toddler, Steve had been exceedingly happy. Things went wrong as soon as he started school. He was slow, with undefined learning difficulties, but given enough time to think things through, he could be surprisingly astute. However, no one except his mother realised this. At school, his peers teased his mercilessly, calling him 'simple', 'stupid', 'mad', 'crazy', 'dim', 'a joke', and those were just the polite names. In many respects, his mother, Brenda, didn't help. She knitted all his sweaters for him, in garish colours, which, to be fair, Steve loved. She chose all his clothes for him, too, and she was no fashion guru. She fed him far too well so that he was considerably overweight. Worst of all, she cut his hair herself. Whether in fact she put a pudding basin on his head to affect his haircuts, no one knew, but it certainly looked as if she did.

But perhaps the worst disservice Brenda visited on her son was to believe, passionately, that he was the cleverest, best-looking, most marvellous boy in the whole world – which, sadly, he was not. However, what far outweighed the many attributes Brenda awarded her son was the fact that, given half a chance, Steve was both kind and loving – and he had loved Jenny Rowe and now she was dead.

While Steve was sobbing in his kitchen, Merrin was locking horns with Inspector Peppiatt in hers. 'You didn't say last night that you thought Jenny was in danger,' Louis said. It was almost an accusation.

'I told you exactly what Jenny told me,' said Merrin, outraged. 'She said she was leaving St Ives to escape an abusive relationship and that the man in question frightened her. Your response, if I recall correctly, was to say that there was a great deal of domestic abuse around. It was your decision not to start looking for her last night – had you done so, you might have saved her life.'

'That's a bit harsh, Merrin Trip,' said Jack, who was looking extremely uncomfortable at this exchange between his boss and his childhood friend.

'We would never have found her camper van in the dark,' said Louis. 'In fact, we didn't find it this morning. Someone walking along the street where she had parked noticed that the door of the van was open. He looked inside and called us straight away.'

'How did she die?' Merrin asked.

Louis hesitated. 'She was stabbed. I'm not releasing that information to the press so I would be grateful if you could keep it to yourself.'

'I'm a lawyer, Inspector. Blabbing to the press is not something I do.'

Merrin was now close to tears and suddenly Louis realised why. 'Do something useful, Eddy, put the kettle on,' he snapped at Jack. He pulled out a chair and, taking Merrin's arm, guided her into it. 'I've done it again, upset you dreadfully without stopping to think, haven't I?'

Jack Eddy stopped fiddling with the kettle. 'What's the boss said to upset you, my maid?' he asked. 'I don't understand.'

Merrin looked up at Jack and managed a small smile. 'It's OK, Jack. My husband died as a result of being stabbed and I think your inspector, knowing this, believes he could have been a little more tactful in telling me about Jenny's cause of death. It's over, I'm fine; I'd like a tea please, Jack.'

'Me too,' said Louis. 'I have no excuse for what I said, and the way I said it – and just to make things worse, I feel certain Adam would be horrified.'

'He would understand you are under a lot of pressure. Two murders in a town like St Ives, just before Christmas and New Year, when everyone is so dependent on the revenue from visitors – this is a case that needs solving quickly, though I know I don't have to tell you that, Inspector.'

Jack distributed three mugs of tea and they sat round

the kitchen table, William having hogged the best place in front of the fire. 'What are you doing?' Horatio suddenly piped up. It broke the tense atmosphere and they all laughed.

'You may well ask, Horatio,' said Louis, 'you may well ask.'

While they drank their tea, Louis wanted to know whether there were any other details Merrin could remember that might lead them to finding Jenny's boyfriend.

'No, apart from him being a fisherman. Oh, sorry, there was one other thing. She said he wasn't local, he'd been a fisherman up north but liked Cornwall better. It would be worth talking to Clara Tregonning, though; she might know more about Jenny's private life than me. You have to remember, I only knew her for forty-eight hours – actually, less than that. I have told Clara that Jenny was leaving Cornwall but obviously Clara doesn't know she is dead – poor woman, I just can't believe it.'

'The restaurant is where I'm off to next,' said Louis. 'I have men already in St Ives and Newlyn asking all the fisherman about the boyfriend, I'll pass on the fact he is from up north somewhere. Do you happen to know if Jenny had many friends locally?'

'No idea,' said Merrin, 'but again, Clara might know.'

'She did have one friend,' Jack volunteered. 'I spoke to a lad this morning who lives with his mum in the house just by where the camper van was parked. He said he was a friend of Jenny's.'

'Did you ask him about the boyfriend, or is he the boyfriend?' Louis asked.

'Definitely not,' said Jack. 'I hadn't caught up with you then, boss, so I didn't know anything about a boyfriend. I really called in to find out if they had seen or heard anything during the night as they live in the nearest house to the scene. They said they'd heard nothing but the lad was very upset.'

'But could he be a suspect?' Louis asked.

'I'm certain he isn't, boss. He has learning difficulties and gets easily upset, his mum said. She told me a little sparrow crashed into their window the other day and died. The lad was in a terrible state for hours, apparently.' Jack hesitated. 'I say "lad" – I would say he is probably in his forties but he's very childlike. To be honest, I can't see him hurting anyone.'

'Mrs McKenzie, have you time for Jack to just take a brief statement from you?' Louis asked.

Merrin nodded.

'Thank you, and then, Eddy, could you go back to this lad's house and ask about Jenny's boyfriend. What's the lad's name?'

'Steve Matthews,' said Jack.

'And, Eddy, just because he's not the brightest spark and lives with his mum, it doesn't mean he couldn't be our killer. Check police records and take his fingerprints. Forensics are removing the van shortly.'

CHAPTER THIRTY-TWO

Inspector Peppiatt ended the call and slammed the phone down on his desk. He had just finished a tiresome phone conversation with Dr Graham Bennett. 'Why oh why, Louis, do your stiffs always turn up at the beginning of a weekend?' Graham had shouted. 'When do you need the postmortem on this woman who's just come in – the stab victim?'

'By Monday first thing at the very latest,' said Louis.

'There's a surprise – another golfing weekend ruined, all thanks to you. What on earth's going on in St Ives? Have you got a serial killer on the loose? And who's coming to ID the body and when?'

'For both our sakes, let's hope it's not a serial killer. The ID is going to be carried out by a Mrs Tregonning, who can't come in until Monday afternoon as she runs a restaurant and obviously weekends are very busy. She's the former employer of Miss Rowe. We can't find any trace of immediate family for the deceased at the moment. Her mother is dead and no father was mentioned on the birth certificate. I am hoping the dental records might at least throw up the area of the country she originates from.'

'OK,' said Graham. 'I'm surprised you didn't ask that nosy Mrs McKenzie to do the ID. She would have loved it.'

'Well, thank your lucky stars, Graham, that I didn't. I'm sure Mrs McKenzie would have been happy to oblige at any time, in which case, I would have asked her to ID today and therefore requested the PM results for midday on Saturday.'

Louis glanced at his watch; he just had a few minutes before a FaceTime with Larry Pearson, James's closest friend at St Andrews. The university had been very helpful. After an initial conversation with James's tutor, his best friend had been identified and as the students had come down for the Christmas vacation, the university had contacted Larry's parents, who had asked to be present when Louis interviewed their son. The boy was very upset, unsurprisingly.

Larry Pearson was a nice-looking boy but to Louis's mind, so very young. *Never mind policemen looking younger*, he thought morosely. *University students look like they ought to be in nursery school.*

Having introduced themselves, Louis said. 'Firstly, Larry, I understand you were a good friend to James Allnut and I am so very sorry for your loss. At your age, in particular, I know it must have come as a huge shock.'

'It has,' his father interrupted. 'You will go easy on Larry, won't you, Inspector. He is very shaken up by what has happened.

'Of course,' said Louis. 'This won't take long, Larry, but I would really appreciate some help from you. To start with, would I be right in assuming you only met James this term when you both arrived at St Andrews?'

'Yes,' said Larry. 'We met our first day; our rooms were on the same floor and we were both reading history of art. We became good friends pretty much straight away; we had a lot of interests in common.'

'I'm surprised James was reading history of art. I thought his parents were in commerce and, therefore, maybe he would follow them into the business.'

'He didn't think much of his parents and from what he told me, neither do I,' said Larry.

'Why's that?' Louis asked.

'I don't know if you are aware that James's parents are tax exiles?'

Louis nodded.

'They live on an island off Singapore. They can't even go to the mainland for fear of extradition, so James was sent off to boarding school there at four years old because there were no suitable education facilities on the island. He was an only child, and from what I understand, his parents weren't that interested in him and I think he had a pretty miserable and lonely childhood.'

'That's very sad,' said Louis.

'What's even sadder,' said Larry, 'is that he was loving uni. He felt really happy for the first time in his life, at least that's what he told me. He loved the course, too.'

'I gather he was a keen surfer, is that right?' Louis asked.

'Absolutely, which is why he went down to St Ives. He was also not keen on spending too much time with his aunt; she sounded like a right old misery. He asked me to go with him to St Ives, but to be honest, I didn't feel like plunging myself into the sea in December and I've never surfed. I wish to God I had gone with him now, of course. He might still be alive.'

'Have you any theories as to why someone might have killed him?'

'None,' said Larry vehemently. 'He was not the sort to pick a fight; he liked a pint but I never saw him truly drunk. He was a little chap and looked much younger than his age. People liked him; he was friendly, bright and very funny.'

It was the perfect opening for the real question that Louis wanted to ask. 'Larry, do you think James was ever involved in drugs in any way, dealing or taking them himself, or perhaps both?'

'Absolutely not!' Larry looked outraged.

'Think very carefully. It's no problem if he was – it won't reach the press, even his parents don't need to know. I am thinking specifically about cocaine.'

'I don't have to think carefully,' said Larry angrily. 'Like all universities, there are plenty of drugs around but James was very against drugs of any sort – he wouldn't even try a spliff, never mind something like cocaine. I know he never touched a drug of any sort.'

'Thank you, Larry, that's all the questions I needed to ask you. I really appreciate your time and you have been most helpful.'

The young man on Louis's laptop screen leant forward and looked astutely at him. 'That last question was the one you really wanted to know the answer to, wasn't it? The rest was just waffle.'

Louis inclined his head. 'Yes,' he admitted. 'When we find James's killer – and we will – I'll let you know. Good luck, Larry.'

By the time Louis reached home that evening, he was both exhausted and frustrated. The flat was cold; he turned up the heating and poured himself a hefty Scotch. He knew he should eat something but he had no appetite. It was Friday night and there was little to be achieved until Monday. The postmortem would be available then and forensics would at least have a preliminary report. Officers had completed house-to-house in the street where the van had been parked but with no results. Jack was still trying to track down Steve Matthews, 'the lad', who was at work apparently on a driving job, so out of contact, according to his mother. This evening, officers were touring the bars and restaurants of St Ives to see if Jenny had gone to any of them on leaving Merrin McKenzie's cottage. No progress had yet been made in finding Jenny's boyfriend but then no one really knew who they were looking for.

Louis had tried to ring David Brownley, the sergeant at Thames Valley who had interviewed Roberta, only to find that he was already off on Christmas leave. In any event, Louis felt that Roberta, and the Oxford end of the inquiry, were the least of his problems at the moment. He had two murders on his hands, in a town where violent crime practically never happened. The holiday season was just over a week away. The pressure was on – Merrin McKenzie was certainly right about that.

CHAPTER THIRTY-THREE

Merrin stood on Porthgwidden Beach. The tide was on the way out and the gulls were paddling about on the edge of the sea – at least they were until William decided to give chase. They rose in a cloud of white feathers and William looked back at Merrin with a proud expression on his face. 'Honestly, William, that was a bit mean,' she suggested. William was unrepentant. She toyed with the idea of popping into Tristan's Fish Plaice but decided against it. She and Clara had spoken on the phone about Jenny's death and agreed to meet on Monday morning for a coffee. It was also launch evening for the takeaway at Tristan's – she would wait until then.

It was a dull day but rather beautiful. The sea was the colour of pewter and slightly translucent. The breakers, as they crashed ashore, were snowy white, creating a lovely contrast to the dark sea. Despite the fact that rain was in the air and a particularly vicious little wind was blowing, normally Merrin would have still enjoyed her walk. But not today. All she could think about was Jenny – a lost childhood, a lost baby, a lost lover, a lost life. It seemed so cruel that so much tragedy should be heaped onto the shoulders of one person. Merrin wished she'd known her better, wished she'd had the chance to perhaps make Jenny a friend. She was an odd person, clearly a very damaged one, but somehow Merrin felt there was real goodness at the heart of her.

Jenny's misfortunes made Merrin think of her own life. Tragedy had struck her too, but she'd had the enormous luck to be loved for thirty-five years by a truly wonderful man and, between them, to have produced a beautiful, healthy, clever, mostly happy daughter. She would give anything for Adam to have lived a long life, for them to have grown old together, to have just had more time for each other – but she could not deny that she had been blessed.

William was clearly bored by so much introspection and began tearing round her in mad circles. 'Come on, then, you crazy dog, let's go home and ring Isla.'

'Hi, Mum, how're you doing?' Isla sounded more upbeat than she had done since the run-in with Roberta.

'Well, not too great,' said Merrin. 'We have another dead body.'

'Oh my God,' said Isla. 'That's awful. Did you find this one too? Who is it? Do we know them?'

Merrin recounted the whole sad story of Jenny – both her life and death. 'So, in a nutshell,' she said, 'I believe that Jenny put James in the bed at Elsie's cottage and because of that, for some reason, she herself was killed, probably by the same person who killed James.'

'And does your inspector agree with you?' Isla asked.

'I don't really know. We haven't spoken since he and Jack came to tell me of Jenny's death. At the time, he was very cross with me.'

'Because you'd asked him to look for Jenny the night before, which could have saved her life?' Isla suggested.

'That, and the fact I had so few details for him – of the camper van and of the boyfriend. I could hardly ask her for the registration of her van, could I, and when I began asking too many questions, she clammed up and left immediately. There was no way she was going to tell me anything more than she did. Maybe I blew it by coming on too strong with my questioning but, honestly, Isla, I think I was lucky to get as much information out of her as I did.'

'It seems to me that you need some moral support,' said Isla. 'Between Clara and Inspector Peppiatt, they're not being particularly kind or supportive. I wish I could come down on Monday, as we originally planned, but I must try and prise Maggie away from her horrible man, whoever he is. Also, we've had no luck finding anywhere to live as yet.'

'No worries,' said Merrin, 'just don't leave it until too near to Christmas or the traffic will be awful. Tell me, did you ask Maggie about the drug business and Roberta?'

'Yes, I did,' said Isla. 'She was a bit funny about it, actually. She swore blind she had seen no drugs on the premises nor any reason to suppose Roberta took drugs either. She just seemed a bit cagey about it all but then she's a bit cagey about everything at the moment.'

'Well, just come down as quickly as you can. I miss you, darling.'

'I miss you too, Mum.'

After speaking to Isla, Merrin realised that she had the perfect excuse to ring Inspector Peppiatt to report on the fact that the girls had seen no evidence of drugs at Roberta's. Her real reason, of course, was that she was desperately anxious to know if any progress had been made with the investigation. The two deaths had naturally shaken her badly but it was the fact that she felt the victims, in both cases, were somehow particularly vulnerable that upset her so much.

She spent the rest of the morning in a state of prevarication – should she ring the inspector or not? Finally, by mid-afternoon, she could stand it no longer and made the call.

'Sorry to call you on a Saturday,' Merrin said.

'No problem, Mrs McKenzie. I don't need to tell you that weekends don't exist for police officers if something major is going on – and this is certainly major.'

'My reason for calling is a little trivial in the circumstances. It's just to tell you that neither Isla, nor her flatmate, Maggie, have ever seen any drugs in the house, nor do they seem to think that Roberta herself takes drugs.'

'Thank you very much for the information. To be honest, I have temporarily binned that end of that investigation. The Thames Valley officer in charge of the case is on holiday until after Christmas and, obviously, what is going on down here is so much more important.'

'Have you made any progress with the investigation?' Merrin asked, expecting to get her head bitten off.

'Just one thing of significance that I imagine will not come as a surprise to you,' Louis said. 'Jenny Rowe was a diabetic, so I think it is probably safe to assume she was likely to be the source of the insulin that killed James.'

'I'm not surprised but I honestly don't think she killed him. She was clearly a troubled soul but I don't think she was a murderer, particularly of a boy of about her son's age.'

'Means, opportunity – we just have to find the motive. I'm sorry but she has to be seriously in the frame for the murder. I agree it makes no sense, particularly since she went on to be killed herself.'

'Surely, Inspector, you have to agree that the two murders are likely to have been committed by the same person?'

'Not necessarily. The murder weapons were different for a start,' said Louis.

'That's true,' said Merrin, 'but I can see we're not really going to agree over this. How is the rest of the investigation going?'

'It's a waiting game,' Louis admitted. 'By Monday I will have the results of the postmortem and also the forensic findings. House-to-house enquiries around the town have produced nothing and we are no further forward with finding the boyfriend.'

'What about the chap who knew Jenny, the one whose house was right by the murder scene? What was his name?'

'Steve Matthews,' said Louis. 'He's away overnight on a driving job and his mother says she can't get hold of him. He is supposed to be back in St Ives tomorrow evening. For some reason, he left his mobile at home so we can't track him either. It might be because he is avoiding us or it may be simply that, according to Jack, he has learning difficulties and he may just have genuinely forgotten his phone.'

'He must be quite important, I imagine, because he told Jack that Jenny was his friend. You may know differently but I got the impression that Jenny didn't have many friends. Sorry, I'm interfering.'

'Not at all, and you're right. She seems to have had no friends – well, none in St Ives, at any rate. Mrs Tregonning is of the same view, Jenny was a loner – except, of course, for the wretched boyfriend. Incidentally, I would like to apologise again for being so blunt about how Jenny was murdered. I can offer you no excuse other than I had just come from the murder scene.'

'Inspector,' said Merrin sternly, 'don't you think it's time we called some sort of truce on apologies. We seem to say "sorry" to one another an awful lot. Shall we declare a moratorium on all apologies going forward – deal?'

'Deal,' said Inspector Peppiatt.

CHAPTER THIRTY-FOUR

Jack Eddy was waiting in his car when he saw Steve Matthews arrive home. It was past almost nine o'clock and Steve arrived on foot. Jack checked his watch again and sighed. His wife, June, was already furious. Tonight they were supposed to be putting up the Christmas tree, which Jack had bought yesterday but was still sitting in the garage. June was in a considerable flap. Their only child, a son, David, was coming down for Christmas on Thursday and staying for four nights. David was bringing his wife, Polly, who was a good-looking girl but neither Jack nor June could really take to her. June said Polly was too posh for them and she was probably right. Still, work had to come first, and it was an anxious time for Jack. He was not sure the boss really rated him much these days. This talk with Steve could provide the breakthrough they needed and maybe improve his usefulness in the boss's eyes.

Jack climbed wearily out of his car and knocked on the front door. It was answered by Steve's mother, Brenda. 'Sergeant Eddy, how nice of you to call round. Do come in; you look perished,' said Brenda. 'Come on, quickly, or you'll catch your death. Shall I make you a nice hot cup of tea?'

A few minutes later, Jack was seated at the kitchen table with a mug of tea and a large piece of lemon drizzle cake, which he knew he should refuse but also knew he wasn't going to. He had established that Steve was in the shower and would be down shortly for his tea. When he appeared, Steve was dressed in pyjamas and a plaid dressing gown.

'Oh hello,' said Steve, 'you're the man who came to see us when Jenny died.'

'That's right,' said Jack. 'I just wanted to ask you a few questions. Would you mind?

'Can I give Stevie his tea so he can eat while you talk? Only he's had a long day,' Brenda asked.

'Before you do, Mrs Matthews, could I take Steve's fingerprints? It's just for elimination purposes, in case there are any of his in or around the victim's camper van.'

Jack had expected trouble but Steve enjoyed the whole process, almost as if it were a nursery game. Clearly, he was oblivious of any implications that fingerprinting might mean. After washing his hands, Steve sat down to his tea.

'So where have you been today, Steve?' Jack asked.

'All over,' he said, starting to attack a large plate of

shepherd's pie. 'Why do you want to know where I've been?'

'Just interested,' said Jack.

'Stevie does a lot of driving; he's very clever with cars,' said Brenda. 'You remember when we used to have two garages in town?'

Jack nodded.

'Well, Stevie started by cleaning cars on the forecourt and then he learnt to change the oil and tyres, all sorts of things.'

Steve remained silent, concentrating on his food. 'So where does Steve work now?' Jack asked Brenda.

'I told you already,' said Steve, 'I work all over.'

Jack was trying hard not to lose his patience. He'd imagined interviewing Steve was going to be easy – that because of his learning difficulties, his answers would be straightforward. He now realised it was going to be much more complicated than that.

'Why are you here, asking me and my mum questions?' Steve suddenly demanded. 'I just want to eat my tea and go to bed.'

'I need to know what work you do, Steve, and whereabouts you do it.'

'Why?' Steve stopped eating and was now looking decidedly belligerent.

'You're upsetting him, Sergeant,' said Brenda. 'He's done nothing wrong. He's hard-working and a good boy. Please leave him alone.'

Jack ignored her. 'Steve, I'm not saying you've done anything wrong. I just want to know what you do. Do you deliver things to people and, if so, what sort of things?'

'I'm not telling you,' said Steve, 'not ever. Rick told me not to tell anyone anything about what we do, so I won't tell you.'

'Who's Rick, your boss?'

'I don't know; I don't know anything. Leave me and Mum alone – go away.'

Jack's patience was at an end. 'I'm not stupid, Steve, of course you know who your boss is and where you work, so just tell me please, now.'

Steve stood up. 'I'm not stupid, I'm not, everyone thinks I'm stupid, but I know I'm not and Mum knows I'm not.'

'I didn't say you were stupid, Steve, I just said you shouldn't think that I'm stupid.'

This was too complicated for poor Steve. 'Stop saying "stupid", I'm not, I'm not, I said go away.'

'You're going to have to leave,' said Brenda, 'I don't know why you're here but you have no right to upset my boy like this. I thought you were coming to tell us you'd caught whoever killed that poor woman, Jenny.'

'Jenny's dead,' said Steve, starting to cry.

For a moment, Jack was tempted to take Steve into custody but looking at him, he quickly abandoned the idea. Steve looked exhausted, frightened, bewildered and was now sobbing. In his pyjamas and dressing gown, he cut a pathetic figure. It would be cruel to take him in and, in any case, Jack was fairly sure nothing would be achieved by locking the poor man in a cell.

'I'll go,' said Jack to both mother and son. 'We'll leave things for now, Steve. Don't worry, you have a good sleep and I'm sorry for upsetting you.'

Back behind the wheel of his car, Jack pondered over what he should have said differently. Obviously, mentioning the word 'stupid' was a big mistake and if it became necessary to interview Steve again, he must remember to tell his boss to avoid any similar words. Clearly, as a result of his difficulties, it appeared that Steve took any such word out of context and saw it as a term of personal abuse. Poor man, he must have been called stupid or worse all his life. Jack also remembered that the boss had told him to try and find out from Steve any details about Jenny's boyfriend, which, in the heat of the moment, he had failed to do.

Still, one thing had been achieved. He now knew that Steve's boss was called Rick. Jack tried to get his tired brain in gear. Steve knew Jenny. Merrin Trip thought Jenny had put James into the bed in the cottage. *Steve also knows Rick – maybe Rick was Jenny's fisherman boyfriend, maybe* . . . Jack's tired brain gave out.

As Jack drove home, to what he knew would be an icy reception, one idea did come to him. Now he had a name, he would go back to Old Tom in Porthleven at lunchtime and see if he knew a fisherman called Rick.

CHAPTER THIRTY-FIVE

Inspector Peppiatt sat at a desk in Graham Bennett's lab trying to make sense of the information before him. Graham, in a slightly less disagreeable mood than normal, confirmed the cause of Jenny's death as multiple stabbings, one of which had torn into her aorta and was the wound that killed her. 'Could a woman have done this?' Louis asked. 'It does seem an incredibly vicious attack for a female perpetrator.'

'Women can be vicious, too, Louis,' said Graham with a smile, 'though in this case, I think it highly likely that the attacker was a man.'

'Why are you so confident of that?' Louis asked.

'I didn't say I was "so confident",' Graham said, always pedantic to the last. 'I think it is highly likely to be a man because poor old Jenny was a big lass – big and strong. She put up quite a fight as it was, as you can see from the defence wounds. I think for a woman to have taken her on, she would need to have been – well, Amazonian. It was a vicious attack, as you say. I would go so far as to say it was frenzied, resulting from extreme passion or, more likely, rage.'

Louis picked up the preliminary forensic report. 'This is a puzzle,' he said.

'Yes,' Graham agreed. 'I've speed-read it – we need all the DNA results in order to form a clearer picture but it's still puzzling.'

Louis had read the report several times and was still trying to clarify what he had learnt. There were three sets of fingerprints in the van. One, of course, was Jenny's. There were two smudged sets that matched James's, as far as they went, and were probably just good enough for identification purposes in a court of law. The third set of prints was everywhere – all around the van, on Jenny's clothing and also on some of the empty pens of insulin found in the bin. The police database had identified these prints as belonging to a man named John Lumley. John Lumley was a well-known villain from Tyneside and forensics had made enquiries with Northumbria Police, who knew of him only too well. Apparently, he had been heavily involved in drug-related gang warfare. The only problem was that he had disappeared off the radar some four years ago and was believed to be dead. Also found in the camper van were some strands of black hair, which, when compared with James's hair, looked identical. They had been sent off for DNA matching, which would provide additional proof that James had been in the van as well – whether dead or alive.

Louis looked up at Graham. 'So, on the bright side, it looks like we are going to be able to prove that our two murder victims and their likely killer were all in Jenny's camper van at one time or another. This chap, John Lumley, is a bit of a worry, though.'

'Yes,' agreed Graham, 'according to forensics, Northumbria Police believe he ended up in the sea off Whitley Bay about four years ago – and very relieved they were too. He was a right piece of work, apparently.'

'I wonder why he's turned up here,' Louis mused. 'I suppose it's a nice long way from Tyneside and, of course, his history with the drug trade all ties in with our case.'

'Before you become too despondent, Louis, there is one other piece of good news. Forensics called me to say they had neglected to put in their report that Northumbria Police had told them that John Lumley was a fisherman.'

Merrin arrived at Tristan's Fish Plaice early in the morning, accompanied by William. 'We don't allow dogs in the restaurant,' said Clara, trying to look stern.

'He's not just a dog,' Merrin protested, 'he's William, and anyway the restaurant's closed.'

The two women embraced and smiled sadly at one another. 'Poor Jenny,' said Clara. 'She was a strange person but I liked her and she was a damned good worker.'

'Did she only work for you on Fridays and Saturdays?' Merrin asked.

'Yes,' said Clara, 'but she had other cleaning jobs, she told me. I don't know where, though. We didn't speak much really. She used to come in on Saturday afternoon to collect her wages but we were always frantic getting ready for Saturday night, so we just exchanged pleasantries.'

'She told me about her baby,' said Merrin.

'Yes, she told me about him, too. I remember her asking if Tristan and I minded not having any children so I explained we had made a conscious decision not to have any. It was then that she told me about her lost son. I think she minded terribly not being able to keep him; it still preyed on her mind, all those years later. She didn't have much luck in life, poor old Jenny, did she?'

'No,' said Merrin thoughtfully. 'Now you've calmed down, you're being very nice about the fact that she was planning to leave you in the lurch again.'

'She's dead, poor girl, and I'm alive. I have a lovely husband and, from what you have told me, she was being knocked about by some awful man, who probably ended up killing her. How can I not be nice about her, when I have so much and she now has nothing at all?'

'Did you know anything about this boyfriend of hers?' Merrin asked.

'Not a thing. The first I heard of there even being a boyfriend was when you called me with the news she was leaving. I don't think your inspector friend was too impressed with me. I think he thought I was a pretty irresponsible employer not really knowing anything about Jenny.'

'He's not my inspector and he can hardly be described as a friend,' Merrin said firmly. 'He does get very uptight about things at times and has a tendency to throw accusations around, but I can't imagine him thinking you were a poor employer.'

'Well, I thought he was pretty accusing,' said Clara. 'He told me that apparently Jenny had been regularly beaten up by this guy and said he was surprised I hadn't noticed any bruises on her, or mood swings.'

'So you told him you rarely saw Jenny except to hand over her pay each week?'

'Yes, I did but he gave me the impression that he thought that was a poor excuse. He can be a bit harsh at times, can't he?'

'Don't worry about it,' said Merrin. 'The only reason he knows about the violent boyfriend is because I told him. There was no detective work involved, so he shouldn't be throwing his weight around. But, yes, he can be a bit harsh at times.'

'Heaven knows why we're fussing about Inspector Peppiatt when the person we should be thinking about right now is poor old Jenny. Did you know I've been asked to ID her body this afternoon?'

'No, I didn't, poor you. Do you want me to come with you?' said Merrin.

'Of course I don't, darling Pearl. You had to ID your husband, then you found poor James; there is no way I'm letting you near another dead body. Besides which, Inspector Peppiatt would be furious if I did.'

'Why?' asked Merrin.

'He asked me to do it because he felt you shouldn't – for all the reasons I've just given. And though it pains me to say it, in this instance, the grumpy old sod is right. I've never seen a dead body before but he has promised he will be there in person for support. I must admit, I'm dreading it – I still can't believe Jenny is dead.'

They sat in silence for a few moments, William with his head on Merrin's knee. He was already adept at sensing when she was sad. At last, Merrin spoke. 'On a practical note, I suppose I'm back to doing changeovers for the time being?'

'There's nothing to do at Elsie's for two weeks. The guests who arrived on Saturday are staying for Christmas and the New Year. So it is just Rupert's on the 23rd and the 30th and I promise to find someone to take over by the end of the year.'

'Isla was supposed to be coming home today but her flatmate is having problems,' said Merrin. 'She has promised to be down by the 22nd at the latest, so I can enlist her help; she is a far better cleaner than me.'

'That's not especially difficult, my darling Pearl,' said Clara. 'Do you think Isla will have forgiven me for my so-called exploitation of you?'

'I very much doubt it,' said Merrin cheerfully. 'On the subject of Isla, I have Christmas sorted but not New Year. What are you guys up to?'

'We only open the restaurant at lunchtime normally but if your takeaway idea works, we were wondering whether to operate that – not until midnight, maybe until ten. Then we could join everyone in the celebrations.

Why, were you thinking we should dress up as fairies yet again? I suppose I could legitimately go as the Fairy Godmother!'

New Year's Eve had always been a huge event in St Ives, with most people dressing up, and attended by crowds which put August to shame. There was a period when a lot of the younger girls dressed up as fairies and as it quite often rained at some point during the evening, as little girls, Merrin and Clara regularly became seriously bedraggled, with drooping wings, but they'd loved it all. As the night wore on and the drink flowed, impromptu house parties developed. Merrin remembered one year when she was home from university, coming downstairs in the morning to find a member of the French Foreign Legion stretched out on the sofa, a small pixie curled up rather sweetly in the log basket and an octopus fast asleep in the bath. The fireworks were great and although rowdy, on the whole, the crowds were very good natured.

'I definitely think our days as fairies are over,' said Merrin, firmly, 'but I was thinking about Isla and her friend, Maggie, if she comes. Isla has never been in St Ives for New Year and I think she would love it. So, Fairy Godmother, over to you!'

Merrin spent the next hour setting up Your Plaice Takeaway, which was going to be served through a window beside the front door of the restaurant. She had delivered the menus and had now put up the posters. Tristan and Clara came out to look.

'I really like this,' said Tristan. 'You've done a great job, Merrin, thanks so much.'

'What happens if it goes really well? How will you cope?'

'God knows!' Clara and Tristan chorused.

Merrin had a nasty feeling in the pit of her stomach that if she wasn't very careful, she would find herself serving takeaways all over the festive season.

CHAPTER THIRTY-SIX

Sergeant Jack Eddy was driving to Porthleven in the hopes of finding Old Tom in the pub again. He felt relatively confident that Tom was a regular visitor to The Ship at lunchtime. He knew the boss had Tom's mobile number but Jack didn't want to alert the inspector as to what he was doing. He was anxious to demonstrate that he could use his own initiative.

Jack was in luck – Old Tom was indeed propping up the bar when he arrived. 'Hello, Tom, can I get you a pint – Proper Job, isn't it?'

Tom did not look particularly pleased to see him. 'It's you again. Where's your governor? I prefer talking to him.'

Jack ignored the slur and ordered Tom's pint and a half lager for himself. He leant close to Tom's ear. 'There's been another murder and we need a bit of advice.'

They sat at the same corner table. 'I know about the

murder of that poor woman in her camper van. Visitor, was she?'

'No,' said Jack, 'she was local. I'm sorry to disturb you again, Tom, but two murders in St Ives is just terrible and who knows, we may be heading for a third.' As he said the words, it suddenly struck Jack that they could be true. By interviewing Steve, by trying to get him information out of him, was Jack putting him in danger? That poor vulnerable man – the thought that Steve could be the next victim filled Jack with horror.

'What is it? What's wrong? You've just thought of something bad; you've gone quite pale, boy,' said Old Tom, who was something of a student of human nature. Tom gave Jack a shrewd look. 'You've just thought of who could be next, haven't you?'

It was useless denying it. 'Yes,' said Jack, 'it just occurred to me as I was speaking to you. This is a horrible case, Tom; we've never had anything like this before in St Ives. The boss isn't here because he's working night and day to try and solve it, but the trouble is, we have so few leads. The two people who could really help us are both dead.'

'Look, boy, I didn't think much of you when you came over here last week because I remembered you from the George Jenkin case. That was a dog's dinner, if ever there was one. I know you weren't in charge but in my view it was a stitch-up – why, I don't know, don't want to know now, but I can see you care about what's going on in St Ives, so I will help you if I can.'

'Thank you,' said Jack, 'I really appreciate your offer

of help. We now know the name of a person of interest in this case. His name is Rick.'

'Don't talk in riddles. Do you mean that you think this Rick could be responsible for the murders.'

'He could be, yes,' said Jack.

'Was he a fisherman?' Tom paused and took a large slug of his pint. 'Well, it stands to reason he has to be, or you wouldn't be wasting your time talking to me, now would you?'

'Yes, you're right,' said Jack, 'we're fairly sure he's a fisherman.'

'I need your word, as a gentleman, that you will tell no one that the information I'm about to give you came from me. That Rick was a brute and if you're right that he's your murderer, he's not going to behave nicely to anyone who helps you find him, now is he?'

'I will have to tell my boss,' said Jack.

'That's alright, I like your governor, a decent bloke, but it's to go no further, mind. Do you swear to me that you will tell no one else you got the information from me?'

'Yes,' said Jack, 'I swear. Think how many fishermen there are in West Cornwall. The information could come from anyone.'

'True,' said Tom. 'A chap called Rick appeared in these parts about the same time as George Jenkin's boat went down, not that I'm saying Rick had anything to do with the scuttling of George's boat – though, of course, he could have done, come to think of it.' Tom was silent for a moment. 'I am trying to remember the name of

Rick's boat but I can't right now but I might be able to find out for you. He wasn't from round here; he came from somewhere up north – it was a difficult accent to understand. He was a nasty piece of work, good looking, the ladies liked him but there was something really bad, almost evil about him but ask me why and I can't tell you, exactly.'

'Have you seen him recently?' Jack asked.

'No, I haven't seen him for at least a couple of years. We were all mightily relieved when he moved on. We were sure he was up to no good but I don't think anyone round here knew what exactly. All I would say is that we never saw a fish in his fishing boat. We all kept our distance when he rested up in the harbour here, which wasn't very often. He would disappear and then there would be sightings of him out Lizard way, Mullion particularly. Then one day, he never came back, thank God.'

'Do you know where he went?'

'Well, it ties in with your murders. I hear he is still seen in Penzance, also Newlyn and Hayle. He fishes now for lobster and crab, sets up his pots off Hayle somewhere I believe. Maybe that's all he is now – a fisherman. Who knows, but whatever he's up to, he's not a bloke to mess with, mark my words.'

'This is very helpful, Tom. I suppose you don't know his surname?'

'I'm trying to remember that, along with his boat. I'll ask around and let you know if anyone remembers. Give me your number.'

The two men exchanged phone numbers, shook hands and Jack started to leave. He was almost out of the door when Old Tom called him back. 'Jack, I've just remembered something else.' Jack was back beside Old Tom in seconds, moving across the bar with uncharacteristic speed. 'It's his ear,' Tom continued, 'one of his earlobes is missing, ragged, like someone has bitten it clean off. I remember once being in the pub, this pub actually, and someone asked him what had happened to his ear. Rick really fancied himself and replied something like it had been bitten off "either by a very angry man or a very excited lady". Bloody idiot.'

Jack could hardly contain himself as he drove back to the office. The fact that he had learnt the name of Steve's boss and now knew his possible whereabouts was great but the missing earlobe was a real bonus. It had to be an easy way to identify Rick. Also, Jack thought excitedly, it was very significant that Rick was in the Porthleven-to-Lizard area when George Jenkin died. Jack had always felt bad about the fact that George's killer had never been caught. An injection of insulin was an unusual way to kill someone and now they had proof that Rick was in the same area for both George and James's murders. He could not imagine how the boss would not be impressed with his investigations.

Louis was suitably impressed with Jack's findings. He listened carefully as Jack described his talk with both Steve Matthews and Old Tom and agreed, with a smile, that the chewed-off ear was a great help.

'There are two important factors on an immediate basis that come out of your findings, Eddy. The first is that we have to get some more information out of Steve without frightening the poor fellow. I have dug up some background on Steve's family. His father was a drunk and was in the habit of coming home from the pub and knocking seven bells out of his wife and son. Finally, having put Brenda Matthews in hospital, he was done for GBH and sent to prison. As soon as he came out, he headed for the nearest pub, got blind drunk, stepped out in front of a car, and died. A merciful release for all concerned, particularly his wife and son. Steve was terrified of his father, according to social services, and if Rick is our killer and the nasty piece of work Old Tom describes, Steve will be terrified of him, too. In fact, chances are he is frightened of men in general. We are going to have to be very careful with him but he is our only chance of finding out where the drug operation is located, assuming there is one, which seems increasingly likely. It may well be that he even knows if Rick is responsible for the deaths of James and Jenny. Despite your assurances, I had Steve in my mind as a credible suspect for the murders. However, having spoken at length to social services, I'm sure you're right, Eddy. Steve is caught up in something that is way out of his depth and he is certainly no murderer.'

'I'm glad we agree on that, boss, but I was thinking when I was over at Porthleven, we could be putting Steve in real danger if this Rick learns we've been interviewing him. I know you need to know what he knows, boss, but he's so vulnerable. If you decide to go ahead with another interview, we're going to have to be very careful or Steve could be murder victim number three, in my view.'

'Don't even go there, Eddy. I'll think very carefully about what you've said; it's a good point – we certainly must not risk putting the poor man in danger. Now, the second thing is this – it seems likely that this Rick's real name is John Lumley.' Louis then explained to Jack about the fingerprints and the talk with the Northumbria Police. 'If you remember, Mrs McKenzie reported that Jenny had said her fisherman boyfriend came from somewhere up north. Old Tom's description of Rick tallies with what Northumbria Police told me, so it looks increasingly likely that Steve's boss Rick is also Jenny Rowe's abusive boyfriend. It would be good to confirm just one more detail to tie up things nicely.'

'What's that, boss?'

'Whether John Lumley had a chewed-off ear.'

CHAPTER THIRTY-SEVEN

Merrin's phone rang just as she had settled down in front of the fire with a cup of tea. Although it was only just 4 p.m., it was virtually dark and that old favourite 'the Cornish mizzle' had set in – a steady drizzle, accompanied by a thick sea mist. Although she had not consulted William, she was completely certain that they were of one mind – an evening walk held absolutely no appeal.

It was Max on the phone. 'Merrin, my dear girl, I've just heard the news – another dead body. I popped in to see Clara and Tristan just now and had Clara sobbing all over me because she'd just had to identify the body of her murdered cleaner. Honestly, what on earth is going on?'

'Where have you been, Max, just when we all needed you?' asked Merrin.

'I'll tell you all about it when I see you, which I hope is tonight – and before you say you are not in the mood for cooking, I thought I would bring over two of Tristan's takeaways, which I understand was your brainchild.'

'I'll get in some wine,' said Merrin.

'No need, I'll bring some of that, too. Tristan's not charging us for the takeaways – it's a thank-you present for all your help.'

Merrin had barely put down her phone when it rang again. It was Inspector Peppiatt. 'Just a quick call, Mrs McKenzie, because I promised to keep you informed,' he said. 'We've made a connection between the boss of the likely drugs operation and Jenny's boyfriend. We believe his name is almost certainly Rick, he has a disfigured ear, he's a fisherman and comes from Tyneside. You did say, didn't you, that Jenny's boyfriend came from up north?'

'That's right, Inspector. It sounds like you're closing in. Well done and thank you for letting me know.'

Merrin ended the call, and for the first time since finding James's body she felt a mild sense of relief. It really looked as if the police might be getting somewhere. William jumped onto her lap, always more aware of her feelings than she was herself. The last few weeks had been unnerving, she acknowledged, but surely she should be used to tales of violence and murder having been married to a policeman for so long? She had found a dead body, she was probably the last person to speak to the second murder victim and both murders had taken place within half a mile of her own front door. Therefore, it was perhaps not unreasonable to feel upset by recent events.

* * *

Merrin was expecting Max at six o'clock but it was after seven when he arrived. 'Blimey, Merrin, you've created a monster!' he said.

'What do you mean?' she asked.

'The reason I'm so late is because I've been queueing for your bloody takeaways – there's a queue right down the Wharf. In the end, I snuck into the kitchen and got Tristan to give me a couple of dishes direct. We've got fish pie and a prawn curry.'

'That's amazing but also a little worrying,' said Merrin.

'Why?' Max asked.

'You know they're massively understaffed and I'm worried about getting roped in to help. I love them both, dearly, and I so want to see their business survive, but Isla will be arriving in the next couple of days and this is an important Christmas for us – our first since Adam died. I can't leave her on her own to go and serve takeaways, even for the Tregonnings.'

'I'm doing nothing special over this Christmas period. I'll help them if they need it. If they approach you, just tell them I'm their man.'

Merrin laughed. 'It's very kind of you, I just can't somehow see you dishing out takeaways.'

'It might be fun, and how difficult can it be? I'm serious, Merrin. Even without Isla coming down, your first month back in St Ives has not been without incident – heavens above, it must have been nothing short of a nightmare.'

'It's not been easy,' Merrin admitted. Very anxious

to change the subject, she said hurriedly, 'Now, Max, while we've been struggling here, tell me what have you been up to – pursuing some lady, I assume?'

'Actually, no, it was work. A big development company in London are wanting to build some affordable housing, just on the outskirts of Carbis Bay. They want me to market and sell the properties for them. It's a big deal, actually. I should earn a lot of money, hence the bottle of champagne I'm clutching and am about to open, if I can have some glasses, please.'

Merrin produced the glasses, frowning a little. 'Are you sure they really are affordable houses?' she asked. 'Only you hear all the time about developers promising planning committees to build affordable housing and then the houses end up anything but.'

'I think so,' said Max. 'There are a few larger houses in the development but not many, as I understand it.'

'What do you mean by larger houses?' Merrin asked.

'Five bedrooms, I guess.'

'Five bedrooms! No one in West Cornwall can afford a five-bedroom house, Max. I bet you're being had. They want your up-country mailing list to sell their wretched houses as second homes.'

'Does it matter so much, if that's true? The building of them will provide work for the locals and second homes bring in more custom for hospitality in the area.'

'But what about you?' said Merrin, exasperated. 'You have a truly terrible reputation so far as women are concerned but in your business dealings, despite being an estate agent, you are much respected. You come across as an honourable chap but flogging pretend affordable housing could ruin all that.'

'I refuse to be deflated by your negative attitude. Let's drink the champagne and be merry.' He raised his glass, 'To no more dead bodies,' he said.

Merrin refused to comment. She did find the champagne a comfort but could not let the matter drop. 'You don't think developers are going to turn their attention to St Ives, do you? she asked.

'I don't see how they can,' said Max, 'there's no room. Whether it's the old fishermen's cottages or the Victorian terraces, they are so well built, they'll last for ever.'

'Someone was telling me the other day,' said Merrin, 'that these new houses being built around Cornwall will only last about twenty-five years. As well as being thrown together with insubstantial materials, it is the salt in the air which does the damage. Is that true?'

'I'm rather afraid it may well be the case, you can't beat granite to survive pretty much anything. Our town has some wonderful old buildings, some date back to the 16th and 17th century but there would have been a lot more but for the fire – in 1689, I think it was, and it destroyed so much of the town.'

'I knew there had been a fire but I hadn't realised it had done a lot of damage,' said Merrin.

'It was devastating, but the town survived – hence all the Victorian terraces. You know, Merrin, I've travelled a lot, seen some wonderful properties but I couldn't live anywhere but St Ives. There's something so reassuring and comforting about the place – maybe it's to do with being battered by the sea on all sides and yet always managing to stand firm. It really is the perfect port in a storm. And you're the living proof of that, my girl. You had your own terrible storm in the form of Adam's death and what did you do? You came home.'

It was nearly midnight by the time Merrin had cleared up and taken William outside for his final ablutions of the day. She was just climbing the stairs on the way to bed when her phone rang yet again. This time it was Isla.

'Mum, I'm so sorry, I expect I've woken you up.'

'Normally you might have done but tonight I had Max round for supper and he's only just left. Are you alright, darling?'

'I'm alright but I'm really worried about Maggie; she's not been home for three nights, if you include this one. I've tried calling her mobile but she's not replying, which is not like her. You know I told you that awful man of hers knocks her about and I just wonder whether this time he has gone too far and really hurt her. I just don't know what to do.'

'So you have no idea who he is or where he lives?' Merrin asked.

'Absolutely not. She is so secretive about him, apart from admitting he's married with children. I don't understand how he gets away with spending whole nights with her; you'd think that wouldn't be too popular with his wife.'

'No, indeed,' Merrin agreed. 'What about contacting Maggie's parents?'

'They're useless,' said Isla dismissively. 'I'm just wondering whether I should contact the police and report her as a missing person.'

'A city full of students, Christmas parties everywhere, I'm not sure the police are going to take much notice but it's worth a try, I suppose. I would wait until tomorrow morning and then report her missing. At this time of night, the police will be very busy, I imagine.'

'OK, I will. Mum, I'm going to come down to St Ives on the 22nd, with or without Maggie, I promise. This isn't going to be an easy Christmas for either of us and I do realise how much we need to be together.'

CHAPTER THIRTY-EIGHT

Maggie Faulkner's childhood had been idyllic until the age of ten – at least that is how she remembered it. Her mother and father were loving, both to her and to each other. They lived on the outskirts of Henley-on-Thames, in a converted farmhouse. Maggie had a pony and the family kept a dayboat on the Thames, which involved frequent picnics on the water, enjoyed immensely by all three of them. Although clearly the family was comfortably off, as Maggie recalled their time together then, they enjoyed the simple things of life – like the picnics. Holidays were never exotic trips abroad but involved hiking in the Lake District, boating on the Norfolk Broads and camping in Cornwall.

Everything changed shortly after Maggie's tenth birthday. She would remember all her life coming home from school one day to find her parents sitting in the drawing room, her father home from work unusually early. 'Come here, darling,' her mother said, patting the sofa beside her. 'Daddy and I have something to tell you.'

Maggie looked from one parent to the other. It almost appeared as if her father had been crying but obviously, that was impossible. She sat down obediently beside her mother, who put an arm round her shoulders. 'I'm afraid I have just been told I have cancer, darling, but you're not to worry. I'm sure I will be fine.'

Six months later, her mother was dead.

Within a year, much to everyone's astonishment, her father had remarried, a woman named Anna, who was seventeen years younger than him. Anna did not prove to be a wicked stepmother, quite the contrary; she was kind to Maggie when she was reminded of her existence, but she appeared to have absolutely no real interest in the child.

Anna's idea of fun was very different, too. She liked eating out, going to the theatre, the ballet, weekends in Paris and holidays where the sun always shone. Maggie was largely excluded from this new lifestyle and a mother's help was employed to care for her when her father and stepmother were otherwise engaged. She had few friends because she never wanted to invite them home – home wasn't really home any more.

Everything changed for Maggie when she was awarded a place at Oxford to read history. Within days, she had a friend named Isla McKenzie, who was fun and kind and, without knowing it, helped Maggie to rebuild her confidence in herself. When Isla's father was killed,

Maggie was able to repay Isla's kindness by supporting her in every possible way she could and the girls became very close. If having a best friend wasn't joy enough, Maggie also fell in love.

And now, once again, Maggie's life was in ruins. Through tear-stained eyes she looked at her watch – it was 3.15 in the morning. She was sitting on the steps of the Martyrs' Memorial in the centre of Oxford. It was cold and every part of her body seemed to hurt. There was something definitely wrong with her shoulder from when he had flung her against the wall. At the time she thought her nose was broken but she had been able to blow it just now and it didn't feel broken, just very sore. She knew her face was a mess where he'd slapped her and he'd pulled her hair so hard, she knew some of it had come out . . . and that was only the things she remembered.

She wanted to go home to Jericho, to Isla, but she had been so horrible to Isla recently, she wasn't even sure she still had her as a friend. Maggie's phone and bag were still in his rooms so she had no money, no ability to contact anyone and no strength to try and walk home. She also only had one shoe – in her panic to escape, she had lost the other one on the stairs. She felt so helpless and began to cry again.

Just then a police car drew up on the side road by the memorial. A policewoman stepped out. 'Are you alright, love?' she called out. She began walking up the steps towards Maggie. 'You can't stay here, it's perishing. We'll take you home; where do you live?' By now the policewoman had reached her and gasped. 'What on earth has happened to you? Has someone beaten you up?'

'Yes,' Maggie managed.

'Have you been raped?' the policewoman asked gently.

'No,' said Maggie, 'I just want to go home.' She attempted to stand up and swayed dangerously.

The policewoman steadied her. 'Have you been drinking?' she asked.

'No,' said Maggie, her voice anguished.

'I really think we should take you to the hospital,' said the policewoman, as she helped Maggie down the steps.

'Please, no,' said Maggie. 'I just need to get home. My flatmate has a car. She'll take me to the John Radcliffe in the morning if I need to go. I promise I will.'

'Alright, but I'm not leaving you alone. We'll see if your flatmate's at home. What's your address?'

Maggie told her.

'I know where that is; the house belongs to a Miss Allnut, is that right?'

'Yes, Roberta Allnut is our landlady,' said Maggie, as she gingerly climbed into the back of the car.

'Me and my sergeant visited her. It was about her nephew. I'm WPC Jessie Andrews, by the way, and the chap in the front who is going to chauffeur you home is PC John Trevor. What's your name, love?'

'Maggie Faulkner,' Maggie said. She leant back in the car seat. Obviously the heater had been full on full blast;

it felt marvellously warm and, above all, safe. She could have gone to sleep, there and then, but Jessie Andrews was full of chat.

'So, is it your mum who lives in St Ives and found the body of Miss Allnut's nephew?' she asked.

'No,' said Maggie, 'it's my flatmate, Isla's mum.'

'She's a bit feisty, that Miss Allnut. She was very cross that your flatmate called us in to check up on the nephew. She was only trying to help, I'm sure.'

'Yes,' Maggie managed.

'Give it a rest, Jess. The poor girl's exhausted,' said John Trevor, much to Maggie's relief.

They were soon in Jericho. 'I'm coming in with you to make sure your flatmate can take care of you.'

Maggie started to protest.

'It's that or the hospital,' said Jessie firmly.

They crept up the stairs and knocked on Isla's door. She opened it in a second. 'Oh my God, Maggie, what has he done to you!' said Isla.

In the light from Isla's room, for the first time Jessie could see the full extent of Maggie's injuries. 'I wanted to take her straight to hospital,' she began.

Maggie looked beseechingly at Isla and shook her head. 'It's OK,' said Isla, 'I'll look after her tonight and take her to the hospital in the morning, if necessary.'

'I will need to talk to you tomorrow, Maggie. Can I come round at midday?' Jessie said.

'That'll be fine,' said Isla.

The relief when Jessie had gone was huge and Isla knew just what to do. She helped Maggie out of her clothes and into her nightie. She tucked her up in bed with a hot water bottle and then fetched some cotton wool and bathed the dried blood away from round Maggie's eyes, nose and mouth. Then she made Maggie take some painkillers and turned out the light, saying, 'I'll wake you up at nine in the morning so we can decide what to do.'

Sitting on the edge of Maggie's bed the following morning, drinking a mug of tea, Isla listened as Maggie told her that the affair was over and that the wretched man in question had beaten her up for the last time. Isla almost believed her.

'Who is this guy?' Isla asked after a lengthy pause. She could hardly bear to look at Maggie's face. This morning it was swelling up hugely and the bruises were starting to come out.

'I daren't tell you,' Maggie began.

'Listen to me, Maggie, please. At midday today, the police are going to return to ask you questions. Between now and then you have to decide whether you want to press charges or not. You need to be clear in your own mind as to what you want to do before that meeting.'

'You have no idea how complicated it is,' said Maggie.

'This is true, I have no idea because you won't tell me,' said Isla. 'Look, we've had our differences recently but, Mags, I love you to pieces, I'll do anything you want to help you get out of this awful situation but you must trust me. You have to share this with someone; you absolutely cannot deal with it alone and I honestly believe I am the best candidate.'

'You are,' Maggie admitted and then began to cry again.

Isla found her some tissues. 'Careful how you mop up; your face is like a battlefield. Look, I tell you what we'll do, I'll ask you questions and you just answer them. OK?'

Maggie nodded.

'Right, question one, who is this awful man?'

'This is the hard part: it is Professor Christopher Barlow, our revered tutor.' Maggie let out a ragged sob.

'Creepy Chris! You are kidding me. He's old enough to be your father, at a pinch your grandfather, and he's awful.'

'I knew this wouldn't work. You'll never understand; you just think I'm an idiot and you're probably right – but I love him, Isla, I really do, though perhaps not as much as I did, after last night.' There was a fresh batch of crying.

Isla pulled herself together, putting firmly to the back of her mind the idea of Creepy Chris and Maggie together. 'Question two – how long as this been going on?'

'It began this academic year, soon after he became our tutor, so we've only been seeing each other for a couple of months. It's been lovely though, until now,' said Maggie. There was a worrying note of pride in her voice.

'Question three – how on earth do you see one another, sometimes all night, without his wife realising?'

'He has rooms in college, as you know. We meet there.'

'Blimey,' said Isla, 'he's brave – "entertaining" one of his own students in his rooms! He could be chucked out for that.'

'I know,' said Maggie, 'it's why I've told no one about him, not even you.'

'OK,' said Isla, 'question four – I know he has been knocking you about in recent months but why did things turn out so much worse tonight? You must have been aware that it was a serious assault, or you wouldn't have run away.'

'This is where it gets really complicated. Christopher snorts cocaine on a regular basis but I didn't realise he was an addict until last night.'

'Go on,' said Isla grimly.

'He'd run out and his normal supplier isn't able to provide him with any for at least another week. He went mad when he found out and started drinking, knocking back the malt whisky like it was lemonade. It was awful. He does drink, of course, but he's much more reliant on cocaine, so he got very drunk, very quickly. Then he started hitting me.' Maggie paused for a moment and drank some tea. 'This is the awful bit, Isla. I told him to stop and then he shouted at me, saying something like, "It's your bloody landlady's fault, inefficient, full of excuses, at Christmas as well." So I asked him if Roberta really was supplying him and he replied that she supplied him and half of Oxford with cocaine; she's a major dealer, Isla. Can you believe that?'

'It is absolutely awful, Mags, but it does tie in with the murder of that poor boy in St Ives, her nephew, doesn't it?'

'Yes,' said Maggie, 'and the trouble is I blurted it out to Christopher. I said something like – "So Roberta's nephew died because she had asked him to bring cocaine up to Oxford for people like you." He went absolutely mad; I thought he was going to kill me. He wanted to know how I knew about James and who I'd been talking to – so I just ran for it. The porter must have thought I was a bit mad, dashing out of college at three in the morning with just one shoe, but I made it, thank God. I just hope Christopher doesn't come round here.'

'Question five,' said Isla, in a slightly shaky voice. 'Are you wanting to press charges with regard to the assault?'

'Absolutely not, I don't want him to lose his position at college.'

'Even though, without a shadow of doubt, he will do this again to someone else, another young student?'

'Hopefully she will be more sensible than me,' said Maggie quietly, tears dried now.

'We do have to tell the police about Roberta, though,' said Isla. 'I've been thinking while you were talking. She always keeps her bedroom door locked, even when she's inside it. I bet you that's where she keeps her supply of cocaine, which, I suppose, normally comes up from Cornwall via county lines. For some reason, she asked James to bring up a supply – perhaps there was a shortage of couriers – and somehow the poor chap became embroiled in the whole beastly business and ended up dead.'

'But that means me having to tell the police that Christopher buys cocaine,' said Maggie.

'It does, but it involves a much lesser charge than seriously assaulting one of his students on university premises – just you remember that. After all, he's not a dealer; that's the important thing.' Isla suddenly stared at Maggie with a look of horror. 'You've never collected any cocaine from Roberta to give to Chris, have you?'

'I swear not,' said Maggie. 'I didn't even know Roberta was his supplier until tonight. There is one thing I haven't told you, though, Isla, because I'm so ashamed.'

'Tell me – it's so important we have no more secrets,' said Isla.

'Here goes,' said Maggie. 'There is a reason why your last couple of essays have, how shall I put it, not been well received. Christopher and I had an awful row a few weeks ago. I told him that I'd needed to explain to you why I was coming home so late and was spending much less time with you. I told Christopher that I admitted to you that I was having a relationship with a married man but, of course, did not divulged his identity. He went mad and even madder when, stupidly, I then said you did not approve of such a relationship and had begged me to end it. That's why he must have been marking down your essays – a sort of revenge. I am so very, very sorry.'

Isla grinned. 'Don't be; it's great news! I truly believed

the first one he marked down was really good and I just couldn't understand why he was so ghastly about it. Now I know, it's such a relief. Come on, let's get you dressed and packed.'

'Packed? Why, and where are we going?' said Maggie, starting to panic.

'Why? Because, from bitter experience, we don't want to be here when Jessie arrests Roberta, which she will do when you tell her what you've just told me. Where? Well, Cornwall, of course!'

'This is probably the moment I should tell you that I think I've a broken collarbone,' said Maggie. 'I fell off my pony when I was about eight and broke it then and this feels exactly the same. So, we will have to stay in Oxford to go to the hospital and, while we're here, perhaps we can persuade Jessie not to follow up on Christopher's cocaine habit – after all, she will have Roberta, who is the real villain.'

'We are not staying in Oxford, Mags. I'm going to fill you full of painkillers and, once we've talked to Jessie, I'm going to drive you straight to Treliske hospital in Truro. Can I remind you that the reason we have to visit a hospital at all is because it was Christopher who broke your collarbone.'

'I'm sure he didn't mean to,' said Maggie plaintively.

'Words fail me,' said Isla.

Suddenly Maggie's battered face broke into a real smile, the first Isla had seen in weeks. 'Well, that's a first!' she said.

CHAPTER THIRTY-NINE

Inspector Peppiatt sat at his desk, pointlessly shuffling around pieces of paper. He had put in motion everything he could and now it was a question of waiting – something he was extremely bad at doing.

He ticked off in his mind what had been achieved in the last twenty-four hours.

Firstly, the laboratory had confirmed that the hair found in Jenny's camper van did belong to James Allnut. So, most likely he had been killed in there with an insulin injection and then transferred to Elsie's cottage. If, as seemed increasingly likely, it was Jenny who had taken him to the cottage, she would have been more than able to carry him up the stairs – she a big strong woman, he a small, slight boy. The question was, had Jenny killed James, or had it been Rick – who left Jenny to dispose of the body?

Secondly, it was now absolutely certain that Rick was

indeed John Lumley from Tyneside, who, obviously, had contrived to make it appear he had died at sea. John Lumley had a missing earlobe and his fingerprints were all over Jenny's camper van. For the time being, though, they had decided to keep his Cornish name of Rick as being the man they were pursuing, because that was the name by which he was known locally, to all those involved in the case.

Thirdly, enquiries had led to two fishermen from Newlyn having some knowledge of Rick. One of them was sure Rick owned a trawler, having spotted him out at sea, and both had seen him come into Newlyn in a small dayboat. Louis had passed on this information to Border Force. Their view was that, assuming Rick was smuggling drugs, he was using his trawler to meet a larger vessel out at sea. Then, according to the size of the load, he would either take the trawler direct to some unmanned deep-water jetty for unloading, or transfer the cocaine to his dayboat, and chose his moment to unload at different locations. Either way, all involved were assuming that wherever the drugs were unloaded, Steve would be waiting with his van.

Louis's contact at Border Force was a very helpful man called Tim Granger. 'It's a tortuous route involved in getting cocaine into Cornwall, but worryingly successful,' he said. 'Most cocaine is manufactured in South America and is then very often transferred to the Caribbean. From there, it is usually loaded onto a container ship and then, somewhere in the waters around the UK, it is transferred to a fishing trawler or sometimes an innocent-looking yacht. All round the coast we patrol the seas, we monitor who comes in and out of ports on a regular basis, but these boys are so clever and constantly change the methods and locations of how and where they land the goods. It doesn't surprise me at all that this Rick uses more than one boat and that the local fishermen don't really know him. He probably spends most of his time at sea.'

So, it was agreed that the best way to break up Rick's operation was to follow Steve, literally everywhere he went. It had been Tim Granger's idea and Louis was much relieved because it provided an alternative to trying to interview Steve again. The more he thought about it, the more certain Louis was that Jack was right – any police contact with Steve again could put him in danger.

Steve was a creature of habit. Every morning, he left his mother's house and went to collect his van at Porthgwidden car park, where he seemed to have a permanent parking space. Louis was taking no chances. He had a man following Steve on foot from his house, and, in the car park, he had both an unmarked police car and a motorbike waiting for him, in the hopes that with two vehicles tailing Steve, there would be little chance of losing him.

It was only seven in the morning and still pitch dark but Louis was restless; he felt he needed to be nearer the action, whatever that meant. He contacted everyone concerned and told them he was driving into St Ives, where he would wait with Jack Eddy for news. 'Please keep me informed of every development,' he repeated several times, unnecessarily.

When Louis arrived, Jack was in radio contact with everyone and also had the kettle on. 'Coffee, boss? You look like you need one,' he said.

Louis nodded. 'No news, I take it – I hope our lad hasn't missed Steve leaving the house?'

'Impossible, boss, it's a really narrow street; he couldn't be missed.'

'Nothing's impossible,' said Louis morosely.

The two men were drinking their coffee in silence when suddenly the radio crackled into life. 'Steve's on the move, heading to the car park now. I'm following at a safe distance; he hasn't seen me, I'm sure.'

A few minutes later, confirmation came through that Steve was in the van, heading as if he might be leaving town. 'He's going past the Tate, up the hill, left to Stennack, looks like he's going out on the Coach Road.' There were a few minutes' silence, then, 'No, he's heading towards Zennor.'

'Damn,' said Louis, 'it looks like wherever he's heading, he's not going to be meeting Rick.'

'Why do you say that, boss?'

'There's no coastline for miles where it would be possible to unload a boat in broad daylight unless the cocaine was very cleverly disguised. I just don't get it.'

There was silence for several minutes. Louis grabbed the microphone. 'Have you still got him?'

'Yes, sir, we've just reached the T-junction and he's turned left, still heading for Zennor.'

'Are you sure he hasn't seen you?' Louis fussed.

'Quite sure, sir, I've fallen right back and Ben, who's on the bike, has overtaken him. There's not much traffic on the road, so we're being very careful.'

'I know what's wrong with you, boss,' said Jack, with an unusual moment of insight.

'What?' growled Louis.

'You wish you were there because you're worried they might mess it up. You want to be on the spot to make sure nothing goes wrong – which it won't if you're there. I'm right, aren't I, boss?'

Louis smiled at Jack. 'You are, of course, right, Eddy, though it pains me to admit it – I deny the bit about me not messing it up, though, because I'm as capable of doing that as the next man, but I do wish I was there.'

'Sir, sir, he's turned off, up a long driveway, towards the sea. Hang on a moment, the place is called Towednack Hall. Shall we follow up the drive? There's a huge great pile of a house at the end; I can just see it.'

'Just get Ben to follow up the drive a little way on his bike, making sure he can't be seen from the house or the van, then come back and report. Be very, very careful. Ben must not be spotted, and you in the car should drive on past the entrance and park up.'

'I know Towednack Hall,' said Jack.

'I knew you would. Tell me all about it,' said Louis.

'The house belongs to some people call Stebbings – Sir Clive and Lady Stebbings. I think the lady of the house is called Amanda. They have three grown-up children, and London was their main home until Sir Clive retired early. He was in business of some sort and sold out, making a fortune, I understand. The house has been in the family for several hundred years, I believe, and they have always spent a lot of time down in Cornwall. They even kept a permanent staff in Cornwall, while they still lived in London. Sir Clive used to be master of the local hunt until it was disbanded and they are very much part of the Cornish gentry scene, if you know what I mean.'

'That's absolutely perfect, Eddy. You did leave out details of Sir Clive's inside leg measurement but apart from that, I feel I almost know the family. Well done.'

'I don't quite follow you, boss.'

'Never mind, just a feeble joke, not worth repeating. Come on, I've had enough of this. Let's go and join them.'

Everyone pulled back from the entrance to the Hall. Louis and Jack's car was parked out of sight down a farm track. They waited. An hour went by and there was still no sign of Steve. *Maybe I've got this all wrong,* Louis thought. *Maybe Steve helps out with odd jobs for the family and Rick is just an autocratic head gardener, who wouldn't dream of committing murder, except perhaps on the slugs and snails who have the temerity to invade his greenhouse. Having 'died' in Whitley Bay as John Lumley and then been reborn as Rick in Cornwall, maybe he is a reformed character and has nothing at all to do with Jenny Rowe.* Except, no, that didn't work because his fingerprints were all over her camper van. Hell!

'I wish I'd brought my lunch with me,' Jack said plaintively.

'Don't moan,' said Louis. 'Just thank your lucky stars that you're not poor Ben, stuck out there on a bike. He must be freezing. Just be quiet for a few minutes, would you, Eddy? I want to think.'

It was reasonable, Louis mused, to understand why James had to die. He must have discovered the cocaine that was in the back of his car, and instead of reporting it to the police he had made a fuss about it – perhaps even returning to the place from where he had collected it. So, why did Jenny have to die? Yes, she had chosen a stupid place to dispose of James's body because it was found so quickly. Surrounded by sea, as St Ives is, wouldn't that sea have been a better place to dump a body? Then Louis remembered the harbourmaster of St Ives telling him that if a body was thrown or fell into the sea from any point near St Ives, even on the cliffs, it would end up on a local beach – usually Bamaluz Beach. 'You'd have to take a body out to sea, beyond Seal Island, to make sure it doesn't come back,' he'd told Louis. 'Then, if it doesn't get eaten by crabs, or caught up in a net, it usually ends up in Padstow.' A cheerful thought. Maybe Jenny knew that or maybe, as Mrs McKenzie believed, it was all connected to her lost son – she simply could not bear to just dump the body anywhere; she had to, effectively, lay it out and give James the respect she thought he deserved.

Still, choosing a silly place to leave the body was surely not a good enough reason to get herself killed.

She had to have done something else to anger Rick, assuming, of course, that it was Rick who had killed her.

'He's on the move,' said Ben.

'Right, you two follow Steve wherever he goes. Jack and I are going to wait a few minutes and then we are going to see Sir Clive Stebbings.'

CHAPTER FORTY

Twenty minutes later, Jack drove the car through the gates of Towednack Hall and carried on down the long drive. The house was not traditionally stunning in that it was made from the same granite that was scattered all over the moorland. It felt almost as if it had grown out of its surroundings but it was, nonetheless, imposing. More spectacular was the view because beyond the house the land fell away to the cliffs, exposing an enormous expanse of sea. 'Nothing between us and America,' said Louis. 'What a view!'

It was reluctantly agreed by Jack that he would stay in the car so he could be kept up to date with Steve's movements. Clearly, he was dying to see inside the house but Louis was not convinced he mightn't say something inappropriate.

The door was opened by a fairly elderly, stern-looking woman, who Louis took to be a housekeeper.

'I've come to see Sir Clive Stebbings,' Louis said.

'I will see if he's free,' said the housekeeper. 'Can I ask who you are?'

'Inspector Louis Peppiatt,' said Louis, holding out his warrant card.

'Oh, I see,' said the housekeeper, clearly a little flustered. 'I won't be a moment.'

Louis was shown into a large drawing room, a comfortable room, expensively decorated but in no way flash. One side of the room was completely given over to three sets of French windows, which opened out onto a large terrace with the wonderful uninterrupted view of the sea.

'Inspector Peppiatt, how do you do?' Sir Clive strode across the room, hand outstretched in greeting. He was a tall man, who Louis judged to be of a similar age to his own. He had lost most of his hair but he was still striking to look at, with a set of piercing blue eyes. Immediately, for some inexplicable reason, Louis did not like him.

'Good afternoon, sir, I'm sorry to trouble you.'

'No problem, Inspector. Can I interest you in anything – tea, coffee, something stronger, perhaps?'

'I'm fine, thank you, sir,' said Louis. 'This is a very brief call. I'm enquiring about a man named Steven Matthews. I've been told he works for you, is this right?'

'Matthews, Matthews, it doesn't ring an immediate bell but we do employ people from time to time on a temporary basis, to help with the land and the garden. It's possible that Matthews is one of those. I don't personally deal with any of that, but I can ask my estate manager and see if he knows of him.'

'Perhaps I could have a word with your estate manager, sir, to save you the trouble,' Louis suggested.

There was a slight pause, too long a pause, Louis judged, for this clearly erudite man. 'I'm afraid he's having a couple of days' leave. I'll get hold of him as soon as he returns and let you know. Steven Matthews, you say? What's he done to interest the strong arm of the law?'

'Obviously, sir, I can't tell you that,' said Louis, with some relish. 'It's nothing serious, nothing that would make it unwise for you to employ him. Here's my card. I would be grateful if you could let me know as soon as you have spoken to your estate manager. Thank you for your time.'

On his way back to the car, Louis considered the impressions he had formed of Sir Clive Stebbings. He was lying about Steve and about the estate manager, but because he was an intelligent man he also knew that Louis was aware of this. He had a cruel mouth; his light blue eyes, although arresting, were as cold as ice. He was also sniffing, not a lot, but enough to notice. It could be a cold – or maybe not.

'How did it go?' Jack asked as Louis climbed into the car.

'He's lying,' said Louis. 'The question is why is he lying? Any news from the boys?'

'Yes,' said Jack. 'Steve has parked his car back at Porthgwidden and has gone home. It doesn't look like he's going anywhere else tonight.'

Louis sighed. 'I want Towednack Hall under surveillance all night. I want to know if anyone visits Steve, and if he leaves his house, I want him followed. I'll drop you off in St Ives, I'm going back to Truro now, but make sure I'm kept informed of any movement. Is that clear?'

'Yes, boss. Apparently, a Constable Jessie Andrews has been chasing you. Do you know who she is?'

'Not a clue,' said Louis.

'I've texted through her number to your phone, boss.'

'Thanks, Eddy, I'll give her a call when I get home.'

All the way home, of course, Louis mulled over the case, becoming increasingly concerned that he was putting too much emphasis on the supposed cocaine smuggling and not enough on the two murders themselves. On what was he basing the link to cocaine – a teenage boy who had spilt some in the back of his car and a knight of the realm who was doing rather a lot of sniffing? Not much to go on – he definitely needed some sort of breakthrough.

On reaching home, Louis collapsed into his armchair. He badly wanted a large whisky but he needed to call the unknown constable first. Wearily, he pulled out his phone but before he could make the call, it rang. It was Merrin McKenzie.

'Mrs McKenzie,' he said, 'how are things?'

'You sound exhausted, Inspector, but I have some very good news that is going to cheer you up – a lot, I think.'

Louis sat up straight, and pulled out his notebook. 'Fire away, Mrs McKenzie; good news is something I could really do with this evening.'

Merrin told Louis the full story of Maggie, Roberta, Christopher Barlow, the police constable and the fact that Maggie and Isla were on their way to St Ives, via Treliske hospital.

'Why have they gone via the hospital?' Louis asked.

'Because wretched Professor Christopher Barlow beat up Maggie so badly that she has a broken collarbone.'

'The brute, I hope she's reported him. Has she given a statement?' Louis asked.

'Coercive control is central to Maggie's relationship with Christopher so, of course, she refuses to report him for her injuries, despite Isla and the police doing their very best to persuade her. However, the good news is that she has made a statement to the effect that Christopher told her Roberta was his supplier. As a result, Roberta has been arrested. She has a little room off her bedroom where she bags up her merchandise. There was not a great deal of cocaine in evidence there at the moment, but plenty enough to prosecute. Of course, she has hardly any stock and Creepy Chris, as Isla calls him, has run out of cocaine, because James never arrived in Oxford with the intended supply.'

'So these two murders really are drug-related; I'm not going mad,' said Louis, more to himself than to Merrin.

'Of course they are,' said Merrin soothingly, 'and no, Inspector, I have never considered you deranged, at least not seriously.'

'That's a relief,' said Louis. 'It's odd, you know, but this case seems to be riddled with coercive control. As well as Maggie, there is Jenny, under the thumb of her boyfriend, Rick. Also, poor Steve, his sidekick, is also terrified of Rick. Still, we are making progress and, thanks to you, I think confidence is restored. I'm not quite sure what tomorrow will bring, but if I may, I would like to come and see the girls sometime, when Maggie feels up to it.'

'Yes, of course,' said Merrin. 'I don't think they'll be out and about very much; Maggie is pretty badly beaten up by all accounts. I'm hoping they will be arriving in the next hour so I can make a fuss of them.'

'Do you happen to know if the constable who helped Maggie is called Jessie Andrews?'

'Yes, I think so, no, I'm sure. Isla mentioned Jessie by name several times,' said Merrin.

'I'll give her a ring and thank her,' said Louis.

'It's a wicked old world out there, Inspector. You take care.'

'I will, and thanks again.'

CHAPTER FORTY-ONE

The call came through at 4.33 a.m. Although exhausted, Louis had found sleep evaded him since his mind was swimming with details of the case. Eventually, he'd fallen asleep in the early hours of the morning – so 4.33 a.m. was not an ideal time to be roused from his slumbers.

It was Tim Granger, his contact at Border Force. 'Rick motored into Newlyn harbour about twenty minutes ago,' he said. 'One of the fishermen there does some surveillance for us from time to time. Rick was in his dayboat. He moored up and then left the yard. He drove off in a black saloon; that's the best my contact can do for us, I'm afraid. He was too far away to get the reg number, or even the make of car. At least Rick is here on dry land but the trouble is we have no idea where he's going. I should have had a car at the yard but, of course, I had no idea where he was going to make landfall.'

'I think I know where he might be heading but it's too soon to be sure – and if I'm wrong, we're going to have egg all over our faces, big time,' said Louis, now very much awake.

'You intrigue me. Why would that be?' Tim asked.

'Because the place I think Rick may be storing the cocaine, and from where he might also be distributing it, is the home of Sir Clive Stebbings.'

'You're kidding me, Louis; are you sure about this?' said Tim.

'Pretty sure but not certain and that's the problem. Steve, Rick's sidekick, spent some time there yesterday but Sir Clive denied knowing him. If Steve sets off for Stebbings's place again today, I think he might well be meeting Rick there.'

'Where does Sir Clive live?' Tim asked.

Louis gave him the details.

'Look, I don't want you and your sergeant playing heroes. This man, Rick, we all believe to be a killer, he's very dangerous. From what I hear, he's wanted for all sorts of violent crime up on Tyneside, under his real name, John Lumley. I'll move some men into position, near St Ives, and the moment Steve is on the move – even if it turns out he's just going to buy a pasty – let me know. Also, can you put the Stebbings place under surveillance?'

'It already is, Tim,' said Louis.

'Excellent – now remember, this is a Border Force issue; I don't want you taking any risks. Understood?'

'Understood,' said Louis meekly.

Hurriedly, Louis made two phone calls. Firstly, to faithful Ben, who, after a few hours' rest, was now back on his bike at Porthgwidden car park. Having established that there was also a car containing two PCs in the car park, ready to follow Steve if he emerged, Louis told Ben to drive to Towednack Hall, relieve the current surveillance team and conceal himself as before. 'Ben, you're looking for a black saloon car arriving at the Hall – it could be coming from either direction. The moment you see it, call me. This is really important: the man driving the car is almost certainly our killer. Do nothing, just call.'

He then dug Jack Eddy out of bed, which was most unwelcome and produced a great deal of grumbling. 'Concentrate please, Eddy,' he said. 'Rick is back in Cornwall and on the move. I've sent Ben over to Towednack Hall. Get hold of our man outside Steve's and the car at Porthgwidden and make absolutely sure they are alert. I think Steve will be leaving quite soon, although it's early, so call me the moment he does. I'm on my way over shortly to pick you up, so be ready.'

By nine o'clock, Louis's confidence was ebbing away. Steve had made no move at all and there had been no sightings of Rick. The traffic was already heavy, which didn't help, created by last-minute Christmas shopping and visitors arriving early to avoid the Christmas holiday exodus to Cornwall. Tim had called twice to see if anything was happening and there was an awful lot of moaning emanating from Jack, who wanted his breakfast. He and Louis were parked up on the Zennor road, about two miles short of Towednack Hall. 'OK,' said Louis, 'we'll drive back to the Co-op but I want you in and out of there in seconds; just grab a sandwich. I don't want you fading away from lack of food, Eddy.'

The irony was lost on Jack. 'Thanks, boss – do you want anything?' he asked.

'A bottle of water would be good,' said Louis. He felt sick with nerves; eating was out of the question.

It was on Jack's way back from the Co-op that the first call came in. 'Steve's on the move; he's heading for the car park,' he said.

Moments later, Ben rang in. 'The black saloon has just arrived; the driver is definitely alone and definitely male. He's parked round the side of the house, outside what looks like a stable block.'

Jack relayed the message.

'How can he possibly see that?' said Louis. 'I told him to stay well away, out of sight, like yesterday.'

Jack had put his phone on loudspeaker.

'It's OK, sir, I'm up a tree. They can't see me but as the land slopes away to the sea, I can see them from this height. Also, I've got a better signal.'

'Good lad, remember to tell us the moment Steve arrives in his van.'

'Will do, sir.'

Moments later, the call came through to say that it looked as if Steve was following the same route as the previous day. 'We'll move up a bit nearer,' Louis said to Jack. 'I'll park in the entrance to Towednack Church so we'll see Steve go by, assuming he's coming this way.'

He then called Tim and updated him.

'I'll move the boys forward now, Louis,' Tim said.

While they had been sitting in the car for what seemed like days, rather than hours, a worrying thought had been forming in Louis's mind. Assuming he was right about Clive Stebbings and he was involved in cocaine smuggling, then the first thing Clive would do on Rick's arrival would be to tell him about Louis's visit yesterday to enquire about Steve Matthews. How would Rick react to that? He had almost certainly killed both James and Jenny, presumably because he saw them as a threat to his business. Working under a false name and having committed a number of crimes on Tyneside, Rick couldn't afford to be caught – so he therefore eliminated anyone who he saw as a threat. Surely that would mean Steve was now in danger, and if so, Louis realised, it would be entirely his fault. With his focus on catching Rick, he had inadvertently put Steve in a very dangerous situation – far worse in fact than simply interviewing him again, which Rick might never have known about.

Jack broke into his thoughts. 'Steve's van has just gone past, boss; he must be going to Towednack Hall', too.'

Louis called Tim. 'Steve will be at the Hall in about five minutes. Where are your boys?'

'I was just about to call you, Louis. They started to drive through St Ives but a large lorry got stuck in the marketplace. Our boys are right behind it; the traffic has backed up behind them so they can't move. They'll sort it but it could delay them by ten to fifteen minutes. So hold back, Louis, until they arrive.'

'I can't,' said Louis. 'I've just realised I have put Steve in terrible danger. We're going in.'

'I forbid it,' yelled Tim.

'Sorry,' said Louis, 'but you have no authority over me and mine. There will be five of us altogether. I am not prepared to leave Steve unprotected. Just get your men here as quickly as you can.'

'Louis—' Tim began but Louis had cut the call.

CHAPTER FORTY-TWO

Merrin couldn't sleep so she had risen early and taken William for a walk in the dark. Many of the cottages kept their Christmas tree lights on all night and Merrin loved peering into the windows as she passed by. No one was about yet and as she walked up Fore Street, over the cobbles, she could hear the sea pounding on both sides of the town. The absolute silence, except for the sea, gave her a sudden profound sense of the past. Over centuries, men and women of her blood must have walked over these same cobblestones and heard the same sounds of the sea. It was a strangely comforting thought, and now with Isla home she felt childlike about the forthcoming Christmas festivities. For the first time since Adam's death, she realised that she was almost happy.

Isla was making tea when Merrin quietly let herself back into Miranda's Cottage. She gave her daughter a kiss. 'How's Maggie?' she asked, as Isla fussed over William.

'I think she slept a bit because she was so exhausted but her shoulder really hurts so I'm going to take her up some more painkillers with the tea and hope she goes back to sleep.'

'Good idea,' said Merrin, 'but how are you? You've also had very little sleep, a long drive and all the worry of the situation.'

'I'm fine,' said Isla firmly. 'It's lovely to have my friend back and she does understand now why I reacted as I did – but I am still so angry about Creepy Chris. I can't bear the idea that he is going to get away with abusing Maggie and hurting her so badly, but she is absolutely adamant that she's not going to report him.'

'You could take some comfort from the fact that CC will not know yet that Maggie isn't going to report him. Hopefully, he will be worried sick and believing it's likely she will tell all and therefore his career will be at an end. He could be extremely worried and frightened at this moment – bullies are easily frightened.'

'I'll hold that thought, Mum – good one, I just can't bear injustice.'

'Sometimes, Isla, you are so like me.'

'Worrying, isn't it?' said Isla with a grin.

Louis stopped his car by Ben's tree. Ben shinned down the tree with impressive speed and agility. 'Morning, sir. Are we going in to get them?'

'This is plan,' said Louis. 'I am going to take the car

as far up the drive as I can, without being seen from the house. I want you to come with us now and then you and Jack are to stay in the car while I go in and find out what's what. Get the two PCs in the other car to join you and if I am not out in ten minutes, then the four of you should approach the stables, but cautiously. Remember, we are dealing with a vicious character who will almost certainly be armed. Listen carefully as to what's going on before making an entrance and stay under cover if there is no immediate danger. Ideally, we should wait for Border Force officers to arrive, but they're stuck in traffic. We dare not wait for them because I'm worried Steve may be in serious trouble.'

'With respect, sir,' said Ben, 'I don't like the sound of that plan at all. I really don't think you should go in alone. With five of us, however much of a villain this Rick is, we must be able to disarm him.'

'And if he's got a gun and we rush him, how many of us is he going to kill or maim before we get him? Trust me, I know what I'm doing. Remember, we are not even sure that this is a drugs raid – they could all be talking about horses or the price of fish.'

Louis drove halfway up the drive and stopped the car. He turned to Jack and Ben. 'Call the other two; tell them to leave their car by Ben's bike and to join you here on foot. Ten minutes, I said; ten minutes is what I mean.' He stepped out of the car.

'Good luck, sir,' said Ben.

'Take care, boss,' said Jack.

The two men sat in silence watching Louis walk

purposefully round the bend in the drive and out of sight. 'Call the PCs, Jack,' Ben said, 'tell them to come and sit in this car and then wait ten minutes before coming up to the stables, but we're going to follow the boss now.'

'But he told us . . .' Jack began.

'Don't be daft,' said Ben. 'We're not going to sit in the car like a couple of frightened kids while our boss gets killed. Come on, man, pull yourself together, make the call and then we're off.'

As the house came into sight, Louis felt strangely calm. There was no need to worry any more as to whether he had judged the case correctly. The die was cast, there was no going back; in a few moments he would know whether he was right or wrong.

A black BMW was parked outside the main entrance to a large stable block. The doors to the stables were open; Louis walked through them and he turned right, following the sound of voices.

At the end of the building, the individual stalls had been removed to create a large room. The tableau in front of Louis took a moment for him to understand. Against the far wall were a considerable number of apparently full compost sacks. There was also a large table, on which were scales, smaller compost sacks and a variety of jugs, scoops and spoons, all neatly laid out. In the centre of the room was a chair. In the chair was a man tied to it, his head drooping; there was blood on his shirt and jeans. Beside him, a knife in hand, was

Rick. Louis had seen a photograph of him sent down by Northumbria Police but even without that, he would have recognised him. He was tall, muscular, with a mop of dark hair and a ring through one ear, but not the other – because the lobe was missing.

Sir Clive Stebbings was sitting at the table.

No one spoke for a moment. 'Well,' said Rick at last. 'I guess, Clive, this is Inspector Peppiatt, who came to see you yesterday, at the invitation of this useless piece of lard.' He kicked out, viciously, at the man in the chair, who yelped and raised his head. It had to be Steve, of course. Louis had never actually met him, until this moment, but the colourful jumper and the terrible haircut identified him immediately, and Louis was relieved to see that the blood seemed only to have come from his nose. He was also pleased to see that Clive Stebbings was looking decidedly uncomfortable and appeared to be going to say nothing at all to confirm or deny his own identity.

Louis addressed Rick. 'John Lumley, I am here to arrest you on two counts of murder and the smuggling, possession and dealing of large quantities of cocaine. You do not have to say anything but—'

'Oh, shut up,' shouted Rick. 'If you think you stand a chance of arresting me, you have to be crazy. Look at you, look at me, and who's got the knife?' He brandished the knife in Louis's general direction.

'Then just let Steve go,' Louis said. 'He has nothing to do with me being here today. In fact, when my sergeant interviewed him, he was fiercely loyal to you and would answer no questions.'

'Ah, but why was he even being interviewed by the police? Tell me that, if you can, Inspector,' Rick sneered.

'Because you murdered Jenny Rowe in her camper van right outside Steve's house and when he heard she was dead, he was very upset and told us she was his friend. He did not betray you; just let him go, Rick.'

'You really are a joke, Inspector. Can you honestly imagine that I'm going to say "Fair cop, Officer" and hand myself over? This creature' – he kicked Steve again – 'is my passport out of here.' He hesitated. 'No, on second thoughts, he'd be too much of a burden. You, Inspector, fetch a chair and bring it over here.' He put the knife to Steve's throat, who whimpered, pitilessly. 'And don't try anything clever, or he dies.'

Louis walked slowly over to the table and picked up a chair. He looked straight at Clive Stebbings, who had still not said a word. 'So, Sir Clive, do you condone this sort of behaviour in what I assume is your colleague?' He nodded towards Rick. Clive simply looked away; his face, though, was ashen. He seemed in shock. 'So you're just going to sit there, are you?'

'Inspector, if you don't come over here this moment, Steve dies. I'd be doing the world a favour; he's useless. In fact, I might just as well do it now.'

As Rick was speaking, he had removed the knife from Steve's throat and was waving it in the air. In that second, Louis realised it was his only chance to save Steve, and maybe himself. He lunged forward, thrusting the chair legs into Rick's chest. Rick lashed out and the knife sliced deep into Louis's forearm, forcing him to drop the chair. Louis clutched his arm, which was bleeding profusely; Rick straightened himself and threw aside the chair. He was still holding the knife.

'That was a very stupid thing to do, Inspector,' he said, advancing towards Louis.

There was a sudden whirl of activity behind Rick and a large Cornish shovel made contact with the top of his head. He fell to the ground. Louis stepped forward and hurriedly picked up the knife Rick had dropped as he fell. Then, looking up, he saw Jack, shovel in hand, smiling at him, and looking very pleased with himself.

There was a movement behind the table. Clive was up and running for the doorway. 'After him, Jack,' shouted Louis, but there was no need: Ben was waiting for him.

By the time the two police constables arrived, followed almost immediately by six members of Border Force, both Rick and Sir Clive were handcuffed and waiting for them – Rick, now semi-conscious and very angry, Sir Clive, scared and apparently in some sort of bewildered trance.

Ben had removed his shirt and wrapped it tightly round Louis's arm. 'They're all yours,' said Louis to the Border Force.

'What about the man over there?'

'Not him,' said Louis. 'Untie him please, Jack, and Ben, could you go and fetch my car. I'm not sure Steve can walk very far.'

'But isn't this Steve one of the gang?'

'Only by default – he's staying with me.'

'Honestly, sir,' said the Border Force spokesman, 'he needs to come with us. The boss told me to bring in everyone connected with the drug smuggling; this matter is certainly under our jurisdiction.'

'And,' said one of his colleagues who had been examining the compost sacks, 'this is a huge haul, a really important drugs bust – there must be millions of pounds of cocaine involved in this lot.'

'Exactly,' said Louis, 'this is, as you say, a serious drug-smuggling operation that, in my view, has been carried out in front of your collective noses for some time – several years certainly. But for me and my men, these "millions of pounds of cocaine" would have been distributed around the country. So, this is my case and I'm the one who makes the decisions.'

The man looked at Louis. Blood was now pouring down his hand and onto the floor, to which he seemed completely oblivious. His face was drained of colour, he looked exhausted but there was no point ignoring the steely look in his eye and the aura of absolute authority. 'My boss is going to furious,' he said lamely.

'I couldn't give a toss about your boss and his state of mind,' said Louis. 'I'm going to take this man home to his mother.'

CHAPTER FORTY-THREE

Rick was now fully conscious and causing trouble. Despite the handcuffs and being held by two burly Border Force officers, he was putting up quite a fight, swearing and shouting, mostly at Louis. 'Put him in the van, for God's sake,' said the Border Force spokesman.

'Just remember, I want him on two counts of murder,' said Louis. 'It would be good to think you lot will have taught him the error of his ways by the time I come to interview him, but I have to admit, I'm not holding my breath.'

'He's certainly a very nasty piece of work. Look, I'm sorry if I was throwing my weight about just now. My name's Simon Burnett.' The two men shook hands. 'That's a very deep cut,' said Simon. 'You need it fixed quickly; you're losing a lot of blood. A good thing it's your left arm, assuming of course that you're right-handed.'

Louis nodded, suddenly becoming aware of his

injury, which immediately started throbbing, as if to remind him of its existence.

'You and your men get off, you via a hospital, I trust,' said Simon. 'We'll secure the site. Is there anyone living in the main house, do you know?'

'There is a Lady Stebbings, Amanda, I seem to remember. I've no idea if she's in residence. When I called in yesterday, there was no sign of her but there was a housekeeper. There are some children too, I think my sergeant mentioned, but I imagine they're all grown up.' Louis smiled suddenly. 'They're unlikely partners in crime, those two, aren't they?' he said, nodding towards Rick and Clive as they were led away. 'When I interviewed Sir Clive yesterday, there was a lot of sniffing going on. My guess would be that he has a serious cocaine habit, which was why he allowed Rick to use his stable for his smuggling enterprise.'

'That sounds about right,' said Simon. 'Look, Inspector, I haven't yet said thank you for uncovering all this and I'm so sorry we weren't here in time to stop you being hurt. We got stuck in traffic in St Ives marketplace, would you believe?'

Louis grinned. 'That I really would believe; the marketplace is something of a quagmire for lorries and especially camper vans.' He started for the door, and raised his good arm. 'Good luck, Simon, nice to meet you.'

Louis found Jack and Steve sitting in his car and the logistics were quickly sorted out. Jack was to drive Steve home and explain to his mother what had happened and tell both her and Steve not to worry – Louis would be in touch in the morning. 'Then, Eddy, park my car at Stennack and I'll see you next on the 28th,' said Louis.

'Where are you going, boss?' Jack asked, looking aghast at Louis's arm.

'I'm going nowhere. It's you who's going home to Mrs Eddy to help her get ready for your son and daughter-in-law's arrival and thereafter to have a very happy Christmas.'

'Really, boss, that's great, thank you. Mrs Eddy will be pleased.'

'And make sure you tell your wife that you are a hero. Oh, and Eddy, thank you – I think you probably saved my life.'

'Mr Inspector,' said Steve, leaning forward in the car to see Louis properly. 'Thank you too for saving my life; I – I thought I was going to die.'

'My pleasure, Steve, you were very brave, and you remember to tell your mum that.'

It was arranged that the two police constables would run Louis to the West Cornwall Hospital in Penzance and leave him there. Ben was to take the bike to St Ives, pick up a police car and return to Penzance in order to collect Louis once he'd been patched up.

'And then I'm to drop you home to Truro?' Ben asked.

'I'm not sure yet,' said Louis.

While Louis was being stitched up in Penzance, Jack took Steve home and then dropped the inspector's car at Stennack, as requested. He decided to walk through town to his home at the top of Baileys Lane to give himself a chance to think through what had happened. In all his years in the police force, Jack had never experienced anything like it. He'd just reached the slipway, close to the Sloop Inn, when he spotted Merrin hurrying towards her home with a large carrier bag. 'Merrin Trip!' Jack called.

Merrin saw him and crossed the road. 'Hello, Jack,' she said. 'How's the case going?'

'Brilliantly – we've caught the villains and Border Force have taken them away. I've just dropped that poor lad, Steve, home and explained everything to his mum. Heaven knows what's going to happen to him. Oh, and the boss has been stabbed.'

For a moment, Jack thought Merrin was going to faint. She went white as a sheet and grabbed his arm to steady herself. Confused, he ploughed on. 'He's alright, little Merrin, don't you worry, just a nasty cut to his left arm. He's at West Cornwall now, no doubt he'll need some stitches, but nothing to worry about, my little maid. He's given me five days off work, too. I reckon it's because I saved his life.'

Merrin, still feeling shaken, was forced to ask, 'How did you manage that?'

'I hit that villain, Rick, over the head with a Cornish shovel. A right bash I gave him and serve him right. He'd already hurt the boss and I reckon he was going in for the kill. So did the boss. He thanked me for saving his life – what about that, Merrin? – and I'm to tell Mrs

Eddy that I'm a hero, apparently. I'm on my way back home just now to tell her.'

'I won't hold you up, then. Thanks for the news, well done.' Merrin continued her way home, a sick feeling in the pit of her stomach.

Ben arrived at West Cornwall Hospital and was told by the receptionist to wait and Inspector Peppiatt would be with him shortly. When Louis arrived, he was preceded by a nurse carrying two bottles of pills. Louis had his arm in a sling and was looking defiant. 'Oh, good,' said the nurse. 'I hope you've come to arrest him, Officer; he's caused no end of trouble here.'

Ben grinned at Louis. 'I am sorry, nurse, what's he been up to?'

'He made an awful fuss when he arrived and jumped the queue because he said he was in the middle of chasing villains. Then he said he didn't need stitches, just a big plaster. I ask you, have you seen the size of that knife wound? Plasters, ridiculous. Then he said I was being slow with the stitching, behaving as if he thought I was just hemming up some curtains. The doctor threatened to admit him to hospital, he was so fed up with him. It's where he should be, in my view. He's had a nasty shock and lost a lot of blood.'

The nurse's tirade finished, Louis did his best to look contrite. 'I am so sorry but there's still a lot to be done today. Thank you for all your help and your very excellent, if lengthy, embroidery.'

The nurse raised her eyes to heaven and handed Ben

two bottles of pills. 'He's had a shot of antibiotics and a tetanus jab. The doctor also gave him a shot for the pain. So these pills should not be started until tonight. Take him home directly and make sure he goes straight to bed.'

'I am here, you know,' said Louis. 'I'm not a child.'

'Then you shouldn't behave like one!' said the nurse, turning on her heel to return to the wards. She stopped halfway across the reception area. 'Inspector,' she called. 'Well done.' And with that she disappeared.

'Well, sir,' said Ben, as they walked to the car, 'you certainly made yourself popular in there!'

'It was all so slow, and such a fuss about nothing. Now I want you to take me to Camborne Police HQ. While I was sitting around in the hospital, I rang and made an appointment to see the chief super.'

'My instructions were to take you straight home,' said Ben, knowing already that arguing the point was futile.

'And those instructions have been overruled,' said Louis firmly. There was a slight pause. 'Ben, you did very well today but on the subject of instructions, you and Jack didn't wait the ten minutes I asked you to do.'

'No, sir,' said Ben, bravely. 'We followed you almost immediately and found that back entrance in the stables, which enabled Jack to surprise Rick from behind.'

'While you cut off anyone trying to escape from the front. It was an excellent plan but completely flouted the instructions of a senior officer.'

'Yes, sir,' said Ben humbly.

'Thank God you did,' said Louis, smiling. 'Just don't do it again.'

'No, sir,' said Ben, smiling back.

The two men climbed into the car and Ben drove out of the car park. 'You'll need to keep talking to me while we drive to Camborne,' said Louis, 'otherwise, I'll fall asleep.'

'Maybe you should have a nap, sir. At this time of day, it will take us at least half an hour to reach HQ; a nap would do you good.'

'God almighty, Ben!' said Louis. 'You're sounding just like that nurse. Tell me, have you started thinking about your sergeants' exams yet? If, and only if, you learn to obey orders, you have the makings of a very fine police officer.'

'Thank you very much, sir, I thought I was a bit young to try for promotion just yet.'

'Not in my view – you have natural leadership qualities already,' said Louis. 'Anyway, think about it. You'll have my full support if you decide to go ahead.'

'Decide to go ahead!' said Ben, braking rather sharply at the traffic lights. 'I don't need to think about it, sir. That's great, I'll apply and start studying right away.'

'I rather thought you might,' said Louis.

CHAPTER FORTY-FOUR

Chief Superintendent John Dent was a good man but inclined to be rather set in his ways. He liked everything done strictly by the book. Since, on many occasions, this conflicted with Inspector Peppiatt's police practices, there had been some fine old battles between them over the years, which, of course, the chief super usually won. The situation, however, did not interfere with the fact that both men liked and respected one another.

'Hello, Sally,' said Louis to John Dent's elderly, long-suffering secretary, of whom he was very fond. 'How are you and what is the state of the climate next door?' He nodded in the direction of Dent's office.

Sally stood up and came round from behind her desk. 'Louis, look at you, poor wounded soldier,' she said, patting his good arm. 'You're the talk of the station, beating Border Force at their own game and, I'm told, discovering millions of pounds of cocaine.' She smiled at him. 'I'm proud to know you, young man.'

'That's made my day worthwhile, Sally dear. I particularly liked the "young" bit. So, am I going to get the same reception next door?'

'Yes, up to a point,' said Sally cautiously.

'And what point is that?' Louis asked.

'He knows you want something and whatever it is, he imagines it is going to be awkward and probably upset the Border Force. I presume he's right.'

'Of course he is, completely right!' said Louis.

'He said you are to go straight in as soon as you arrive. So, in you go and put the poor man out of his misery – or not.'

The two men shook hands and John Dent gestured to the two easy chairs at the far end of the office. 'Would you like some coffee, or maybe a sandwich? Have you eaten anything since your adventures?'

'I'm fine, sir, thank you, on both counts. I had a sandwich and a coffee from the machine at the hospital, which for the time being has put me off eating or drinking anything ever again.'

'I can imagine; and are you in much pain from the knife wound? By all accounts, you had a lucky escape but I hear it's a nasty cut. Tell me exactly what happened; I understand you and your men did very well.'

Louis told his story in every detail. John Dent listened in silence until Louis mentioned the involvement of Clive Stebbings. 'I know Sir Clive Stebbings,' he said, 'not well but we have met at various county events over the years. I never liked the man, without quite knowing why. Now I do. So presumably you are going to interview this man, Rick, real name John Lumley, and try to pin the murders on him?'

'That's my problem, sir. I am certain he is the person responsible for the murders but at the moment, I only have only one person who can tell me exactly what happened.'

'And that person is this chap Steve Matthews, who you refused to hand over to the Border Force?'

Louis nodded.

'I've already had Tim Granger on the phone moaning about you.' John Dent sported a rather fine set of bushy eyebrows, which Louis always believed appeared to bristle when the chief super disapproved of anything. There was a hint of bristling already.

'There are two reasons why I need to hold on to Steve. The first is the practical one I've just explained. At the moment, apart from Clive Stebbings, Steve is the only person left alive who can provide the evidence to nail Rick. Secondly, he has quite severe learning difficulties. I genuinely believe he had no real idea as to what was going on – at any rate until the murders took place. He's a child, sir; prison would destroy him and, with a good lawyer, I reckon community service would be the right course of action at the very most. He lives with his mother; he's not a danger to anyone.'

'Are you going soft, Louis? What's the matter with you? This man is part of a gang that has been bringing cocaine into Cornwall for some time and as a result of their activities, two people have died.' The eyebrows were definitely bristling now.

'Alright, sir, look at it another way,' said Louis. 'Accept, if you will, that this man has learning difficulties and is very vulnerable. If he's chucked into the cells and interrogated by Border Force officers, he will never make a credible witness to send Rick down for the murders. He will simply fall apart. So, the end of this case will be star-studded so far as cocaine smuggling is concerned but we will be seen as having failed to get a conviction for the murders. I am hoping there is a possibility that Sir Clive knew something of the murders and if so, in my view, he will soon be singing like a canary. We could see the panic in his eyes before he even left the stables and, certainly, there will be no loyalty shown to his partner. But we can't rely on that – Steve knows the truth and also the details of exactly what happened, I'm certain of it.'

'Very well,' said John. 'Interview him tomorrow morning and offer him the duty solicitor. We'll see what comes out of it. I'll hold off Tim Granger for twenty-four hours – actually, you have the luck of the devil, Peppiatt. In reality, that probably means until after Christmas, I suspect.'

'With respect, sir, the duty solicitor won't work. Steve is terrified of men. His father apparently used him as a punch-bag growing up and, of course, he was justifiably frightened to death of Rick. He will just about tolerate me interviewing, I think, because he believes I saved his life but he will have to be supported by a woman.'

'What are you suggesting – a social worker? That'll never work, mark my words. Going that route, in all probability we won't be allowed to interview him at all, if he genuinely does have learning difficulties.'

'No,' said Louis. 'I was thinking of a female solicitor. I do know someone who has practised family law for many years. If she would do it, she would be ideal. She lives in St Ives and in fact was the person who discovered the body of the first murder victim, James Allnut.'

'Surely,' said John, 'that's going to introduce a conflict of interest.'

'I don't think so,' said Louis, 'but we can rely on her – if she sees it as a problem, she won't take the case.'

'You're putting a lot of faith in this woman – who is she?' John asked.

'Sir, you must know about the killing in Bristol of Chief Inspector Adam McKenzie?' said Louis.

'Yes, of course I do, a terrible business – a good man, an excellent officer in every way.'

'The lady in question is Merrin McKenzie, his widow. Not only is she a much respected family lawyer, she also has a unique understanding as to how police procedure works. She's ideal.'

'Alright,' said John grumpily, 'but who's going to pay for her services? It's particularly awkward since we don't even know if this man is going to produce anything worthwhile and I'm damn sure he won't be able to afford her, if she's as good as you say.'

'I can't speak for her, obviously, but I think in the circumstances, she will be prepared to offer pro bono –

that is, if she feels she can take the case at all.'

'Well, Adam McKenzie was a remarkable man so let's assume he was married to a remarkable woman. But you only have tomorrow because then it's Christmas, so what's going to happen to Steve Matthews then? You have to charge him with something so he'll still end up in a cell.'

'It depends what he says but I am thinking of charging him with either something very minor, or preferably nothing at all. I am very anxious to keep him out of the cells for the reasons I've explained.'

'And, of course, your Mrs McKenzie will then produce enough evidence to support the fact that he was too frightened to report what was going on at the time, so, ultimately, there will be no case to answer.'

'I hope so,' said Louis.

'Louis, you did a splendid job in tracking down and exposing the drug smuggling, but I was not at all happy with the way you unnecessarily exposed yourself to danger. You should have waited for back-up, but then you know that, don't you?'

'Yes, sir,' said Louis.

'Just don't do it again, for God's sake. You were very lucky this time but if you try this sort of stunt again, the fates may not be with you. Can I remind you that you're not a young man any more – it's time to settle down and behave yourself.'

CHAPTER FORTY-FIVE

Merrin was sitting up in bed with a cup of coffee, ticking off in her mind the things she still needed to do in order to try and make this Christmas special, in its own way. She knew it needed to be low-key and relaxed but at the same time, she wanted it to be perfect. The obstacles for achieving this were considerable – she and Isla were in a new family home without their beloved husband and father for the first time, and poor Maggie was nursing the injuries from a toxic relationship, yet finding it preferable to be with her and Isla than with her own father. William, taking advantage of her preoccupation, had crept up the bed and was now lying beside her. This was a recent phenomena of his, which Merrin knew she should resist but somehow couldn't because it was so comforting. She glanced at her watch; it was nearly seven and she needed to get up for it was changeover day at Rupert's Cottage. 'Please, please let the current incumbents be tidy people,' she murmured to herself. Just then, her phone began ringing. She frowned, wondering who on earth it could be at this hour.

'Mrs McKenzie, it's Louis Peppiatt. I hope I haven't woken you. I do apologise for ringing so early but it is important.'

'No problem, Inspector. I'm already into my first cup of coffee.' She didn't admit she was still in bed, nor how cross she was with him for putting himself into the position of getting stabbed, bringing back the horror of Adam's death.

Louis told Merrin as much as he knew of Steve Matthews's story and how he believed Steve was essentially innocent, but also had a vital role to play in helping the police to reach an understanding of how, where, why and above all, who was responsible for the murders. Louis explained he had managed, at least temporarily, to have rescued Steve from the jaws of Border Force but on this, the day before the Christmas festivities began, it was vital that he was interviewed.

'The thing is, Mrs McKenzie, Steve is frightened of men, and I wondered whether you would represent him. The duty solicitor is male, and to be honest, not especially good. With your background in family law, it seems to me that you are just who Steve needs to help him through the ordeal of being questioned. He's very fragile.'

'So, he's frightened of men but you're going to be the one questioning him? That doesn't sound quite right, Inspector,' said Merrin.

'He believes I saved his life, so I think he trusts me and

I'll have a woman PC sitting in, though not questioning him, of course. Also, I would like his mother to come with him to the station but hopefully not be present in the interview room.'

'And is he right?' Merrin asked.

'About what?' said Louis.

'About you saving his life,' said Merrin.

'It's possible,' said Louis noncommittedly.

'I'm supposed to be doing a changeover for Clara this morning but I think Isla will do it for me, if I ask nicely,' said Merrin. 'So, how and where are we doing this?'

'Just a few things I need to say before you decide,' said Louis. 'I have cleared this with the chief superintendent but when I mentioned that you had found the first body, he did ask if this presented any conflict of interest.'

'That's not an issue. Obviously, finding poor James's body was awful, but he was not a relation, nor a friend and I had never even met him. No conflict there.'

'The other problem is that I'm sure, ultimately, we will get legal aid. However, if for any reason the case collapses, would you be prepared to act for Steve on a pro bono basis just for today?'

'Anything else?' Merrin asked drily.

'We need to conduct the interview in Truro. I would come and fetch you myself but I can't drive at the moment. So, I can organise a police car to pick up you, Steve and Steve's mother at about 10 a.m., if that suits?'

'So, the deal is this – I spend the last day before Christmas in Truro – when I should be spending it with my daughter and her friend – assisting you with the interview of a very vulnerable man, and I'm not going to be paid for it? Have I got that right?'

'Perfectly,' said Louis.

'I think you should organise the pick-up of us all from Steve's home at ten-thirty. If you give me his address, I will go round at about ten so I can spend a little time getting to know him and his mother and hopefully reassure them about what's going to happen. If he's frightened and worried, he'll clam up. We need him as calm and as trusting in us as possible. However, Inspector, I'm not on your side; I'm on Steve's. If you start upsetting him, in any way, or asking questions that I consider to be out of order, you'll certainly know about it.'

And that was the moment when Inspector Peppiatt knew for certain that he couldn't have chosen anyone better than Merrin McKenzie to deal with this vital, yet very sensitive interview.

Merrin showered and, still in her dressing gown, went to wake Isla, which she managed to do without disturbing Maggie.

'What's up, Mum?' Isla whispered, rubbing her eyes as she tiptoed from her bedroom.

Merrin explained the situation in broad outline. 'I was wondering, therefore, if you would be prepared to do the changeover for me at Rupert's Cottage this morning? It's only just round the corner and I'll ask Clara to show you what to do.'

'Inspector P seems to have taken over from Clara in

making unreasonable demands on my mother's time,' grumbled Isla. She watched Merrin as she flew round the kitchen, toast in the toaster, feeding William; her notepad, containing several jottings already, was out on the kitchen table. 'You're enjoying this,' she said shrewdly, 'I told you it was a mistake to give up the law, particularly to replace it with scrubbing other people's loos.'

Merrin stopped and looked at her daughter, sitting at the kitchen table, so pretty and with a look of triumph on her face. 'You're right that I'm excited about this case. I can see there's a situation here that can be resolved and help a number of people. But you're wrong about family law in general – I couldn't bear to go back to all those ghastly parents scrapping over who should have custody of their children, just to score points off one another.' She grinned at Isla. 'You're also right about the loos and the whole cleaning thing, though. I do need to find something to do that I'm actually good at.'

By 9 a.m., Isla had been dispatched to meet Clara at Rupert's Cottage. Clara was absolutely delighted. 'Thank heavens, Pearl. Wonderful to have a cleaner who can actually clean.'

'Both rude and ungrateful,' Merrin retorted, 'but so true.'

By 9.45 a.m., William had been walked and a note, explaining all, left for Maggie when she woke up. Merrin was now dressed in her work suit and crisp white shirt, her briefcase packed and she was ready for action. She had to admit, but only to herself, of course, that she was immensely looking forward to the challenge.

CHAPTER FORTY-SIX

Brenda Matthews opened the door. 'Come in, love,' she said. 'The inspector told us you would be coming and I can't believe you've turned into a lawyer.' Merrin was not quite sure how to respond to this but she needn't have worried, as Brenda continued. 'Little Merrin Tripconey – I remember you and your brother playing in the harbour, on the sand. Lovely kiddies you were, and now look at you – so grown up.'

Merrin smiled warmly at her. This was a good start – his mother remembering her as a child, it had to be reassuring for Steve. 'Well, I should be pretty grown up by now, Mrs Matthews; I'm fifty-four,' she said.

'Never! Well, you certainly don't look it, my maid.'

Brenda led Merrin into the kitchen. As well as being so warm and friendly, Brenda was a pleasure to look at – small and round, with pink cheeks and the bright little eyes of a robin. She seemed also to have a permanent smile on her face. The same could not be said of her son. Poor old Steve looked a fright. He had two black eyes and a hugely swollen nose. He was wearing a shirt and tie, over which he sported an obviously hand-knitted waistcoat in all the colours of the rainbow. Unfortunately, this garment served to emphasise his seriously large stomach. He stood up as Merrin entered the room. 'Hello, Steve. You've been in the wars – I am sorry, poor you.' She extended a hand to shake his but this was clearly difficult for him, so she hastily withdrew it.

'Coffee, my maid, and some cake?' Brenda asked.

'Just coffee, thank you, Mrs Matthews, that would be lovely.'

They settled round the table. 'Steve, I don't want you to be worried about today. I'm here to represent you, to help you in every way I can, and Inspector Peppiatt is a good man, a fair one—'

'He saved my life,' Steve interrupted. 'Rick was going to kill me. He said I was a burden and he was going to kill me, just like Jenny.' He began to cry and his mother offered him a large handkerchief. After a few minutes, during which time Merrin had the good sense to say nothing, Steve rallied. 'Mr Inspector stopped him. He hit Rick with a chair and then Rick was going to kill Mr Inspector as well, but the other policeman hit Rick over the head with a shovel.'

'The inspector told me that he thought you had been very brave, Steve,' said Merrin.

'I know he thought that because he told me,' said Steve proudly, and for the first time, he smiled – the sweet, innocent smile of a young child. And in that moment, Merrin knew exactly why Louis wanted to save him.

Over coffee, they talked about Christmas. Steve was very excited and showed Merrin their tiny sitting room, dominated by a large Christmas tree, underneath which were an impressive number of presents.

'Go upstairs now, Stevie, brush your hair and visit the lavvie. Then it will be time to go to Truro,' said Brenda.

'I'm glad of a few moments on our own,' Merrin said to Brenda. 'Both Inspector Peppiatt and I think it is a really good idea for you to come with Steve to Truro but not for you to sit in on the interview. We think he needs to do that on his own. I do hope you understand.'

'Of course I understand, Merrin – may I call you that? The thing is I talk too much and often answer for Stevie. It goes back to his childhood; he was very slow to talk – not much speech until he was seven and, even now, any difficult questions he takes his time to answer. I've never got out of the habit of speaking for him, I'm afraid. I'll be outside if he gets very upset and needs me.' This was not the answer Merrin was expecting and she was mightily relieved. 'And just one more thing, Merrin dear: Stevie is unable to lie. He can be stubborn and refuse to answer a question, but when he does it will always be the truth – remember, though, it will be the truth as he sees it.'

'Thank you, Brenda, you're being an enormous help,' said Merrin, just as Steve started down the stairs towards them.

* * *

297

Steve enjoyed the journey to Truro and became quite animated. He sat in the front with the police driver, who showed him how the siren worked. However, as they stopped in front of the police building, he became very anxious. 'Are they going to be cross with me?' he asked. 'Will they shout at me?'

'None of those things, I promise,' said Merrin. 'And remember I will be with you all the time to make absolutely sure they are nice to you.'

While mother and son waited, Merrin was shown into Inspector Peppiatt's office, which was very far from palatial, but serviceable. 'Would you like a coffee?' asked Louis.

'No thanks, I am already awash with coffee and I don't think we should leave them too long or Steve is going to get very nervous.'

'I agree,' said Louis. 'How did things go this morning?'

'Good, I think. Brenda Matthews knew me as a child, which helps, though, I must admit, I don't remember her. The important thing is, she completely endorses the need for you to interview Steve without her being present.'

'That's a relief,' said Louis.

'A couple of pointers – we mustn't rush him into answering difficult questions. He may take some time to reply and we need to be patient. Also, Brenda says that he cannot lie. However, we need to be aware that he tells the truth only as he sees it.'

'Very helpful,' said Louis. 'One tip I picked up from Jack Eddy is that we need to avoid using any derogatory terms that might reflect on his learning difficulties. For example, Jack said the word "stupid". It was not aimed at Steve but Steve went mad because he immediately thought Jack was talking about him. In other words, he takes out of context the sort of words that the poor bloke has been called all his life. Anything else?'

Merrin shook her head. She was trying not to notice Louis's sling, nor his obvious pallor and the dark circles under his eyes. 'Oh, just one more thing,' she suddenly remembered. 'Don't attempt to shake his hand – he doesn't appear happy with physical contact.'

Louis stood up with surprising vigour. 'Noted. Come on, then, let's do it,' he said.

CHAPTER FORTY-SEVEN

In all, the interview took a gruelling five hours. Early on, they all realised that food was very important to Steve and also helped to calm him down. So, there were breaks for a pasty, saffron buns, a piece of heavy cake and the contents of a large lunchbox, which Brenda had thoughtfully brought with her.

The tale that unfolded was a sad one. Louis was anxious to get on tape Steve's miserable childhood, believing it would help build a case for recognising his difficulties. Initially, Steve was very resistant to talk about school but Merrin was able to coax him as they had been to the same local school, just over a decade apart. They started to have a laugh about various teachers they'd had in common. Louis let the tape run and, when he judged it to be the right moment, said, 'So how was school, Steve, did you enjoy it?'

It took a long time to extract the information but

it was clear that throughout his school days Steve was bullied unmercifully and given very little support by the teaching staff. He was regularly beaten up in the school playground, often set upon on his way home. He was teased for being 'thick' and fat, and for his rather odd appearance. He was always left out of games, never picked for a team and had no friends. By the time he left school, his reading and writing skills were wholly inadequate and any sort of work with figures completely floored him.

During one of their breaks, Louis said to Merrin, 'I know there is still an awful lot wrong with society, but I do believe in today's schools, Steve would have done better.'

'Maybe,' said Merrin, 'but the trouble is the bullying still exists – it just happens more on social media than in the playground.'

'Academically, though, his difficulties would have been recognised and dealt with better, wouldn't they?'

'I'd like to think so,' said Merrin, with a sad smile.

They then heard a little about Steve's father. How Steve and his mother used to hide when they heard him come back from the pub. Steve was clearly more concerned with the beatings his father gave his mother than the ones he received himself.

'I'm no psychiatrist,' said Louis, during the second break, 'but it seems as if Steve felt it was perfectly acceptable for his father to beat him up – I assume that was because he had no sense of self worth. While he loved his mother and was desperate to protect her, he also thought he deserved the beatings he received because he was so hopeless.'

'Desperately sad, but probably true,' agreed Merrin.

What followed was the happy period in Steve's life. On leaving school, he picked up a number of part-time jobs in garages, both in and around St Ives and Hayle. He loved cars and working with them, and, after a while, took his driving test and passed first time. As the years went by, he managed from his wages to buy first a little car and then the van he still owned. His mum was apparently very proud of this and loved being driven around by him.

'Why did you decide to buy a van, Steve?' Louis asked.

'I started moving things for people,' he said.

'Like what?'

'People moving house, sometimes the garages wanted me to pick up spare parts. Also, I would take things to the dump that people didn't want no more. It was hard work, doing it as well as the garages, but I liked it.'

He had met Rick in a pub one night. Steve struggled with time but it seemed to be about eighteen months ago. Steve was obviously impressed that Rick had bought him a pint. They had got talking and Steve had explained what he did. After a few drinks, Rick offered him a driving job. At first Steve had declined the offer but Rick had promised him double the money he was currently earning and so Steve had said he would ask his mum.

During another break, Merrin asked Brenda whether

she had been in favour of Steve working for Rick. 'At first, yes,' said Brenda. 'I hadn't met the man but the fact he was offering Stevie so much money seemed a good idea. We've always struggled with money.' She hesitated. 'Quite soon I regretted it, though. Stevie went back to how he used to be at school – miserable, not very talkative, depressed I suppose.'

When the interview reconvened, Steve agreed that he had not been happy working for Rick almost from the beginning. Once, after just a few weeks, he had suggested to Rick that he should go back to working at the garages and Rick had responded by hitting him. Clearly Rick saw that physical violence worked well when it came to controlling Steve, for from then on, the beatings continued.

'So what were you delivering for Rick?' Louis asked.

'Compost,' said Steve, and then looked uncomfortable. 'I thought that was what we were selling, just compost, for a long time.'

'And when did that change, Steve? When did you think it might not be compost?' said Louis.

'Last summer, I think, it was a hot day. I loaded the van and I broke one of the bags. I was tired and I threw it in the back of the van too hard.'

'And what was in the bag?' Louis asked.

'White powder in bricks, except one of the bricks had broken too. Rick was very angry, more angry than ever. He hit me and hit me and called me names. He made me take everything out of the van and after I had cleared up the powder, I had to hose the inside of the van. It took a long time.'

'Did you ask Rick about the white powder? Think carefully, Steve, this is really important,' Louis said gently.

'I didn't ask him but he told me. He said it was special feed to put on plants and crops to make them grow quickly, which is why it was called compost.'

'This is another very important question, so please think about it, don't rush to answer if you don't feel like it. Did you believe Rick when he told you what the white powder was for?'

There was a very long pause during which both Louis and Merrin waited in suspense. 'I wasn't sure,' said Steve at last. 'The deliveries I make are in towns – like Exeter, Plymouth and Oxford, and once I went with Rick to London to make a delivery. There aren't any farms or gardens in those places, not many, I don't think. In Oxford, I deliver to an old lady who doesn't have any sort of garden. I deliver into her bedroom.'

Louis and Merrin did not dare look at one another – Roberta, of course. 'And so when did you know for certain that the white powder wasn't for growing plants?' Louis asked. This time, he and Merrin were definitely holding their breath.

'My friend, Jenny, told me,' Steve said, and promptly burst into tears.

They had yet another break. While Brenda dried her son's tears and offered him some more food from the lunchbox, Louis and Merrin took the opportunity to slip into his office for a few minutes.

'It gives me considerable pleasure in this otherwise very sad story,' said Merrin, 'to learn that Rick had underestimated Steve. I'm really proud of my client for working out that the customers were not obvious candidates for bulk plant food. Go, Steve!'

Louis smiled. 'I agree, but now we come to the tricky bit. How much does he know about the murders, and do you realise it has taken us three hours to get to this point? I'm worried he'll become too tired to continue.'

'Remember, he has the advantage of Brenda's tender loving care and endless nourishment. I think he will probably last longer than us. I will stop the interview, though, if I think it's too much for him.'

'I expect nothing less,' said Louis.

CHAPTER FORTY-EIGHT

Although Louis was concerned about keeping the interview in chronological order – which he believed was probably best for Steve – he also felt it made sense to talk some more about Jenny first, to see how she fitted into the whole picture.

'Jenny was very kind to me,' said Steve simply. 'She was Rick's girlfriend but sometimes he hit her, just like he hit me – and he shouted at her, which wasn't fair because she was nice.' Steve looked close to tears again.

'Did Jenny also work for Rick?' Louis asked.

'Yes,' said Steve.

'What did she do?'

'Sometimes she made deliveries for Rick, like me, and he bought her the camper van. Mostly, she packed the white powder into small bags.'

'Did she do that at Towednack Hall, in the stables?' Louis asked.

'Yes, she was very quick at it. I tried to do it once to help her but I was too clumsy.'

'When did Jenny tell you what the white powder really was?' Louis asked.

'The day she died. She told me it was a drug, called cocaine, and that what we were doing was bad. She said that we had to get away from Rick, that she was going to run away in her camper van but she was worried about me and Mum. I said we had nowhere to go because we didn't have a camper van, and then she started to cry.'

'Just give Steve a moment please, Inspector,' said Merrin.

No one spoke in the room for some minutes. Then, Steve suddenly sat up straight and looked Louis in the eye. 'Jenny told me Rick had killed that boy and she was worried he might kill her and me as well. And she was right, wasn't she, Mr Inspector? Rick did kill her and he nearly killed me but you saved me. Thank you very much.'

Gradually, painstakingly, the whole story emerged. Knowing some background about Roberta and James helped to unravel the sequence of events. It seemed – and this was partially guesswork on Louis's part – that a particularly large consignment of cocaine had been landed by Rick, brought in directly by trawler, which, according to Steve was landed at Dynamite Quay in Hayle. This was possibly why Jenny had handed in her notice to Clara, because there was so much bagging up to do.

Roberta wanted a supply of cocaine for her customers

during Christmas and New Year. For some reason – maybe everyone was too busy to deliver to her, or perhaps she had offered to have it collected as her nephew was in St Ives – James called at the Hall stables to collect what it appeared he thought was a sack of compost; that was certainly what he asked for. Steve was there and had been told not to let James into the stables, which he didn't. Steve put the sack in the boot of James's car and James left immediately.

What happened next was uncertain. Maybe James was curious or maybe, once again, Steve had been rough with the bag and it had burst open when he put it in James's car. Either way, James discovered what was in the bag and recognised it as cocaine. Why he didn't go straight to the police is unclear, except, perhaps, he had only been in the country for a few months and didn't want any trouble – or maybe he was afraid of the incident being reported to his university, where, according to his friend Larry, he had been so happy. So he returned to Towednack Hall, went into the stables and saw exactly what was going on there. Jenny had joined Steve by this time and she was busy filling bags of cocaine. James told them he didn't want any trouble but he wasn't prepared to carry drugs up to Oxford. He handed the sack back to them.

Jenny became very worried at this point, concerned that as James now knew all about the operation – and clearly did not approve – he was in danger if Rick found out about him. She told James this and he said he couldn't leave St Ives as he had run out of money and was waiting for his parents to transfer some funds to his bank, which had not yet arrived. James also had to collect his clothes from the B&B in St Ives where he had been staying.

Jenny hatched a plan, which unfortunately she explained to James in front of Steve. She and James would both drive in their respective vehicles into St Ives and park at Barnoon car park. She would go to a cashpoint, draw out enough money for James's petrol while he collected his things, and they would then go to Wetherspoons and buy James a burger to keep him going on the journey.

Rick arrived at Towednack Hall shortly after Jenny and James had left. He asked Steve where Jenny had gone. Steve tried not to tell him but Rick started slapping him about and threatening to kill both Steve and his mother. Bearing in mind that Steve could not lie, once he was forced to tell Rick what had happened, the whole story came out.

From what Jenny told Steve later, it seemed that when they arrived at Wetherspoons, James said he was anxious to get going on his journey to Oxford, so he took his burger with him. He said goodbye, thanked Jenny for her help and promised to refund the money he had borrowed. He then returned to his car. Jenny stayed behind and had something to eat and drink.

Steve, of course, loved cars and was able to tell Rick exactly what car James was driving. Therefore Rick had no problem in finding James eating his burger in his car at Barnoon car park. He hit him over the head in his car, where traces of his blood were later found, and then transferred him to the camper van. Now unconscious, James was killed by Rick with two lethal doses of insulin, which Jenny kept in her van, because she was a diabetic. Jenny returned to her camper van, to find James dead in her bed with a note from Rick saying she was to dispose of the body, as he was going back to sea again that night.

Jenny and Steve met at the Sloop the following evening. Jenny told Steve about James being killed and how she had put the body in Elsie's Cottage – but not why. Her reason for doing so, therefore, died with her, but Merrin's theory that James had been about the same age as her lost son was a plausible one.

Assumptions also had to be made as to why Jenny had asked Clara Tregonning for her old job back. Presumably, Louis surmised, it was because, having disposed of James's body, she believed she would be in Rick's good books and therefore felt safe. On his return from the sea, clearly Rick was angry with her, possibly about where she had chosen to leave James's body, and maybe during the ensuing row Jenny had threatened to expose James's murder and the drug smuggling. Whatever the cause, the result was that Jenny feared for her life. As well as telling Merrin she was essentially running away from St Ives, she also told Steve. Clearly, she was worried about him and his mum which was why she told him the true nature of the white powder, anxious to try and impress upon the poor bewildered man the danger he was in.

There was now plenty of forensic evidence to back up Steve's story, which he told holding tightly to Merrin's hand throughout. He didn't cry at all and it seemed as if telling the story was something of a relief – for he had not even told his mother everything, never mind anyone else. Heartbreakingly, though, at the end he broke down completely and said it was all his fault that James and Jenny had died. He had told Rick where to find James and he had suggested to Jenny that she park her camper van outside his house.

Louis and Merrin did their best to explain that Rick was a monster who would have found them and killed them both anyway, with or without Steve's so-called help, but he was immovable in his sense of guilt and grief.

The interview finished and while, once again, Brenda did her best to comfort her son, Louis called for a car to take them back to St Ives and he and Merrin went once more into his office.

'Are you going to charge him with anything?' asked Merrin, believing she already knew the answer.

'No,' said Louis. 'In my view he has committed no crime. Alright, he could have told us before today what was going on, but there was very little time for him to do so – only a couple of days. He was terrified, frightened for himself but mostly for his mother, confused and, in my view, incapable of processing what he should be doing. I'm not sure I'm going to be universally popular but, in this instance, I don't really care. I'm confident it is the right decision. I just hope I can persuade the powers that be – after all, Steve's help and co-operation has been total.'

'And I'm sure you're not entirely surprised that I wholeheartedly agree with that decision,' said Merrin. 'You know, while listening to Steve, I've been thinking about poor Jenny. She was a bit like Nancy in *Oliver Twist*.'

'Remind me,' said Louis.

'Nancy was in love with Bill Sikes, the villain of the story – i.e. Rick. Nancy is killed by Bill, when she defies him, in her efforts to save Oliver. The difference is, of course, Nancy did save Oliver, but poor Jenny failed to save James.'

'But, in a way, she did save Steve, and it's our job to make sure she didn't die in vain,' said Louis.

CHAPTER FORTY-NINE

Once again, Merrin was snuggled up in bed with a coffee and a very happy William lying beside her, when her phone rang.

'Mrs McKenzie, I am really sorry to do this to you again,' said a familiar voice.

'Inspector, you've done much better than yesterday – it's eight o'clock, rather than seven – almost civilised,' said Merrin.

'The reason for calling so early is that the station's fairly empty as we are on emergency cover only for Christmas. However, I do have the chance of a lift over to St Ives in about fifteen minutes. I have a lot to tell you and I would like to see the girls. How inconvenient would it be if I turned up on your doorstep at about nine?'

'Not inconvenient at all, Inspector, though I may have to ask you to accompany me on a quick walk on the beach with William.'

'No problem, I would like that. I do have one piece of good news I simply cannot keep to myself until I see you. Sir Clive Stebbings has admitted he knew about the murders. That means—' Louis began.

'That means,' Merrin interrupted, 'that the court will be far more interested in hearing evidence from Sir Clive than a poor chap with learning difficulties – and so, of course, will the press. It may well be that Steve will only be required to provide a written statement to go in the prosecution bundle.'

'My thoughts exactly. See you in about an hour.'

Louis put down the phone and began struggling into his clothes. He'd managed a shower, but putting on socks and doing up buttons one-handed was a slow business. He was just about ready when his phone rang. It was Stephanie, his ex-wife.

'Are you alright, Louis? Your escapades were on *Spotlight* last night but today they've made the national news.'

'I'm fine, thank you. A bit weary and sore but definitely on the mend. Thanks for telling me; I'll be careful not to watch the news, then. How are you and the children?'

'We're good. Listen, would you come for Christmas lunch with us tomorrow? We'd all like it and it would mean a lot to the children.'

'I'm not sure,' Louis began.

'Edward told us what you said to him when you came over the other week,' said Stephanie earnestly.

'Most of it involved baas, as I recall.'

'Stop it, Louis. You know perfectly well what I mean. You told him that you now feel on the outside of the family, as if you shouldn't intrude. It really upset him and it's upset us all, including Andrew. We both made mistakes so far as our marriage was concerned, but, between us, we created these wonderful children who we both love and who love us. Of course you're a part of us all. Please say you'll come.'

'I can't drive,' said Louis lamely.

'That's no problem. Andrew will pick you up and I'll book a taxi to take you back home – early evening, would that suit? I imagine you're very tired.'

There was a pause. 'Actually, Steph, I can think of nothing I would like more. Thank you so much.'

'Excellent,' said Stephanie. 'Obviously, we're only inviting you because of your celebrity status!'

'Naturally,' said Louis. 'I suppose fame is something I'll just have to learn to live with. Maybe you would like to print off a few photographs for me to sign.'

Merrin was all ready to go when Louis arrived at Miranda's Cottage. 'Do you mind if we go straight out?' Merrin asked. 'Only this is later than William normally has his walk and his ability to nag is shocking. It really is easier to do as he says.'

Louis held open the front door. 'Has it occurred to you that, not very subtly, William is taking over control of your household?'

'I do have to agree, regrettably. I now recognise

that my life is largely run by Horatio and William. I'm outnumbered and the sulking that goes on if I don't obey orders is horrendous.' They walked down towards the Harbour Beach. 'Actually, on the subject of horrendous, yesterday was neither the time nor the place, but I am extremely cross with you for getting stabbed.'

'Most people are being very kind, asking after my health and checking that I'm feeling OK and in not too much pain. Apart from some modest criticism levelled at me by the chief super, I think you're the only person to be actually angry with me – what have I done to deserve that?'

'Putting yourself in a position where you got stabbed in the first place, of course. I saw Jack in the pub last night and he filled me in on the full details of what happened. You insisted on going in alone to confront Rick, who had already been identified as the killer of two people. What an idiotic thing to do! To deal with someone like that, you needed full back-up, body armour, armed response officers – literally, all the boys in the band. Can I just remind you again – he was a violent murderer, which you knew, and yet, what did you do? You wandered in there alone and nearly got yourself killed!'

'I'm sorry if I upset you,' said Louis, still slightly confused.

'Of course you upset me. My husband, Adam, is supposed to be your hero. So what do you do? Slavishly follow in his footsteps, even to the point of nearly getting yourself killed? It beggars belief.'

'I couldn't let my officers burst in for fear Rick had a gun, in which case, as we were unarmed, he could have killed several of us. I needed to stall for time, for two reasons. Firstly, I was worried he was going to hurt or even kill Steve, and I was right in that. Secondly, I thought by keeping Rick talking, it would delay his chance to escape. I was worried he would do a repeat performance – get away on that boat of his and probably set up again in a new place and under a new name. He's very slippery.'

'And very dangerous. Anyway, let's not spoil our walk. I just wanted you to know that it upset me very much to think you might have ended up as Adam did.'

Louis smiled at her. 'I will try and be more sensible.'

'Fat chance,' said Merrin sagely. 'I know your type.'

'Let me update you. Clive Stebbings is telling us everything we need to know – how the cocaine has been arriving in Cornwall, and how and when the murders occurred, which completely ties in with everything Steve told us. Clive is desperate not to be associated with the murders and everyone believes he wasn't directly involved. He appears to be prepared to co-operate in any way to help save his skin, though, of course, he'll go to prison. However, as you said earlier, this may well enable us to keep Steve out of court. Strangely, John Dent, the chief super, listened to the tape of the interview with Steve yesterday evening and agrees that he should not be charged with anything, unless any new evidence emerges. He may decide to clear it with the DPP but he is much respected; I don't imagine he will have any problem having his decision endorsed.'

'That's marvellous,' said Merrin, 'well done.'

'I'm not at all sure that it's anything to do with me – you're the one in the spotlight. The chief super was always greatly impressed with Adam and now he's mightily impressed with you. So, Steve may have got lucky through reflected glory, thanks to you and your husband.'

'Who cares, so long as it worked,' said Merrin.

'The other problem that I believe has resolved itself is that I've been worried about Steve's safety.'

'Me too,' said Merrin. 'I was going to ask whether you thought he and Brenda should be put in a safe house until after the trial, though I can't see them ever being prepared to leave their home.'

'No need, I don't think. Originally, I was told Rick was part of a drugs gang on Tyneside but it turns out it was just him and his younger brother. His brother got caught and is in prison. John Lumley, as we know, was thought to have drowned at sea and was reborn as Rick Bolam in Cornwall. I gather the little brother wasn't too bright and the Northumbria Police reckon that the villains of Tyneside don't rate John – they see him as a vicious sod who shopped his own brother. It's interesting: down here, he rather repeated the patten by gathering around him vulnerable people – obviously Steve and Jenny but also Stebbings, in a way, with his addiction problems. I imagine when James, inadvertently, set the ball rolling by discovering the operation at Towednack Hall, Rick panicked and thought he could trust no one and so started killing, aware that his past might catch up with him. He has quite a number of convictions to face up north as well as in Cornwall. His really will be a life sentence.'

'So, what you're saying is that there is no one likely to try and nobble the witnesses before the case comes to trial?' said Merrin.

'Exactly, there doesn't seem to be anyone who has any respect or sense of loyalty towards Rick, certainly not enough to do any dirty deeds for him. Look, if I've got any of this wrong, can I ask if you would be prepared to act for Steve if he needs a solicitor in the future? Certainly, I would be grateful if you would help him with his statement, if you're happy to do so.'

'Do you really need to ask? Of course I will,' said Merrin.

They turned for home. They had walked the length of Porthmeor Beach. The tide was very low and William, clearly bored with their incessant talking about something other than him, had taken himself off to play with a cocker spaniel on the edge of the sea. Louis nodded in William's direction. 'He seems to get on very well with other dogs,' he said.

'Yes, he does,' Merrin agreed. 'It's people he growls at, dogs he rates.'

'Sensible chap. Tell me, as a returning resident of St Ives, what do you think of that?' He pointed up towards the Tate Gallery.

'I love it,' said Merrin. 'When the plans were first on display, I wasn't sure, but somehow it works. I genuinely think the building itself is marvellous, it seems to reflect its surroundings perfectly. And, of course, the Tate brings money and prestige into the town, which we really need.'

'Funny, I don't know why, I thought you would be a traditionalist, preferring the old architecture of St Ives, like your own cottage. Tell me to mind my own business, are you happy to be back in your childhood home?'

'It's a bit early to say,' Merrin admitted. She spun round, arms outstretched. It was a cloudy day but for a single shaft of sunlight hitting the crest of the incoming waves. 'And yet, when you look at all this, what could be better?'

Merrin whistled for William and the three of them clambered up the steps from the beach.

'There is one thing that still upsets me about this case,' Louis said.

'Go on,' said Merrin encouragingly.

'Three years ago, a fisherman named George Jenkin allegedly drowned in Mullion Cove. Dr Bennett did the autopsy and the man died because he received a blow to the head followed by a lethal injection of insulin. Sounds familiar?'

'Heavens, yes. What happened?' Merrin asked.

'Nothing – the police investigation was a botched job. The judge returned an open verdict but said in his opinion it was suicide. The man had hardly any family and few friends so no one made a fuss. The thing is, Jack found out from an old fisherman in Porthleven that a man named Rick, with a ragged earlobe fished in the area at the time – I say fished; no one ever saw him with a catch. The locals believed he could have been involved in smuggling so it looks like George Jenkin may have been as well and was killed by Rick, who saw him as a threat. Presumably, Rick already knew Jenny at that time and used her insulin to kill him. No one would have been any the wiser but Dr Bennett tested George for insulin because he was demonstrating to a group of students. I suppose what concerns me most is that George could have been another innocent victim, like James. Maybe he just saw Rick unloading drugs in one of those coves between Gunwalloe and Mullion, for example.'

'Is there any way of reopening the case?' Merrin asked.

'Absolutely not; there is just no concrete evidence available to charge Rick.'

'It sounds as if you weren't involved in the case,' said Merrin.

Louis stopped walking and gazed out to sea. 'No, I was in charge of a missing little girl in Penzance, so I had my hands full.'

'Did you find her?' Merrin asked, suddenly realising, too late, from the expression on Louis's face, that she was treading on very sensitive ground.

'Yes and no,' said Louis. 'I found her but she was dead.'

Merrin put a hand on his arm. 'That must have been awful; I am so sorry. I realised as I was asking the question it was a very painful subject for you. Me and my big mouth.'

Louis turned and smiled at her. 'It's alright. I admit it is a case that haunts me still. The stepfather murdered her. He'll be in prison until he's an old man, if he lives that long. The mother, of course, will never get over it – a terrible business.' He began walking again. 'Come on,' he said, 'enough doom and gloom, let's go and see if those girls are awake yet.'

CHAPTER FIFTY

The girls were sitting at the kitchen table, drinking coffee, when Merrin, Louis and William returned from their walk. Merrin made the introductions but so far as Louis was concerned, they were unnecessary – Isla was so obviously her father's daughter. A delicious aroma of bacon filled the cottage. 'I made an executive decision,' said Isla, 'that as for two of you a knife and fork are out of the question, bacon sandwiches were the way to go for breakfast.'

Louis and Maggie smiled at one another, both sporting an arm in a sling.

'An excellent plan, thank you,' said Louis.

They gathered round the table and made short work of demolishing several rounds of bacon sandwiches and two pots of coffee. 'Now,' said Isla, 'Mum and I have to start preparing vegetables for tomorrow. So, the wounded soldiers amongst us need to go and sit by the fire with William so that they're not in the way.'

'She's quite bossy, your daughter,' Louis said to Merrin.

'I'm sure, Inspector P, you don't have to look too far to recognise where I get that from,' said Isla.

'I think the only safe response to that is no comment,' said Louis sensibly.

While mother and daughter squabbled in a friendly way over the vegetables, Louis and Maggie did as they were told and settled down by the fire. 'I'm sorry you've had such a rough time of it, Maggie,' Louis said. 'Have you made your statement to the police concerning Christopher Barlow's use of cocaine?'

'Yes, all done,' said Maggie, a little defensively.

'The case against Roberta is out of my hands, Thames Valley will handle it, but I just wanted to say that if you are worried about anything or need any help, please don't hesitate to call me. I don't have any cards with me but Mrs McKenzie will give you my direct number.'

'Thank you, Inspector, but I really don't need anyone else telling me I ought to be reporting Christopher for beating me up,' said Maggie. 'I know all the arguments, like it's my civil duty to make sure he doesn't abuse anyone else, but I just can't face it.'

'I absolutely agree with you,' said Louis.

'What?' said Maggie. 'You think it's right that I shouldn't report him?'

'I didn't say that; I think he should be punished for what he did to you. What I am saying, though, is that I believe I understand why you don't want to report him.

He's a well-known figure in Oxford, as I understand it. The press and the fuss surrounding the discovery that not only has he been unfaithful to his wife, but he has been having an affair with one of his students, abusing her and taking illegal drugs on university premises – it's going to be huge. There would be all the build-up to the case, the statements, the meetings with your legal team. Then, you will have to give evidence in court, in front of him, followed by the fallout. Whatever the outcome of his trial, the case would be notorious and you would never be free of it – or him. So, I agree you shouldn't report him – not because you probably still love him, certainly not because he deserves to get off, but because moving forward without a case hanging over you is the best thing for you. And you are the only person who matters in all of this.'

Louis was suddenly aware of silence in the room. Mother and daughter by the sink had stopped their vegetable preparation and were staring at him. 'Blimey, Inspector P,' said Isla, at last, 'you don't pull any punches, do you? Of course you're right, absolutely right. I'm so sorry, Mags. I've been nagging and nagging you to get the bastard banged up without thinking about what's best for you. What an idiot I am.'

Louis looked up at Merrin. 'I don't seem to be behaving as a very proactive policeman at the moment, what with trying to keep Steve out of prison and advising Maggie not to press charges. I must be losing my touch.'

'Maybe not a very proactive policeman but a very

nice man,' said Merrin firmly.

Louis smiled at her. 'You're probably wrong but it's very kind of you to say so. If there is any truth in it, then I don't have to remind you, I learnt from a master.'

'Who was that?' Isla asked.

'Your dad,' said Louis.

'Really?' said Isla. 'You knew him? You knew my dad?'

'I met him, just once, but he made a huge impression on me. Your mum can tell you about it when I'm not here. I'm a bit embarrassed, Isla, to be honest. I'm supposed to be a grown-up man in his mid-fifties – far too old for hero-worship!'

'Well, I'm slightly confused by all of this,' said Maggie, 'but I would like to say a big thank you to Inspector Peppiatt for making me feel massively better about the whole Creepy Chris thing.'

'You called him Creepy Chris! Amazing, magic, what a result!' said Isla.

'Oh, shut up and just get on with your vegetables – and stop eavesdropping,' said Maggie, smiling.

Louis put another log on the fire and settled back in the Windsor chair. As soon as he had he done so, William leapt up on his lap, sealing in Merrin's mind the proof, if proof were needed, that Louis had said the right thing, as far as Maggie was concerned.

'I think I'm going to find it difficult to think of the professor in any other way except Creepy Chris,' said Louis.

'Creepy Chris is what all the students call him,

except me, of course,' said Maggie, suddenly sad again.

'Putting aside every other consideration, I suppose it is going to take you quite a time to get over him. You won't go back to him, though, will you, Maggie?'

'No, he won't be teaching us next term so that will make it easier. He's a lot older than me; I guess it was some sort of father fixation, though I've never been attracted to an older man before. Mind you, I'm only nineteen so I haven't had much chance, particularly having been holed up in an all-girls' boarding school before I came up to Oxford. Being with him was, you know, my first proper relationship.'

Louis had to fight back the desire to tell Maggie exactly what he thought of her first love – a man in authority, old enough to be her father, taking advantage of an obviously innocent young girl, who was also his student. Not normally a violent man, at that moment, Louis would have welcomed the opportunity to knock Creepy Chris's teeth down his throat.

'What about your father? Do you see him often?' Louis asked.

'I could do, I suppose,' said Maggie. 'The thing is, he really doesn't care about me. My mother died when I was young and my father remarried. He is very focused on his second wife, who is nice enough, but they don't need me in their life. And if you say "I'm sure that's not true", which is what most people say when I tell them that, I might start to scream.'

'I certainly shan't do that, Maggie. Of course it's true, if that is what you think. My mother died when

I was young, as well. Mothers are people who protect you from the world, who would step into the cannon's mouth for you. When they're no longer there, you feel sort of exposed, all at sea, and you are still so very young. You could look on this relationship with Christopher not as a catastrophe but as a lesson in life. You know the old saying: what doesn't kill you makes you stronger. We only really learn about love from experience. This experience could set you up for life, even make you wiser beyond your years.'

'You're right, of course,' said Maggie, 'but another old saying is: easier said than done.'

'Of course it is going to take courage, but I reckon you can get through this with flying colours.'

'When you two one-armed bandits have stopped muttering to one another, I think it's drinks time as it's Christmas Eve,' said Isla. 'Come on, Mags, let's go to the Sloop.'

'I can't, my face, I look like Frankenstein's monster,' said Maggie.

'Have you looked in the mirror this morning?' said Merrin. 'The swelling has all gone; you look absolutely fine. Be off with you and then the inspector and I can have a nice glass of wine in peace and quiet.'

There was a lot of thundering up and down the stairs and eventually the girls were ready. 'Will you still be here when we get back, Inspector P?' asked Isla.

'My car's picking me up at twelve thirty,' said Louis.

'Not a chance, then,' said Isla. 'Happy Christmas, Inspector P, nice to meet you.'

'Happy Christmas from me too,' said Maggie, 'and thank you.'

'One thing I forgot to mention,' said Louis. 'I think Roberta will definitely go to prison but she is currently out on bail. I imagine you and your respective parents would not be too happy about you two living with a drug dealer, nor in fact having anything more to do with Roberta. A couple of ideas – firstly, why not get hold of the university and tell them what has happened and ask them if they can provide you with emergency accommodation for the rest of the academic year? That will give you time to make plans for your final year's accommodation. Jessie Andrews' boss, Sergeant David Brownley, will be back on duty immediately after Christmas and I am sure he will be happy to speak to the university if they require confirmation concerning Roberta's status. Also, Jessie has asked me to tell you that she is not happy for you to go back to Jericho on your own to collect your things. So when you decide to leave St Ives, call her and she will meet you and chaperone you through the process of extracting yourselves from the clutches of Roberta. I think it would be sensible to take her up on that offer.'

'I agree, wholeheartedly,' said Merrin.

'OK, we'll do as you say and contacting the university is a great idea, now we know Roberta is a baddy. Thanks for the heads-up, Inspector P,' said Isla as they charged out of the cottage.

'Youth!' said Louis. 'But one can't help but be a little envious of all that energy. That girl of yours is a live wire. Heaven knows what she will be, but she is going to be something very definite!'

Merrin laughed. 'She is a lot more upbeat than when I saw her last. I don't imagine tomorrow will be easy for either of us but I think she's getting there, so far as her dad is concerned.'

They sat round the fire with a bottle of wine between them. Now Merrin was there, William swiftly transferred himself from Louis's lap to hers.

'Traitor,' said Louis fondly.

'Do you have a dog?' Merrin asked.

'I used to, well I still do, sort of. The family dog is a much-loved, overweight, now extremely elderly chocolate labrador, named Susie. She stayed with my wife and the children when we broke up. It was the right decision for Susie – I couldn't have looked after her properly. She would have been lonely; she is such a family dog. Actually, I'll see her tomorrow. I've been invited over for Christmas lunch.'

'That's great,' said Merrin, 'I'm so pleased for you and I bet the children will be delighted. I was lucky enough not to have experienced divorce personally but heaven knows I have been involved in more divorce cases than I can possibly count. What always upsets me is how often it is the children who suffer most and how they hate their parents fighting. The fact that you and your ex-wife are happy to sit down for Christmas lunch together is marvellous.'

'Thank you. I didn't think it was anything I would feel comfortable doing. We've celebrated Christmas apart ever since the marriage broke up, but having been asked, I am really happy about it. Now, back to work, briefly. You kindly said you're happy to help Steve put together his statement. Obviously, you don't need too much detail as we have the tape but you need him to confirm as much detail as possible surrounding the murders. When it's done, perhaps send it to me as a draft, and then Steve can sign it with Jack Eddy. There's absolutely no rush, though; after New Year will do.'

'OK,' said Merrin. 'I'll take my laptop over to his house and try to type up exactly what he says, which won't be terribly easy, but I'll do my best. When we're done, I'll read it to him and Brenda several times to make sure they're happy with it and then, as you say, I will email it over to you.'

Louis glanced at his watch and stood up. 'Perfect, that would be great. I'd better go; the car will be waiting for me by the slipway. I can't thank you enough for all your help, Mrs McKenzie, I'm truly grateful. I suppose, if we are successful in keeping Steve out of court, I won't be seeing you again. I'm very rarely needed in St Ives.'

'Well, if you find yourself in town, do pop in for a coffee. I would very much like to know the outcome of the trial, though I appreciate it will be a long way off.'

'Of course, I'll keep you informed of developments. It's been a great pleasure and privilege to have met you. Goodbye and happy Christmas, Mrs McKenzie.'

They shook hands. 'Happy Christmas, Inspector,' said Merrin.

Louis reached the front door and turned back. 'If we

do ever meet again, Mrs McKenzie, do you think we might dispense with formalities and go for Merrin and Louis?'

'I will give it some serious thought, Inspector,' said Merring smiling.

CHAPTER FIFTY-ONE

At six o'clock on Christmas morning, Merrin was woken by a phone call. For a moment, her heart sank, thinking it might be Inspector Peppiatt again, which could only be bad news to disturb Christmas Day. In fact, it was her brother, Jago, calling from Australia.

'Hi, sis, how are you? A difficult day for you, my love. Is Isla with you?'

'Oh, bless you for ringing, Jago. I'm fine and yes, Isla is here but fast asleep.'

'Sorry,' said Jago, 'I know it's early. We're spending Christmas Day on the beach and I've just popped back to the house for some more booze, so I thought it was a good idea to call you in a place where there's a bit of peace and quiet.'

They exchanged news and talked for a while, then Merrin reminded Jago of the cost of the call. 'You're right, sis, I'd better go. I wish I could have been with you for Christmas but we just couldn't afford to come to the UK twice in a year, having come back for poor old Adam's funeral. I glad you're back home in St Ives. It's great, we'll come and see you there next year, which will be very special – us together again in St Ives – when did that last happen?'

Merrin felt very bleak, having ended the call. It would have been lovely to have Jago here to help her and Isla through the day. She was also very tired. They had been to midnight Mass and on their return, while the girls went straight to bed, she had stuffed the turkey and then slept badly, tossing and turning for most of the night, or at least, that's how it felt.

After showering and dressing as quietly as she could, Merrin put the turkey in the oven and suggested to a sleepy William that a quick walk would be beneficial for them both. It was still dark outside and Merrin sat on the harbour wall while William snuffled about on the sand below. Already, it felt very different from all the Christmases they had spent in Bristol. Here she was sitting in the dark, watching the tide creeping in, a dog at her feet. Later, Max, Tristan and Clara would be coming over. Entertaining in Bristol had always been a rather formal affair – by comparison, it was so relaxed in Cornwall and, of course, a throwback to her childhood. Was the contrast a good thing or not? She had no idea.

When she and William arrived home, Merrin was about to light the fire when she looked across the room at Horatio and made a decision. It was the perfect moment to let him out of his cage, with no one else around. She told William to sit in his basket and then opened the door to Horatio's cage. He was obviously tired of being shut up as he immediately came to the door and flew straight across the room to the wine rack. William did not move but thumped his crazy tail with apparent enthusiasm. Smiling with relief, Merrin went over to Horatio. 'Toast?' she enquired.

Minutes later, with Horatio and William each in possession of a piece of toast, Merrin, with a coffee in hand, sat down at the kitchen table. Watching Horatio eating his toast from his favourite perch, memories of the morning Adam died flooded her mind. How a life can change in seconds – that awful day, she'd put the toast in the toaster for Horatio, a happily married woman, confident and secure. By the time the toast was ready, she knew herself to be a widow. For the first time in several months, she began to cry, which was how Isla found her moments later.

'Oh, Mum,' said Isla, putting her arms round her mother and then sitting down beside her, holding her hand. 'Christmas without Dad is absolute shit, isn't it?'

'It's not really about Christmas, it's about Horatio eating his breakfast toast on top of the wine rack,' said Merrin, reaching across the table for a piece of kitchen roll.

'Horatio, you're out!' said Isla, then she glanced across at William, who seemed very relaxed in his basket. 'That's brilliant, Mum, it doesn't look as if William is too bothered.'

'I'll have to put Horatio back soon because we need

to light the fire, but at least I now know they appear to be OK together.'

'I don't understand; why did Horatio eating toast make you so sad? It sounds slightly odd, to put it mildly.'

So, for the first time, Merrin told her daughter the details of the moments leading up to knowing that Adam was dead. 'Everything was so normal and then suddenly, it was never going to be normal again,' she said.

'We'll get through it, Mum. Dad would be livid with us if he knew we spoilt a single day of our lives by moping. You know that's true.'

Mother and daughter held tight to one another for a moment or two and then Merrin suddenly sat up straight, wiped her eyes and said, 'You're absolutely right, darling. He loved Christmas and he would be absolutely furious with us if he thought we weren't having a good time. I'll get you a coffee.'

'What time are we expecting Max and the Tregonnings?' Isla asked.

'I said for them to come at about five. Tristan is bringing lots of leftovers from the restaurant so we don't have to prepare anything, and Max says he's bringing – to quote – obscene quantities of wine. It's going to be fun, darling, and we must make sure Maggie has a good time.'

'Yes, we have to make it a lovely day for Maggie,' Isla agreed.

'And we must also ensure that Max doesn't make a play for her; he's free at the moment and you know what he's like,' said Merrin.

'Mum, that's never going to happen. He's so old; he's as old as you.'

'Thanks so much for the compliment, darling. Can I remind you that Creepy Chris is old,' Merrin justly pointed out.

'No worries,' said Maggie, coming down the stairs. 'For the time being, I am totally immune to the charms of the opposite sex and, yes, let's have fun today.'

Andrew picked up Louis from his flat at eleven o'clock sharp. Initially, the two men discussed the arrest of Rick and Sir Clive Stebbings and then Louis's injury.

'It's honestly nothing much,' Louis insisted. 'I had my arm re-dressed yesterday evening and there's no sign of infection. Why on earth I have to wear this wretched sling, I've no idea. I suppose it's to remind me not to waggle my arm about and tear the stitches.'

'You were very lucky,' said Andrew. 'As I understand it, you might so easily have been killed.'

Louis smiled at him. 'Don't you start, Andrew. I've had quite a few lectures on the subject of misjudged heroics. We got the villains, that's the main thing.' Louis kept to himself the call he had received from his chief super on his way over to St Ives the previous morning. Having again reminded Louis of his foolishness, John Dent had also told him that his name had been put forward for promotion to chief inspector. Louis was secretly very pleased but was telling no one until the promotion was in the bag.

Andrew and Louis then discussed Christmas traditions enjoyed by their respective families during their childhoods, the state of the building trade and, in desperation, the weather. As they approached the centre of Falmouth, Andrew stopped the car in front of the Greenbank Hotel, with a view of Falmouth Harbour stretching out before them.

'Why are we stopping?' Louis asked.

Andrew turned off the engine. 'There's something I want to ask you, Louis. It's awkward; I don't quite know how to say it.'

'Whatever it is, just spit it out,' said Louis, not unkindly.

'I want to marry your wife,' said Andrew, 'and I'd like your blessing to do so.'

'You mean Stephanie?' said Louis.

'Yes, of course Stephanie,' said Andrew.

'Andrew, Stephanie is my ex-wife. We divorced years ago. She's absolutely free to marry you, and you certainly don't need to ask for my blessing.'

'I know all that, of course, but I still feel I need your approval.'

'Why?' Louis asked.

'I think Stephanie mentioned that Edward told us about what you said to him when you last visited, about being on the outside looking in. To me that sounded crazy because that's exactly how I feel – on the outside, not really a part of the family. Even the house, where I live now, is really yours and Stephanie's – not mine at all.'

'If we're talking crazy, sorry but you're the crazy one,'

said Louis. 'You give Steph the stability she needs, you're a marvellous father figure to my children, always being there for them. You have a sensible job, which enables you to have uninterrupted time at home, and talking of home, the house has really always been Steph's. OK, we bought it together, but she gave me back my investment when we parted and all the improvements have been her idea, paid for with her money. Forget the house; it's your home now. And most important, above everything else, I believe they're all very happy that you are part of the family.' Louis smiled. 'I can't speak for Susie, obviously, but then she loves everyone!'

'So, you won't mind if I ask Stephanie to marry me? She might refuse, of course.'

'Of course I don't mind; I'm delighted for you both, truly,' said Louis, 'and I'm completely certain she will accept.'

'But will you still feel outside the family? I hate the idea of you feeling like that, Louis.'

'Maybe we need to recognise that we both bring different things to Stephanie and the children. Once you're married, I'm absolutely certain it will make you feel not only part of the family, but in the centre of it. As for me, I'm sure I will fit in somewhere. You're a very decent chap, Andrew, and I really appreciate you talking to me as you have done and I hope it's helped us both.'

'I'm sure there will be someone else for you one day,' said Andrew.

'I doubt it,' said Louis. 'Who'd have me?'

CHAPTER FIFTY-TWO

Brenda and Steven shared a chicken for their Christmas lunch. This was followed by Brenda's homemade Christmas pudding and an impressive pile of mince pies, accompanied by brandy butter and Cornish clotted cream. It was a feast.

Afterwards, they watched the King's Christmas broadcast. Following the dramas of the last few days and a large lunch, Brenda expected her son to fall asleep in his armchair, but instead he was very restless, striding about the room, unable to settle.

Finally, the questions came thick and fast. Would he have to go to prison, would Rick come and kill them both, would he ever get his van back from the police, would he be able to get another job, would they starve without his money? Brenda answered each question as carefully and as patiently as she could, then she found a suitable television programme for him to watch and, in a few minutes, he had fallen asleep.

Was she right to be so reassuring? Brenda wondered. Steve became upset so easily and although she knew nothing about police procedure and the courts, instinctively Brenda was aware that it would be a long time before the case was over. In the meantime, it was her duty to keep Stevie as happy and content as possible.

Maybe she was deluding herself, but somehow Brenda firmly believed the outcome would be good. After all, they had Merrin on their side and Brenda, who was no fool, got the distinct impression that Inspector Peppiatt was really on Stevie's side, too.

All would be well.

Sitting in the taxi, on his way home to Truro, Louis reflected on the day. It was, by far, the best Christmas Day since he and Stephanie had split up. On the occasions, in the past, when it was his turn to have the children for Christmas, it had always been a little awkward, he had to admit. There was this big hole where their mother should have been, particularly when the children were very young. The jollity had been rather forced. But today, it had seemed natural and as relaxed as one could expect, with two overexcited children involved.

Louis realised he genuinely liked Andrew and acknowledged he had been wrong to blame Andrew for his own lack of contact with his children. He was happy for them all but *where did that leave him?* he wondered. Some people would say how lucky he was – appearing every so often as the fun dad, no longer responsible for anything much other than his financial contribution to the children's upkeep. But, of course, it left him rudderless so far as his personal life was concerned. He had friends, both inside and outside of the police force, but he had precious little time to see them. His upcoming promotion would not make that any easier.

Out of nowhere, his thoughts shifted to Merrin McKenzie. He wondered how she and her daughter had coped with their first Christmas without Adam. Now he had come to know her a little, he could see quite clearly what a perfect match she and Adam must have been. She had done a wonderful job with Steve Matthews, steering them through the difficulties of understanding Steve's confused and traumatised mind. Despite the terrible tragedy she had recently suffered, Merrin McKenzie had remained both resourceful and talented. He admired her greatly and wished her well.

Christmas lunch at Miranda's Cottage had been fun. They had eaten and drunk far too much; there had been crackers and stupid jokes. Even when they had raised their glasses to Adam, it was to wish he was with them to enjoy the fun – there were no more tears. While they cleared up and tided the cottage, ready for the arrival of Max, Clara and Tristan, they, too, watched the King's speech.

When everyone arrived, laden with more food and drink, there was universal groaning but it was not long before another bottle of wine was opened. 'I'm just going to take William out for a quick walk,' Merrin said.

'No, Mum, you've haven't stopped all day,' said Isla. 'Come on, Max and Tristan, some fresh air will do us all good.'

After they'd left, Clara and Merrin settled down in front of the fire with a glass of wine. Maggie had retired to her room, asking to be woken up in half an hour. 'So,' said Clara, 'how are you, my little Pearl? I mean how are you really?'

'Not too bad,' said Merrin. 'I had a bit of a wobble this morning but Isla helped me pull myself together.'

'I was wondering how you enjoyed being a lawyer again. We haven't had a chance to talk since you dashed off to help the good inspector, leaving me with your much more efficient daughter.'

'I think we did a reasonable job and it was a worthy cause. So yes, I liked being useful in an environment I knew and understood, but it was a harrowing day, one way and another.'

'I know better than to ask you to tell me the gory details,' said Clara. 'Your inspector has made quite a name for himself, splashed all over the press. I expect you felt a bit squeamish when you heard he'd been stabbed.'

'You know, Clara, you can sometimes be surprisingly perceptive. You are the only person who has made that link, and yes, it did upset me, I must admit.'

'Pearl, my darling, I would have preferred it if you'd taken the word "surprisingly" out of that sentence but I'm glad to be the only one who made the connection. Tell me, what are you going to do now? Did your day back in the lawyer's saddle give you a renewed taste for it? If not, what next?'

'I know what I don't want to be – I don't want to be a cleaner or a waitress and, in any event, if I had aspirations in that direction, my future career would be doomed!'

'I would like to disagree with you, my Pearl, but hand on heart, I really can't.'

Just then, Isla, Tristan and Max returned and Isla was dispatched upstairs to wake up Maggie. They all enjoyed the evening; Maggie, in particular, seemed like a different person. Max behaved perfectly and Merrin suspected that Isla had warned him off so far as Maggie was concerned, despite her disparaging remarks about his age.

At last they all left and Merrin told the girls to go to bed and that she was happy to clear up.

'Are you sure, Mum?' said Isla. 'It's still Christmas Day and look what happened when you were left alone this morning.'

Merrin smiled. 'I'm fine, thanks, darling – it was a momentary lapse.'

Clearing up done, Merrin took William out for his bedtime walk. For some reason, even after a long day, Merrin felt surprisingly energised and so they walked through the town and up onto the Island. Having walked round it, Merrin settled on the bench overlooking Porthmeor Beach, her favourite spot. It had been a cloudy day but it was now clear, stars sprinkled across the sky and a nearly full moon riding high and throwing out a path of moonlight across the sea. It was beautiful.

As she sat there, her thoughts strayed to Louis Peppiatt and she wondered how his day had gone with his ex-wife, her partner and the children. Well, she hoped, especially for the children's sake. He was a funny mixture. In early stages of the case, he had been quite aggressive and then gradually a different side of his character had emerged. Both his desire to help Steve and his understanding of Maggie's predicament were impressive. His obvious distress when reminded of the little girl's death in Penzance was touching, too. And how could she not help liking him for hailing Adam as his inspiration?

Of course, Adam would have a major influence on the lives of both her and Isla for as long as they lived. But clearly, he had touched the lives of many other people, like Louis Peppiatt, and had left his mark. As Louis had said, Adam was his yardstick, and had made him aware of the frailty of life.

So, that was Adam McKenzie's legacy, Merrin realised, sitting with her dog in the moonlight. A life cut short, but a life well lived.

EPILOGUE

12th April

Merrin rose at the usual time, and made herself a coffee and some toast for Horatio. The minutes were ticking away towards the exact time when, twelve months ago, her husband, Adam, had died.

Since then, there had been a great many changes, of course. She was firmly settled in St Ives and knew now it had been the right decision for both her and Isla. Two old ladies had died, many years apart, and left behind their beloved pets, who now, bizarrely, sat cuddled up together in the dog basket – Horatio, the parrot with attitude, and William, possibly the ugliest dog in the world – both much loved. She had renewed old friendships, made new ones and had slipped back, almost seamlessly, into being a part of the community again.

There had been some triumphs, too. The trial of

John Lumley and Sir Clive Stebbings was due to start in two weeks' time; the conviction of them both seemed certain. However, Steve Matthews had not been charged with any crime, nor did he have to give evidence, except by written statement. Roberta had been found guilty of drug trafficking and was now in prison. Tristan's Fish Plaice had survived and they now had the season to look forward to – they reckoned the takeaway business had saved them. The university had found temporary accommodation for Isla and Maggie and they had secured a decent flat in Cowley for their final year. Maggie had not seen Creepy Chris again, nor had she wanted to. She claimed much of her recovery was due to her talk with Inspector Peppiatt. And Max was in love again, though only time would tell if that turned out to be a triumph!

And Merrin herself? Since Christmas, she had done very little. She had painted parts of the cottage, made new curtains and added little touches here and there. She had walked miles with William and felt fitter and altogether better for the exercise and fresh air. Tristan had built her some more bookshelves and she had started reading again, something she had not done in years. She now felt she was almost ready to begin a new phase in her life, whatever that might be.

She looked up at the kitchen clock, eyes on the second hand. She took a deep breath as it reached the exact moment when Adam had been declared dead. She stood stock still, wondering what to do, what to say, what even to think. And then she remembered her courageous little mum speaking the last lines of a Shakespearean sonnet as her father's coffin disappeared behind the curtain. Her parents' marriage had been enormously happy, as had her own. The words were perfect.

For thy sweet love remembered such wealth brings
That then I scorn to change my state with Kings.

ACKNOWLEDGEMENTS

Huge thanks to those who helped and supported me during the writing of this book – to Dr Lucy Mackillop, Sally Cuckson, David Harley, the team at Allison & Busby and, of course, my lovely family.

DEBORAH FOWLER'S first short story was published when she was seventeen. Since then, she has published over six hundred short stories, novels, a crime series and several works of non-fiction. Deborah lives in a small hamlet just outside St Ives and *A St Ives Christmas Mystery* is the first in a new series set against the beautiful backdrop of the West Cornish coastline.